# EXPATRIA

## Keith Brooke

**CORGI BOOKS**

EXPATRIA
A CORGI BOOK 0 552 13725 1

Originally published in Great Britain by
Victor Gollancz Ltd

PRINTING HISTORY
Gollancz edition published 1991
Corgi edition published 1992

This book was set in Plantin by
Chippendale Type Ltd, Otley, West Yorkshire.

Corgi Books are published by Transworld Publishers Ltd,
61–63 Uxbridge Road, Ealing, London W5 5SA, in Australia
by Transworld Publishers (Australia) Pty. Ltd, 15–23 Helles
Avenue, Moorebank, NSW 2170, and in New Zealand
by Transworld Publishers (N.Z.) Ltd, 3 William Pickering Drive,
Albany, Auckland.

Printed and bound in Great Britain by
BPCC Hazells Ltd
Member of BPCC Ltd

Keith Brooke is a young British writer whose
short fiction has appeared in *Interzone*, and
the anthology *Other Edens 3*. His first novel,
*Keepers of the Peace*, is also available from
Corgi Books. *Expatria* is the first of two books
and its sequel, *Expatria Incorporated*, will be
published in hardcover in 1992.

Also by Keith Brooke
KEEPERS OF THE PEACE
and published by Corgi Books

# PART ONE

## *Into the Night*

# Chapter One

The voice seemed to come from nowhere. 'People! Welcome to the Newest Delhi open-air market.' A pause, then: 'Idi Mondata wants you to know about his sea-fish: he has mawfish, doggies, mirrorbait and, *yes*, the finest blue bass you could ever taste. Idi tells me it came in only . . .'

From his concealed position, Mathias Hanrahan didn't notice the effect of his disembodied words on the people who filled the market-place.

He didn't sense the wave of awe that swept over the throng, shopper and trader alike.

He didn't sense the panic.

After telling the good people about Idi Mondata's fresh sea-fish, Mathias moved on to Mica Akhra's newly crafted implements – the finest tools this side of Orlyons, Mica had called them.

As he spoke into the microphone, Mathias marvelled at how his own voice was being transformed into tiny electrical impulses to be multiplied and converted back to sound by the loudspeakers. Now he knew why the book had called them *loud*speakers. Mathias and Mica had constructed the public address system in secret, relying on components and a manual they had found in an abandoned storeroom in the Primal Manse. Technology was not approved of on Expatria, it was a thing of the past,

7

an unwanted relic from the early days of the colony, when the ways of Earth had remained important.

Earlier, Mathias and Mica had placed the two loudspeakers high up on one of the balustrades that were set against West Wall. Concealed cables led back to a heavy-duty cell and the amplifier unit which they had positioned under the back awning of Mica's stall.

When they had finished, Mathias had wanted to search out Greta Beckett and tell her of his plan – explain to her about the little packets of energy that would carry his words – but he had held back. Greta was going through a Conventist phase and she disliked his fondness for the ancient ideas and technologies.

The previous week, Mathias had come across a music box in his rummagings through the closed-off rooms of the Manse. He'd taken it out to Gorra Point, concealed in his cloak; Greta had arrived a short time later and they had stood watching the great brown cutters skimming the sunset-reddened waves. Leading Greta beyond the hearing of their chaperone, Mathias had given his fiancée the box. She had taken it curiously, studying its design, too intricate for a native product. She had tipped it to one side and instantly a coloured ball of light had sprung dancing from the box and strange music had started, halfway through its tune.

When he had found the box, Mathias had thought it beautiful.

Greta had thrown it away and it had broken on the rocks. She had shuddered and tugged her sun-white hair away from her face. 'Thank you,

8

Matti,' she had said sadly. 'But it's not of this world. It's not ours to give or receive.'

And so Mathias had not involved Greta in his plans to modernise the market-place in the city of Newest Delhi. The Convent had clouded her judgement in recent weeks so that now it appeared that her every action had to be considered in terms of the sorority and the lessons of Mary/Deus.

Only Mica Akhra and Idi Mondata had known of Mathias's plans today and neither of them had believed the technology could be made to work. 'Voices in the wires?' Idi had said. 'More like voices in your head. Go see Doctor O'Grade, Matt, you're going crazy!'

Even Mica had not really believed in the public address system. Mica used the old technology every day: a terran microfurnace could cast tools of a higher calibre than any other method, well worth the price the Manse charged for power, as she always said. You can never overestimate the wonders of the old ways, she always said. But she had not believed the wires would carry Mathias's words. That was just too much.

'Vera Lugubé's greens are freshly picked every morning, grown along the banks of the purest mountain streams . . .' Now Mathias was moving on to cover the stall-holders who did not know of his scheme. By next market-day they would be queuing up for his services and the city of Newest Delhi would be one more step into the future.

As Mathias talked – Chet Alpha's walk-in peep-show had a new star and the price was just the same – he marvelled at how clearly his words rose above the clamour of the market-place. His voice sounded so clear, so powerful.

Mica Akhra lifted a flap at the back of her stall and hissed at him. 'I think you'd better look,' she said. Her mid-brown face had turned as pale as Mathias's.

Mathias stopped talking into his microphone and instantly he realized why his voice had carried so clearly. Apart from the occasional cries of caged animals the market-place was quiet. Mathias had never heard such a silence.

With a hollow feeling in his stomach, he stood and raised the flap at the back of Mica's stall.

It all seemed unreal.

He stepped through and stood beside Mica. The market was packed with people, as was always the case. Children, mothers, traders, geriatrics, fathers who normally stood tall and proud, heads above the mass of ordinary folk. All stood pale and open-mouthed. All looked up at the sky, trying to see where the Voice had come from. Clusters of Masons stood plucking uneasily at their neckties, waving Hiram handshakes at acquaintances in the crowd. Even the wailing momma who fronted the Jesus-Buddha stall – 'penny a prayer, a quarter for minor forgiveness' – had halted her Cry of the Hellbound.

A crackle of static came from the speakers and echoed around the gathering. A child's scream broke loose to be muffled by someone's hand.

'Why are they scared?' whispered Mathias. 'Why have they stopped trading?' Mica didn't answer and Mathias wondered if the success of the system had affected her too. He had expected *some* sort of reaction – none of these people had ever heard an amplified voice – but nothing like this. He could see the look on the wailing momma's face: it was a blend of fear and something like rapture, as if her Jesus-Buddha had spoken to her through one of the wooden statuettes she sold from her stall. The others, too, showed fear tinged with awe: a voice they didn't understand, a voice they didn't *want* to understand.

'They're crazy,' he muttered. 'Crazy.'

He turned his back on Mica and returned to the rear of her stall. He picked up the microphone and heard a moan from the crowd as another crackle came from the loudspeakers.

Holding up the flap so he could see, he spoke into his public address system.

'This is Mathias Hanrahan, heir to the Primacy of Newest Delhi. I am speaking to you over a voice-multiplication system. Its outlets are set in West Wall. If the system proves useful it will become a familiar feature of the market-place.'

The crowd was stirring. Ripples of movement ran through the throng, colour returned to faces, noises resumed their babble.

'Listen to the voice and you will find the best bargains, the finest fresh foods, the crispest cloths and linens! Yes, we will have the finest market-place on all Expatria!'

But Mathias had misread the crowd's reaction. The ripples of movement turned into waves that broke against the stalls, the colouring of the faces was fuelled by the adrenalin of rage, the sounds rose to drown out the words carried by Mathias

11

Hanrahan's miraculous public address system.

Bodies pressed against the frontage of Mica Akhra's Finest Metal Implements stall, breaking one of the uprights away so that the striped canvas roof fell in on Mica and Mathias. Struggling free of the stall, Mathias saw that they had not turned against *him*, the perpetrator of the Voice. It was more complex than that. He stared at the frenzied faces. The crowd was a mindless animal, moving under its own momentum, surging around the market-place and bringing down everything in its path. The beast had been awoken.

The first stall to go under was the wailing momma's. She rode free with the flow, clutching an armful of Jesus-Buddha statuettes to her chest; but then, as part of the crowd, she was taken over, absorbed, and she began to throw the carved figures with the rest. Stones, too, were flying, along with greens from Vera Lugubé's stall and chunks of fish from Idi Mondata's.

Mica Akhra clutched Mathias's arm. 'Come on,' she said. 'This is *not* the place to be.' At times the small age difference between Mathias and Mica did not matter, at others it gave her a seniority that he instantly accepted and obeyed. Now, he followed her without thinking into the fringes of the rampaging crowd.

Instantly there were hands pulling at him, bodies pushing, jostling, a current that was pulling him in a direction he didn't want to take. He fought the flow, shrugged free of the hands and tried to follow Mica.

Something wet and heavy hit him across the shoulders, a huge steak of blue bass. Stunned, he looked around but he had lost track of Mica. His head fuzzy, he let the crowd take him, pulling him through the shapes it drew in what had once been the market-place of Newest Delhi.

Rough stone against his face, the taste of it in his mouth. Mathias clung to the wall, realized where he was. He edged along the obstacle, fearful of being crushed by the crowd-creature but fearful, also, of losing contact with the solidity of West Wall.

A hand curled around his face and pulled his head back. He bit hard on an index finger and the hand disappeared. Tasting blood in his mouth, he struggled along the face of the wall and finally he reached the opening that he knew must be there. Without the wall to support him, the weight of the crowd pushed Mathias through the opening and he clambered up the steep steps and away from the madness that he had somehow inspired.

At the top of the steps, Mathias paused for breath. The city's ramparts were wide here, the sea thundering on one side, the crowd on the other. Hands seized him roughly.

'When will you ever learn?' said a tired voice that he instantly recognized. Lucilla Ngota, consort of March Hanrahan, his father; the woman who had sworn to shape Mathias into something that might just be worthy of inheriting March's Primacy when the time came.

The hands – those of a guard – released him and he turned.

'But . . .' The words were suddenly difficult for Mathias to find. 'They shouldn't have . . .'

Lucilla was looking at him with an expression that told him exactly what she thought of him. He would never make it, he would never be a worthy heir.

Rifle shots rang out from around West Wall, fired into the air. Mathias looked at Lucilla and at the mix of Primal Guards and militia troopers that surrounded them on the ramparts. More shots rang out. His shoulders slumped. Why did nobody understand?

'Come along,' said Lucilla. 'The militia can handle the rest. I think March might want to discuss this with you.'

The Primal Manse formed a rough crescent of interconnected buildings close to the market-place and the stone curtain of West Wall. The original prefabricated colony M-frames had been overbuilt with masonry and extended over the years with an array of mismatched blocks and wings, leaving the Primal gardens to the north, and a square known as the Playa Cruzo to the east. Lucilla left Mathias in his room in the private western wing of the Manse, the oldest part of the complex.

He sat on his bed, staring at the shelves of ancient documents, most of which he could not even read. He opened his windows so he could hear the distant swell of the sea. Whenever he was in torment he turned to the sea; its fathomless age helped him to see things in perspective, helped him to shrug things off.

After a time, there was a knock at the door.

He was in another world but eventually the persistent tap-tap-tap broke through and he strode over and opened the door himself. A servant, masked for the customary anonymity of the serving classes, said, 'Sir, the Prime of Newest Delhi awaits your company in the Court of Sighs.'

The Court of Sighs was a high-roofed hall, its sides lined with pillars. March Hanrahan sat casually towards one end, just one of the two dozen or so present, yet clearly marked as different by the people around him. His face was lined and greyed, years ahead of time; his hair was white already. Again, Mathias wondered at the pressures of the Primacy.

The Prime was talking to Edward Olfarssen-Hanrahan, Mathias's half-brother by one of March's early mistresses. March often said publicly that he regretted bedding Natalia Olfarssen. She was a tough negotiator. She had carried his son, only three months younger than Mathias, and insisted that he be recognized as the Prime's second child. Natalia Olfarssen had friends in irksome places and there had been only one way to placate her; grudgingly, Edward had been brought up as a member of the Primal household. Although the clan was large, its growth had been by affiliation and takeover; Mathias and Edward were the only members of their generation to bear the family name.

March Hanrahan ignored Mathias as he approached but all the others in the court paused in their conversations and watched. Mathias felt good. He knew he was about to be publicly humiliated but that mattered little in the run of things.

The Prime said something sharply and Edward backed away, his face pale. Mathias stopped before

15

his father and said, 'You requested my presence, March.'

The Prime stared at his son, as if he was trying to see through him. 'I have warned you before,' he said, spacing his words. 'You are irresponsible. Immature. You have no sense of your own position.'

Mathias looked around. They were all lapping it up. They couldn't wait to slither away and spread word of the hopelessly irresponsible heir. He smiled at them and then stopped, aware that March might get the wrong impression.

His father continued. 'We have yet to discover the monetary cost of your little escapade. Stalls were wrecked, their produce destroyed. People were hurt, fourteen are still under doctor's supervision. Someone could have been *killed* today. And all because you wanted to be louder than anyone else.' The Prime shook his head. 'I sometimes have trouble identifying myself in you, son. You make things difficult for no good reason.'

Mathias spoke into the silence. 'Sir. I see now that I handled it badly. I should have guessed what might happen. But it was the *people* who did this, not me. They reacted out of ignorance and injured themselves in consequence. Confronted with something they didn't understand, they panicked. Next time, things will be different.'

'Next time? Have you heard nothing I have said?' March Hanrahan gripped the sides of his seat and then slumped back. 'These toys you experiment with, they are a part of the old ways. There is no place for this *science*, this *technology*.

'Our ancestors from the Ark ships, they had these technologies, yet they were scared to land on Expatria's surface. They had been confined for too long. When they landed they rapidly changed their ways. They saw that there was no room for the old ideas: they didn't work. Today you provided yet another example of why these ideas do not work, yet still you persist!'

Mathias's light mood was gone. 'Your reasoning is false,' he said. 'You make connections where there are none, you link effects with the wrong causes. *Can't you see, old man?*'

'I can see,' said the Prime, his voice low and unnaturally steady, 'it is time that you faced up to your position as heir to the Primacy of Newest Delhi. You must amend your ways. You must learn responsibility. I will have no more of this stupidity.' He paused. 'This is the last time I warn you, Mathias Hanrahan: face up to your responsibilities. If not, well . . . there are always others in line.' He shrugged and it was clear that he had finished.

Edward coughed and, when Mathias glanced in his direction, smiled and looked towards the Prime. Mathias concentrated on his breathing and managed to remain silent.

The Prime turned to a representative from one of the inland valleys and spoke quietly.

Clearly dismissed, Mathias walked from the Court of Sighs and wandered away from the Manse, heading for the comfort of the sea.

'When the sun bleeds the horizon,' Greta had said. 'At the Pinnacles on Gorra Point.'

17

Leaning against one of the standing rocks, Mathias looked out at the red smear that marked where sea merged with sky and he remembered Greta's words. Cutters skimmed low across the waves of Liffey Bay, heading for their night-time roosts on the cliffs. Mathias envied them their freedom.

His mood had eased upon reaching the shore and he had laughed at the absurdity of it all. Nothing could get him down for long. He had passed the time until sunset locating gin-shells in the sands, and trying to see how heavy a stone had to be before it would trigger the bivalve shell into snapping shut.

When the sky had started to colour he had headed for the group of rocks they called the Pinnacles. They stood the width of Mathias's shoulders and at least three times his height. Once, when he was younger, he had tried to climb one but he had not succeeded, the surface had been too sheer and he could find no grip. March had chastised him for that, told him it was too dangerous an activity for the heir to the Primacy. Mathias had only wanted to find out how far he could see from the top.

Now he waited, leaning against one of the smaller Pinnacles, listening for sounds of Greta or her chaperone.

As the last colours were fleeing the night sky, Mathias heard the sound of footfalls and then he saw the glow of two lanterns. 'Greta,' he called, and stepped clear of his rock. Even in the dim light, she looked as fresh and alive as ever.

'Matti,' she said, and her chaperone melted discreetly into the shadows, the glow of her lantern

18

reminding the young couple that they were never quite alone. 'When will you learn?' said Greta.

Mathias cursed to himself. He had hoped she had not heard, that he could tell it to her in his own way. 'It was the stupid, ignorant people,' he muttered, scared to meet her eyes. A hawk-moth was hovering inside a nearby gin-shell, gathering sweet exudations from the shell's interior without triggering the creature's deadly trap. 'I was doing it for *them*, but they didn't see, they just panicked. What could I do?' He knew it was no good trying to justify himself to her, she was as much against the old ways as his father.

'I was at a Gathering,' she said. 'We were praying to Mary/Deus, repeating the triunes. I could feel the sorority all around me: I felt like a real part of it for the very first time. It was beautiful.

'Then one of the Little Sisters told me about what you had done and it made me want to *cry*, Matti. Do you know what you're doing?'

Mathias hated talk of the Convent, the strange animation it gave to Greta's talk. The Convent had found a gap in Greta's life and Mathias felt excluded. Why couldn't she turn to him instead? Why did she need this substitute for the more conventional teachings of Jesus-Buddhism, if she needed such superstition at all? 'But if people can only . . .'

'No, Matti. Those ways are no good to us now.' She removed the hand he had placed on her arm — he was so rarely able to touch her, he had held her in his arms on only two occasions, each ended by the discreet cough of their chaperone — and gave him a stern look. 'Matti, there is much that is good about you, but there is much that must change. Your father is right, you have to grow into your responsibilities.' She backed away and kissed the air in parting, then left with her chaperone.

Mathias felt terrible. He could easily cope with his argument with March, but not Greta too! Since her father had pledged her troth to Mathias, nearly four years before, their relationship had grown, it had given Mathias something to depend on.

And now she was angry with him.

He had to change, that was what she had said. He had to grow into his responsibilities.

He wandered down to stand by the sea and, skimming stones into the night, he knew that he would do anything Greta demanded of him. He would mend his ways and become a Prime to make the clan proud.

And *then* he would be able to think about the changes he would make.

## Chapter Two

'Make me a Prime March can be proud of,' said Mathias. 'I want to learn.'

Sala Pedralis sat across from him on a balcony that overlooked the inner Manse gardens. Her features were grey and craggy but somehow, beneath it all, she had retained an element of youth. Once, for a brief few months, she had been the Prime's partner; later, she had been elected on to the board of the Hanrahan clan to serve as one of his main advisers. In this capacity she had been responsible for Mathias's education. She had found him ancient books, shown him the wonders of discovery, fed his hunger for knowledge and understanding.

She laughed lightly. 'So the old goat has finally made some sort of an impression on you?' She laughed again.

'Sala, he's my *father*. I don't want to keep fighting him.'

'Or Greta Beckett, hmm?'

Mathias blushed and looked out over the rich greenery of the gardens. The scene was bursting with life: flycatchers darted after fluffy grey moths, froglets clung motionless to the lichen-coated tree trunks, grana seeds parachuted themselves towards the few open spaces that were not paved.

'Mathias, I've been tutoring you for the last five or six years. You know what I mean when I say someone is decent or . . . *moral*. You know I believe in progress but that I also believe advances should be gradual and considered. What more do you want me to tell you, hmm? I can't just snap my fingers and turn you into the right stuff. I can't still your temper or make you less of an impetuous young fool. There's no secret rule of thumb that all good Primes know and others can only guess at.'

Mathias felt a surge of anger at her words but he controlled it. He would have to do it all himself then, if even Sala refused to help. After a few minutes of small talk, he rose and left her on the balcony. It was all a question of will-power, strength of mind.

He closed the door and turned and Edward was standing before him in the corridor with that familiar half-smile on his face. 'Please, Miz Sala,' he said, 'make me a Prime to be proud of!'

Mathias grabbed him by the jacket and pushed him up against the wall. Edward was small and weak and he didn't try to struggle. 'At least I am going to be Prime,' hissed Mathias. 'At least I am not destined to stay forever in someone else's shadow, crawling behind them with my nose up their—'

'So you have changed your ways, have you?' It was the voice of Lucilla Ngota. Her timing was perfect. Mathias guessed that she had been keeping a close watch on him, waiting for the very first sign of deviation.

Slowly, he released his grip on his half-brother. Ignoring Lucilla's comment, he glared at Edward and said, 'I do not like people listening to my private

22

conversations.' Then he turned to Lucilla. 'I do not like being spied upon as a *rule*.'

He turned and marched away, his shoulders braced, his breathing steady. At last he was learning some kind of control over his actions. He grinned. He would cope on his own, he didn't need Sala's help – primacy was in his blood.

Mathias was determined that his new attitude would endure. He found that he felt better about himself now, calmer, more purposeful. The self-discipline was paying off. He had realized that he needed this sort of goal in his life, something to aim at, something to focus his energies upon.

The only thing he resented was the loss of his books and journals. Returning after his encounter with Edward and Lucilla, he had instructed his servants to remove all the ancient artefacts from his rooms. It had been painful, but he had seen it as necessary. He found life difficult without the books, the strange and wonderful world they painted, but it had been a sign that he meant business and at last Greta seemed pleased with him.

Earlier today, she had even suggested he could be her concessionary male at one of her Gatherings.

He had started at that suggestion, but when he studied Greta's face it was clear that her suggestion was innocent. She could never hide anything from Mathias. He had refused, as she must have expected, but now, waiting in the darkness outside the deus house, he began to wonder if he should have accepted her offer.

'Here they comin', ya' highness,' said Idi Mondata, pointing to the blocky building's entrance and pulling a face that might have been a manic grin.

Mathias pushed his friend into the alley and for a moment it felt like they were still children, slipping out without their parents' knowledge, high on the adrenalin of disobedience.

But they were older now, and Mathias's mood was more subdued. The adrenalin was no longer there.

'You coming inside then?'

Mathias could see the whites of Idi's eyes in the darkness. 'Sure,' he answered. He pulled his cloak around himself, the coarse material feeling unfamiliar, the camouflage of the street. 'Come on.'

That morning, Mathias had been gutting fish with Idi. 'I sometimes wonder what goes on in there,' he had said, 'in their Gatherings.'

'Brainwashing,' Idi had said. 'Brainwashing 'n' witchcraft. That's what Rabi always used to say.' Then his eyes had narrowed and he had continued. 'You want to see for yourself, Matt? I know some Dee Krishnas who could get us in if you want. They've been watching them for years – don't trust 'em. You want?'

And so they stood in the shadows as the drizzle began and the first of the Daughters and Little Sisters of the Convent made their way along the Street of the Holy Fountain, their route lit dismally by hanging torches, dampened by the night. They entered the deus house in threes, all bowing their heads, passing through the doorway without pause, carefully stepping on the white entrance stone and

24

simultaneously crossing themselves with geometrical precision.

There was a sound nearby in the shadows and Idi put a hand on Mathias's arm. A short man had joined them.

As his eyes adjusted to the level of the light, Mathias saw that the man was bald, his head and face covered with tattoos – hearts and flowers and eye-centred swastikas – making it impossible to judge his age. The Death Krishna blinked slowly and Mathias saw that caricatured eyes had been tattooed on to his eyelids.

'This is Joseph,' said Idi. 'He's our guide.' The man, Joseph, nodded briefly and then retreated and gestured for them to follow.

The balcony ran the length of the auditorium below. Sounds of the Gathering were louder here, voices chanting, the words indistinct, a chaos of unco-ordinated chants.

They had entered the deus house's basement through a trapdoor, and then they had followed Joseph up a series of spiralling staircases. The place smelt of incense and damp and there were posters still hanging from the walls from when this had been the city's only theatre.

As the three fanned out along the balcony, Mathias looked at the Gathering below. The smell was stronger up here and the first thing that struck Mathias was the banked mass of purple candles burning on a raised platform at one end of the auditorium. Behind the candles was a huge crucifix, easily ten metres high; nailed to the cross was the

25

contorted figure of a woman carved from dove-grey jelebab wood, her face tipped to the heavens, her features settled into a peaceful smile. Mathias stared, transfixed, into the wide-awake eyes of the carved Mary/Deus, almost on a level with his own.

Below, the Little Sisters and Daughters of the Convent stepped forward, three by three, and prostrated themselves, moaning, before the giant crucifix. Behind them the congregation buzzed in excitement; even the Conventist Guards dotted around the wall seemed to be overcome with the experience. Mathias shook his head, glad that Greta had already been to her Gathering for this week.

He glanced to his right, first at Idi, picking his nails and staring at the giant crucifix, and then at the small Death Krishna, looking down patiently over the Gathering. He wondered what it was that drew the Krishnas to the Convent, and then he began to wonder just how much he had been sheltered from, brought up in the Manse, what dark currents lay hidden from him beneath the familiar surface of Newest Delhi.

And then he looked down and saw that Greta Beckett was lying face down before the crucifix, moaning like her sisters on either side.

That sun-white hair was unmistakable.

'Fountain of life, the greater part.' The congregation started to sing. It was a hymn Mathias recognized from the past, from neighbourhood pageants put on for the Prime, although the words had been altered. 'Wet my brow, Sorority.'

He couldn't take his eyes from Greta's prostrate form, the slight, ecstatic movements of her legs, her hips, the arching of her back as she took up the hymn. 'Springing up within the heart' – he was sure he could hear Greta's voice, carrying clear above the rest of the congregation – 'Mary/Deus, Eternity.'

He jerked away, shaking his head in a vague effort to clear his mind of the image from below. He felt dirty, he hadn't come to spy on his fiancée. He would never have been here if he had thought there was the slightest chance that . . .

He'd only wanted to see for himself.

He looked across at Idi and Joseph, still studying the Gathering intently. He couldn't take any more. He peered through a curtained archway that led off the balcony. The corridor was empty so he stepped out, feeling an instant release from the tension Greta had stirred in him.

He walked slowly to the first junction, reconnaissance diverting his thoughts from what Idi would think when he saw that he had been unable to stay.

The way was clear and he turned back to join Idi.

It was then that he heard the voices and he paused. He knew he should return to Idi and the Krishna but instead he took a step, then another, down the right-hand fork in the passageway. At the next junction he determined that the voices were being carried up a nearby stairwell. He stopped at the railing, keeping out of the light seeping up from below, breathing slowly so as not to choke on the candle smoke being carried up by the draught.

' . . . if he will not protect the sorority's name, then we will simply have to make him do so,' said one of the voices.

'We have always had ways,' said another. 'A good woman can control a hundred men, particularly a Valley man.' The two women laughed.

The Convent had recently made representations to the Prime about what they described as their persecution in some of the southern valleys – that must be what the women were talking about. March had not been forthcoming in his response. Mathias was about to return to the balcony when he heard the second woman add, 'The world should remember the strength of the deus.'

He shook his head. Once, the Convent had carried great influence with the Primacies of its day; there had always been a matre or a Little Sister on hand to advise and, eventually, to manipulate. The Convent had grown rich and strong before it had been reduced to its current status. But that had been three, maybe four, generations ago. Now, the Prime's view of them fluctuated between amusement and irritation.

Mathias straightened as he heard a noise from the corridor. Idi and Joseph must be stirring – they would want to be clear before the Gathering broke up.

He turned and then he knew that he had been trapped. Two Conventist Guards blocked his way, a Little Sister standing nervously behind them. The Guards were big and they were wrapped in leggings and jackets of thick black cord. Their hands hung easily by the long knives strapped to their thighs.

The Little Sister stepped forward and called down the stairwell and Mathias knew that this would be his only chance to break free and save face: they were yet to recognize him in his ordinary street clothes.

He raised his hands, said, 'Listen,' and then darted at the gap between the two guards.

But they were ready for him, as he had expected. They caught him easily and held him firm as three more Conventists appeared at the top of the stairs.

Two of the new arrivals were Little Sisters but the third, a thin woman with a large crucifix hanging across her chest, was a priestess, a matre. She looked at Mathias and her recognition of him was betrayed by a brief twitch of her eyebrows. 'They say your diplomacy is non-existent,' she said to him, signalling to the guards to release him. 'But I had not believed it could be so.'

Mathias's skin was burning, adrenalin coursing through his veins. 'I just wanted to see for myself,' he said. He was not going to apologize to a matre.

'And what did you see?' The matre folded her hands across her crucifix and waited.

'An old theatre that could be put to better use.' She had no right to question him, she knew who he was.

'And nobody knows that you are here.'

Suddenly, in the ensuing silence, he realized how vulnerable he was. The matre's statement was not a threat, but it was an observation that cut right through Mathias's defences.

The matre whispered sharply to one of her companions, who then hurried back down the stairwell. After a few minutes of taut silence, Mathias heard footsteps returning up the stairs and then he saw that it was Greta, accompanied by the Little Sister.

He wouldn't meet her eyes. He didn't dare. He knew she had inherited a sharp temper from her father but she had never had reason to vent it on him.

He had never seen her body so tense, the knuckles of her fists so white by her sides. 'Matti,' she said quietly. 'We have to go.'

They walked in stiff silence back to the Manse, chaperoned by a Little Sister. Every step was painful, every silent breath more punishment than her temper could ever have been. He felt like he was drowning in shame, like he was being smothered.

At the entrance he finally looked up at Greta. 'I'm sorry,' he said. 'I didn't mean to . . .'

'I'm sorry too, Matti.' She wiped a tear from the corner of her eye and kissed the air in parting. Mathias watched her figure retreating across the Playa Cruzo, shadowed by her chaperone, and wondered if things would ever be the same again.

# Chapter Three

As Dum drew closer to the slightly larger Dee a new excitement grew. When the two moons at last appeared to touch, clan heads in the city of Newest Delhi initiated the biannual festival of Dumandee.

For the past week, it had seemed that nobody would speak to Mathias. Sala was busy arranging the festivities and Idi was still angry over Mathias's wandering off on his own in the deus house; on the few formal occasions when he had been with Greta they had barely exchanged a word. As Dumandee grew closer it became clear that the Kissing Moons would exert little influence on Greta Beckett.

Mathias had never believed in the superstition, anyway. In reality, the moons' orbits were tens of thousands of kilometres apart and Dum was actually quite markedly smaller than Dee, despite the common perception. The Kiss was an illusion.

The festival of Dumandee always culminated in the grand Primal Ball, on the night when the moons became, briefly, one. Mathias didn't want to go. Instead he sat in his room, trying to filter out the sounds of the revellers arriving at August Hall in the east wing of the Primal Manse, knowing that he should be there, cursing his indecision.

Eventually, his self-discipline won. He rose from his bed and dressed himself with the aid of a masked servant. His leggings were new, his padded jacket old but refurbished with pure golden threads and white sand-pearls from the island of Clermont.

He dismissed the servant and stood for a moment on his balcony, looking up at the single white disc formed by Dum and Dee. 'Exert your influence,' he said to the moons. 'Just this once.' Then he turned back into his room and headed for August Hall.

Already, the music was playing and the Hall was packed with finely dressed clan officials and sheet dancers, costumed servants and a host of representatives from the affiliated valleys. The octet were playing something percussive and new that Mathias didn't like, although it fitted his mood without a seam. The atmosphere was seductive though, free and energetic, smells of heavily spiced food and drinks almost overpowering in their intensity.

Mathias breathed deeply as he strolled around the edge of the dance floor. Edward was there, of course, and then Mathias spotted Greta standing nearby. Her gown was fine and loose, her hair woven high and away from her face. She was laughing and looking all around. Mathias wondered how long her high spirits would last.

Edward had an arm around a solemn, black-maned girl – that kind of intimacy was more accepted on an occasion such as this – but he was looking longingly at Greta. She had always been one of the obstacles between Mathias and his half-brother, another spur to Edward's envy.

Mathias stepped into Edward's line of vision and then moved towards Greta, hoping that things would be all right.

She saw him, she smiled, she held her hands towards him. It was as if there had never been a rift. She kissed the air in greeting and held out a glass for him. He took it and drank, noticing nothing but Greta. 'I'm late,' he said, but she shrugged. Tonight was no night for apology, tonight was the night of Dumandee, tonight was the night of the ball.

The music began to swell and fall away, swell and fall away, and, feeling supremely confident, Mathias gathered Greta into his arms and guided her on to the dance floor. Her body was small and brittle against his own. She smelt of fresh honeysuckle. Mathias had never held her so close for so long, their chaperone had always coughed discreetly and then not so discreetly. In the crowd of dancers they had more privacy than they had ever had alone.

The music changed and still they danced, moving faster, closer. Over Greta's golden head, Mathias saw Edward slipping away with the long-faced girl.

They danced faster, closer, pressing urgently together. Mathias bent to whisper in Greta's tiny ear. 'Greta, shall we—' But she was whispering in *his*, and her words stopped him in mid-sentence.

'The Prime spoke to me today,' she said. 'He asked how my father would react if Edward became heir to—'

'He *what*?' People nearby stopped dancing to look.

'He didn't mean . . . It was only if you . . .' Greta looked around at the staring faces and then dropped her head and tried to move back into Mathias's arms. '*Matti*, not here. I'm sorry.'

But she had said too much already. Mathias barged his way across the dance floor. His father was standing with Lucilla Ngota, just inside the balcony that overlooked the Playa Cruzo.

Mathias grabbed the Prime's shoulder and pulled him round. '*What do you mean* . . .?' Then he remembered who he was mishandling and stopped, stunned by the force of his rage.

The Prime had gone pale, but his control was total. Mathias stepped back, then turned and ran through the shocked gathering. As he ran out of the hall the music faltered back into the silence and then a few voices came back too. In the corridor he saw Edward grinning cruelly, his companion nowhere in sight. Then he saw no more, everything a blur as he ran along the empty corridors and out into the night.

The streets of Newest Delhi were alive with partying crowds and a strange, new tension was caught up in the air.

March was trying, clumsily, to get at him through Greta – that much was obvious once Mathias was alone and more calm, walking through the darkened back streets. He was using the threat of naming Edward his heir to try to force Mathias to conform. But, instead, it had brought the old impetuosity back to the surface.

He stopped thinking and tried to become a part of the darkness. It was a game he had played as a child: ignore the thoughts that keep jumping into your head and try to melt into the night, or the sea, or the cliffs, try to feel yourself a part of the world.

It worked for a time: his mind forgot itself as his body grew calm and tranquil.

He was feeling sedate when partying noises broke through his barriers and reminded him of himself. He was on the Lincolnstrasse, in the poorer part of the city, where serfs lived alongside lowly engineers. The buildings here were low and in need of repair, the streets uneven and unpaved. Bonfire smoke clung to the air.

There was a sudden shout in the street ahead and, with a chilling clarity, Mathias realized that the sounds were not those of an ordinary Dumandee party. A sudden scream confirmed his intuition.

He stopped in the shadows, peered ahead.

Figures moved quickly at the next junction, throwing things on to a huge fire – no ordinary street bonfire – and yelling hoarsely at each other. The smell of smoke was now bitter on the night air as Mathias crouched behind a trader's stall, upturned in the disturbance. A nearby shop had been broken into, its double wooden doors smashed through, its contents looted and vandalised. For the second time he was aware of how little he knew of the real workings of the city.

He let himself give in to an almighty shudder and then he looked all around.

His head was clear now and he looked back along the street. He had to get clear. Quickly, he retraced his steps, cautiously at first and then more boldly, heading for the shore. He needed somewhere to think.

*

35

The waves barely made a sound as they half-heartedly crept a metre or so up the beach and then sagged back. He thought of the disturbances on the Lincolnstrasse, but that was too fresh, too confusing. Instead, he tossed pebbles into the water and thought of Greta, of holding her as close as he had at the ball. That had felt better than he had ever dreamed it would. It was less than a year – fourteen months, he counted – until their wedding. Things would be calmer then. He would have had time to settle into his role, if March ever forgave him for his behaviour this evening.

He moved up the beach and followed the cliff path out along Gorra Point, towards the Pinnacles. Small creatures scuttled in the darkness. Burrowers. He had listed them all when he was younger. The native furworms and gnaws and footies, the terran voles and gophers and jerboas. Each to its own niche, his list had grown long and complex in its details of breeding and possible evolutionary connection. But the list had gone out with his books, locked in some dark cupboard or maybe even dumped in a bio-converter in one of the valley farms.

The Pinnacles loomed against the night sky, brightened by the stars and the almost set moons. He sat with his back against the rocks.

He stayed like that for a long time, staring out to sea, spotting the occasional night-sighted cutterette and, after a time, the skipping forms of a school of terran porpoises. He smiled, then, and rose and headed back along the cliff path towards Newest Delhi.

He followed the deserted ramparts of West Wall around to near the Manse, cautious in case the disturbances had spread. Up on the Wall he could still hear the sounds of the Dumandee Ball, quiet but persistent.

To get to his suite he would have to pass through the corridors by August Hall. Despite – or maybe because of – his calmness of spirit, he did not want to face that; he wanted to preserve his inner peace.

When he was younger he had often left the Manse without permission. March would never have let him out to play with the common folk, not with Mica Akhra, daughter of a lowly engineer, not even with Idi and Rabindranath Mondata, sons of the finest fish merchant in all Newest Delhi. When March grew wise to his son and posted servants to watch over the doors of his suite, Mathias had simply refined his route. It was a number of years now since he had climbed the pillars outside his balcony and he doubted if he could still manage. But there was only one way to satisfy his curiosity and, all of a sudden, he was filled with the adventurous spirit of a child.

The handholds he remembered were too close together for an adult, but there were others in the ancient masonry that were just as good. The two-storey climb made him breathe harder than he had expected, the life of an heir had been too soft on him. His hand caught the top of the balcony wall and he pulled himself up until his other hand joined it. With a heave his elbows were there and his feet found purchase on the outside of the balcony.

Then he looked up and saw the people in his room. 'What—?'

Vice-like hands seized his arms and pulled him over the balcony wall. He hit the floor hard. Winded, he struggled to turn, but the hands were still gripping him, holding him down.

Pulled to his feet, he looked into the face of an officer of the Primal Guard. The man's name was Agrozo; Mathias had never spoken to him before.

'Sneaking in, eh?' said Agrozo. 'Didn't fancy the stairs, eh? Eh?' He prodded Mathias in the ribs.

'You can't treat me like this,' said Mathias, straightening in the grip of two more guards.

'Orders says we can.'

'Orders?' Pernicious thoughts about his father were creeping into Mathias's mind. All he had done was argue, he had committed no crime! 'The Prime would not order you to treat his son in this manner,' he said, trying to sound in control, trying to sound like March. 'Let me speak with him.'

Agrozo exchanged glances with another of the guards. 'You can save that for the Court, sir. Now you can come with us.'

'Court? What are you saying? Just let me speak with the Prime, OK?'

Agrozo set his face and turned from Mathias. 'The Prime is dead, sir. Murdered. My orders are to arrest you, that's all.' The man shrugged. 'Now will you just come along? Or the boys'll have to get physical.'

Mathias went. He didn't know what else to do. The Prime dead? *Dead*?

## Chapter Four

The Manse corridors were empty as Agrozo led
Mathias and his guards to the Administry wing.
On one level, Mathias had already accepted what
had happened: March was no longer alive.

But he tried to distance himself from that thought.

How could he mourn when he was being marched
like this through the Manse, surrounded by soldiers
of the Primal Guard? He felt physically broken,
like when the market-place crowd had threatened
to crush him. Twelve years earlier, when his mother
had been killed in the Abidjan Uprising, Mathias
had felt like this; only now it was worse. The closest
family he had left was Edward. True, there were
Sala and, especially, Greta, but they were not *family*.
Walking through the corridors, he could only think
of his loss; he had no time for thoughts of his
own future or what was happening to him at that
moment.

The fact of his arrest finally hit him when
Agrozo hammered at the door of the Prime's office
and called, 'Prisoner Mathias arrested and awaits
interview.'

The door opened and Agrozo was ushered in.
After a minute or two the door opened again and
Mathias was ordered to enter.

This had been March's favourite room. Here he

had a broad desk and a view over the Manse gardens; on fine days he would open the windows for the scents of the Expatrian herbs. The room was cluttered with mementoes and signs of regular use; the single bookshelf was heavy with hand-bound volumes of Expatrian history, some written by Sala Pedralis, one volume even penned by the Prime himself, back when he had only been heir to his vagabond father.

But now the room had lost its easy atmosphere. Four guards stood by the door, a scribe sat poised to document the proceedings and the Prime's oak desk had been cleared. Seated behind the desk was Lars Anderson, Captain of the Prime's Guard. At his left shoulder stood Lucilla Ngota, staring at the wall and carefully avoiding Mathias's gaze. Mathias could not tell if she would be his ally or not, events were still confusing him.

He looked at Anderson and stepped forward. 'Tell me, Captain. Is it true? What happened?'

Anderson's face told him nothing. The captain had taught Mathias to shoot, shown him the basics of shore-casting for mawfish; they had spent many hours, just the two of them, the world left far behind. And now they were on opposite sides of the dead Prime's desk.

'The Prime is dead,' said Anderson. 'Please, answer my questions. This has to be done. Where did you go after you assaulted the Prime tonight?'

'Then, Captain, am I not now the Prime of Newest Delhi? I demand that you tell me exactly what happened tonight. My father has been murdered and you sit there wasting my time with trivia!'

Anderson did not seem affected by Mathias's outburst. 'Very commendable, sir. I hope you are telling the truth. I hope that in time, too, you will see the necessity of this interview. Yes, you are technically the new Prime. But in the present contingencies I am still an officer of the old Prime and you, sir, are technically under arrest. Forgive me, but we must proceed. Where did you go tonight?'

'Lucilla?' But she was still staring at the wall. He wondered at what there had been between her and his father – she had been repeatedly unfaithful to him, with the women and men of the Court, but she had remained longer than any of her predecessors. 'Lucilla, you know this is wrong.' Then, she finally looked at him and he wished he had kept quiet. There was venom in her eyes, she was directing the naked flame of her hatred directly at his heart. He looked back at Anderson, shaken.

'I learnt of my father's death when I found Agrozo in my suite. After . . . after leaving the Dumandee I wandered in the streets then walked out along Gorra Point to a place we call the Pinnacles – tall needles of rock. I sat for a time, regretting my earlier behaviour, swearing to mend my ways. Then I returned to this.'

'You neglect your somewhat unconventional means of entering your suite,' said Anderson. 'Why did you sneak in? Why did you want people to think you were already in your room when the alarm was raised?'

'You are making false assumptions, Captain Anderson.' Mathias was learning that his self-control was far greater in real adversity than was normally the case. 'I did not know an alarm would be raised, as I had no idea what had happened. My method of return is one developed over years of avoiding parental restrictions. I chose to "sneak in" tonight because I wished to avoid meeting anyone who may have witnessed my earlier behaviour. Captain Anderson, I was *ashamed*. Now, this has gone on too long, you must have more important things to do.' No matter how hard he tried, he could not adopt the same tone of authority his father had used to such good effect; Anderson merely ignored him.

'What did you think when you learnt of the means of death?'

'Nobody has told me any details,' said Mathias. 'Presumably so you could try such amateurish methods of interrogation.'

Anderson ignored the slight. 'Why did—' He was interrupted by a knock on the door. 'Yes?'

Agrozo walked in and put something on the desk. After a muttered explanation in Anderson's ear he retreated to stand by the bookshelf.

Anderson looked at Mathias, something new in his eyes. 'Tell me, Mathias,' he said. 'Why should you have a stolen servant's mask in your possession?'

'I don't know what—'

'*This* one,' continued the captain, holding one out before him, the item that Agrozo had brought in. 'It was found on your balcony. A crude form of anonymity, but one that might work. Why were you carrying it? And why did you drop it when you saw my men?'

Before Mathias could answer there was a roar of rage from behind the desk and Lucilla Ngota had stepped around it and thrown herself at him. The impact knocked him to the ground, and he fought her frantically until two guards dragged them apart.

Disbelievingly, he stared at Lucilla. He had never seen a person so enraged. She would have killed him if she had not been stopped.

'Worthless,' she hissed, still struggling with the guards. 'You'll pay.' Mathias did not like to look at her as she struggled to get to him.

'Enough!' snapped Anderson. 'This takes us nowhere.' He gestured at a guard and Mathias was led out of his father's office. The last words he heard Anderson say were, 'There will be a trial. You must let justice do its . . .' Then the words grew too faint to hear and Mathias dumbly followed his guard through the long Manse corridors.

Dawn was breaking by the time the guard locked the door from the outside. Mathias looked around at the room that was to be his prison. It was an ordinary guest-room, in the south wing of the Manse. He was still shaken by Lucilla's reaction, but he knew that all he could do was wait until events proved his innocence.

At first he had been willing to accept that his arrest was inevitable, after the murder of the Prime. He *had* publicly assaulted March, only hours – *minutes*? – before his death. And Mathias was the person with most to gain from the situation: the inheritance of the Primacy of Newest Delhi, and with it the effective rule of almost half the population of Expatria. It was natural that suspicion should fall on his shoulders.

But the mask cast everything in a different light. Someone was trying to set him up, presumably the same person who had killed the Prime. He remembered the disturbance in the streets that night: the guard had told him it was Black-Handers, out for whatever they could grab while the revellers were distracted by Dumandee. The militia had easily kept control. He thought again of the dark currents flowing through the city he had thought he understood, the cults, the clans, the disenchanted. What did they think they would gain by all this? And then he stopped himself. Speculation would do him no good. Where had his self-discipline gone?

There was a knock at the door and he glanced up to see it open and someone step through.

'Idi!' They rushed together and embraced. 'Idi, how did you get in? Tell me what's happening!'

Idi's face looked serious and hollow, as if he had not slept that night. 'Your sentries don't like what they're doing here,' he said. 'There's a lot of people like that. Word gets around, you know? How much they tell you? Nothing? I figured. Listen, word is your pa was strangled with a power cable. Like a PA cable, they say. They say he left the party after an argument with *you* – yeah, I know you didn't do it, least I did when I just saw your face. After this bust-up he left, then Edward found him dead and you're chin-deep in shit creek. It stinks.' Idi smiled for the first time, but it was obviously an effort.

'You say Edward found him?'

'It's not what *I* say, it's what *they* say. It's what the militia and the guards say when they're letting off steam, it's what servants say who don't like the idea of being under Eddy.' He smiled again. 'It's the word, Matt, the word. They say he was broken up about it, say he was crying when he called the guards. They kept it quiet at first, until they figured they knew what had happened.

'Word also says that Eddy's ma has crawled out of the woodwork, now she's heard what's happening. She's trying to put pressure on for Eddy to be adopted above you as the new Prime. She doesn't care what comes of this, just says it's another proof that you're not the right stuff like her Eddy is.' Idi sighed 'What have they got on you that'll stick?'

'Nothing solid,' said Mathias. 'Not that they've told me. Except for a mask somebody planted in my room; Anderson says I used it for cover. Someone put it there, Idi. Someone wants me out of the way.'

'Good reasoning, Matt. Except it's not just you: they wanted the Prime out of the way, too.'

Someone coughed outside the guest-room door and Idi stepped towards it. 'That's my signal. Time to go. Listen, Matt, try not to worry.' He shrugged. 'Yeah, I know. But you've got friends out here. We're not going to let you go down with this.'

Idi opened the door and Mathias hurried over to stop him. 'Listen, Idi,' he said. 'Will you get word to Greta for me? She has to know what's happening. I have to see her!'

'Hey, there's no *have to*s from where you're sitting, Matt. Yeah, OK. I'll try, I'll do something.' He gave a final grin. 'We'll get you out, Matt. They can't do this.'

*

45

Mathias tried to occupy his mind as he sat imprisoned in the guest-room. He counted the animals that flew past the window, setting terran birds against the native bat-types. The Expatrians were well ahead when he stopped counting. He tried to listen for the sea, but the day was calm and the sea quiet. He even tried to recall his list of cliff-top burrowers but it was no good. Always his mind came back to his lost father. He wished things had been easier between them; the feelings had always been there but it took death to make Mathias see that.

They brought him food – a plate of corn hash – towards the middle of the day. He didn't eat it. He just sat there, working his depression more deeply into his soul, wondering what his half-brother was doing in his place.

Later he sat watching the sun, too low and red to hurt his eyes. The day had been a long one and now it was ebbing away into the nothing of another brief night. At first the sky changed slowly, the sun burning a deeper hue, its colours seeping into the scattering of clouds. Then the change accelerated, the colours spreading, deepening, flowing through cloud and the darkening sky, ever-changing, drawing Mathias up and away.

A knock at the door brought him back down to the reality he had been trying to forget. He had been expecting them all day, another interview, maybe some more planted evidence that would prove his 'guilt' beyond all reasonable doubt.

The door opened and Greta was standing there.

He wanted to rush to her, to take her in his arms as he had at the Dumandee Ball, but instead he held back, feeling suddenly unsure of himself.

The door opened wider and Greta stepped aside to allow the chaperone to follow her into the room. Of course, she would not come to see him alone. Even in this situation – *especially* in this situation – they had to be watched.

Chaperone leaning on the closed door, Greta moved into the room and sat upright on the edge of the wide bed. Mathias wanted to go to her, but he couldn't move, he couldn't even speak.

'I'm glad they still treat you well, Matti.' She gestured around at the guest-room. 'Your cell is rather splendid.'

Greta's lightness of spirit was one of her most endearing qualities, but it was also one of her most infuriating. If ever an argument had gone against her and Mathias had felt close to winning a point, she would joke and the matter would be closed and Mathias would feel angry and elated at the same time. He felt both those feelings now and didn't know which was proper.

'You made me very proud, last night,' he said. 'To be dancing with you at the Dumandee Ball. I wanted to show you off to the whole world.' He shrugged and turned away. He was no good at compliments, no matter how truthful they were. 'It wasn't me. You have to believe me: I could never have done anything like that.'

Greta was staring at her hands. 'Everybody saw the two of you arguing,' she said. 'And they say you climbed into your room to avoid detection.'

'You believe them, then?'

'At the Gatherings we are told that belief is total

commitment. I do not *believe* that you . . . killed the Prime. I simply . . .'

Mathias stood by the window and watched a gull dipping over the roof-tops. 'How can I earn your total commitment?' he asked. 'What must I do?'

'I don't know, Matti. I'm sorry but I . . . Things have changed rapidly, since Dumandee. It appears that Edward will be named at least Prime-Designate, until things become more settled. He is working very hard to keep the clan functioning. He has made many friends by his efforts. Faces are changing too rapidly for me to follow. Captain Anderson has risen with Edward; they complement one another. Sala Pedralis is helping smooth the transitional period, too. I don't think she likes Edward, but she is winning back the dissidents and gaining the clan time. Lucilla Ngota has been disgraced. She won't tell me what happened but she has been suspended from all duties and her staff have been redeployed to cope with the crisis. I have tried to comfort her – the Prime's death has hurt her deeply. Matti, what will they do to you?'

Mathias did not like the news. Sala deserting him – going with the flow, as she liked to say – Edward's rapid rise and, worst of all, Greta's doubts and the fact that she chose to comfort *Lucilla* and not him. 'Just believe in me. Even if only a little. When I'm out of this mess everything else will fall into place. Remember our plans: I will be free again.'

'There have been other changes, too, Matti.' Something in Greta's face made Mathias feel terribly small and vulnerable. 'When father pledged my troth in your name, he did so to bind our two families more closely together. You were going to be Prime one day. He has told me of his own doubts and fears and now he has changed his pledge.

'Matti, I'm so sorry.' She buried her face in her hands as if she wanted to stop the words coming out. 'He has pledged me in the name of Edward Olfarssen-Hanrahan. He signed settlement with Edward's mother this morning. Matti, I'm sorry.'

Mathias was not as surprised as he should have been. In his gut he had known something like this must happen, compounding his loss. He knelt before Greta and took her hand, releasing it in response to their chaperone's soft cough. 'Greta,' he said. 'If I could leave, would you join me?'

'Matti, don't,' she snapped. Then, more softly, she continued, 'My father . . . he has so much to lose. Matti, you are talking ahead of yourself. You must face the Court: innocence wins through. And guilt . . .'

She didn't need to finish. Finally Mathias saw that he had lost everything. He should have seen it sooner and saved Greta from having to go through such an ordeal. He rocked back on his heels, then stood. He walked to the window and watched another gull sliding through the darkening sky.

Behind him, he heard Greta rising to her feet, stepping away from the bed. 'Matti,' she said. 'You're very sweet.' He wanted to jump from the window, but it was locked and he doubted he had the strength left in him to break it. 'Matti, I have to go now. I told Edward to meet me at sunset, we have details to discuss. Matti,' – he turned to face her – 'goodbye.'

Edward. Smiling, laughing, pawing at Greta's breasts. Pulling heavy-duty cables tight around her delicate neck. Pulling them tighter, making her face turn blue and her eyes bug out but she was enjoying it, Mathias knew she was enjoying it and that this was what she had wanted all along. He wanted to get to them, to pull them apart, to carry Greta away from his half-brother, convince her that she wanted only *him*. He struggled to move, but hands gripped his arms, pulled at him, shook him as he watched his love slipping away, strangled by those ancient black leads. Still the hands gripped him, shook him and a voice came across the grey wastes: 'Mathias. *Please*. We have little time.'

He woke and rolled on to his back. He opened his eyes and there was a faint light in the room and the face of Sala Pedralis floating close to his own. 'Sala. What is it?'

He shrugged off the last vestiges of sleep and realized that he had suddenly left everything behind. His grief, his anger, it was all gone. From now onwards he had to look out for himself.

'Come on, Mathias. We have little time.'

He remembered Greta's summary of events beyond the guest-room walls and said, 'So it's *your* turn to question me now, is it? I have no more to tell.'

Sala looked hurt and he added, 'I was told you had changed your allegiance. I was told you were helping Edward secure his throne.'

'I am securing *Newest Delhi*, not Olfarssen. Violent currents have been flowing since the loss

50

of the Prime. Sects and clans fight openly in the streets. If they are not controlled then everything will be chaos. I can only do what I *can*. But that does not mean I like it. Come on. I have transport arranged.' She opened the door. 'Or will you stay here and let Olfarssen take it all?'

Mathias followed her out of the room, pulling the door closed behind him. Two guards stood in the corridor, both staring studiously at the wall. Their gazes barely flickered as Mathias passed by.

As they walked quickly through the corridors and across the Manse gardens Mathias kept expecting to hear voices raised in pursuit, but the night remained still. The guards at the main gate stared right through Mathias, choosing not to see him, and then he was out in the Playa Cruzo, believing at last in what was happening.

'Come on,' said Sala. 'You're not clear yet.'

The streets they followed were empty and it was not long before Mathias realized they were heading for the docks. It made sense: a boat would not have to pass through the unsettled back country where the clans would be at their strongest and Mathias might be recognized by citizens mourning the loss of their Prime.

As they climbed the steps inside West Wall, Mathias thought of his grandfather. He had never heard much of the story, except that the disgraced Prime had fled Newest Delhi under the cover of the night, much as Mathias was doing now. There had been some sort of scandal and his grandfather had fled in an old shuttle, restored in secret in case it should ever be needed. But the scandal had been so great, or the escape so hasty, that the shuttle had been struck down from the skies, ending, finally, the influence of the old ways. Tonight Mathias was fleeing, but there the resemblance ended; he did not expect to be struck down in the sea, he just wanted to be free from all that had happened. March had done well to retain control under the circumstances of his father's demise; he had managed to keep tight rein on the excesses of the transition. Any excesses March had inherited from his father had long been suppressed. As Mathias's feet crunched along the upper reaches of the beach, he felt a sudden affinity with the grandfather he had never met.

Sala stopped ahead of him on the jetty, the dark shape of a barge just visible over her shoulder. She stepped towards Mathias and embraced him. 'I'll pray for you,' she said. 'Maybe someone will hear.'

'Edward will pay for this,' said Mathias. It was a wish more than a threat.

'Edward? You think he killed the Prime? Maybe, but I don't think he would have it in him, he's just capitalising on it. My guess is that one of the clans is responsible. They will make their move on Newest Delhi soon enough and then we will know.'

She released him and nodded at the barge. 'Idi Mondata arranged the boat through his Krishna friends. It will take you to Orlyons, out of Edward's reach. Mathias, you are like a son to me, or a brother . . . I don't know. I'll clear your name, somehow. I'll find out who killed your father and then you will be free to do what you wish. Mathias, look after yourself. Don't be bitter.'

Mathias turned away, confused again. Things

52

should not be like this. A hand reached out to help him on to the boat but he shrugged it off and stepped aboard, clambering over a pile of rope and feeling in his bones the rhythmic beat of the vessel's meth manoeuvring engines. He turned to wave but Sala had vanished. He wondered if he would ever see her again.

As the engines quickened Mathias settled down in the aft cargo hold and tried to get comfortable. He released a long-held breath and slowly the barge edged away from the dock, away from Newest Delhi and into the darkness of night.

# PART TWO

## *MidNight*

# Chapter Five

Kasimir Sukui was not fond of the sea. It was un-
tamed. It followed no internal framework of logic.
It aroused feelings he preferred not to acknowledge:
fear, anger, awe. Fear was perhaps to be expected
– drowning was not something to anticipate in any
other way – but why be angered or awed by slabs of
water, stirred by gravity and by the wind? Kasimir
Sukui disliked such impulses. He was a rational
man.

Facing his fears boldly, he stood at the prow of the
barge and watched the waves. The largest – barely
three metres from trough to tip – were capped with
foam that was green with algae. He tried counting
the waves in an attempt to find some sort of ruling
pattern but there was none and soon he tired of the
activity.

He walked back to the aft hold and sat in his
mahogany chair, under the shelter of a canvas awning. After rummaging in a bag he withdrew a book,
opened it on his lap and wrote down the results of his
counting. He would probably never read this page
of his diary again but he knew that method was the
key to the universe; everything must be recorded,
the failed experiments as well as the successes. This
was science, it had to be carried out in an orderly
manner.

Kasimir Sukui came from the southern fortress city of Alabama, capital of the lands that were ruled by the Andricci clan. He was descended from Expatria's first chief archivist and he had been reared in a lean-to that was crammed with books and diaries, handwritten histories of the first days of the colony and even histories from the Ark voyage that had brought the original colonists from Earth.

Although Sukui did not believe in family precedents – each person must realize their own potential – he recognized that he did not deviate far from what such a tradition might have expected of him. The books had been a formative influence. He had read of inventions and of science and soon, using a borrowed pencil, he had learnt to copy the letters and then whole words.

He had entered the Primal household as a servant but had risen rapidly through the ranks. He had studied the people around him. He had worked out what it was that made people succeed and what it was that made them stay at the same level for a lifetime. Putting his observations to work, he had associated with the right people, he had given his superiors bright ideas and then praised their originality, he had even slept with an ungainly senior vetting officer in order to convince her of his suitability for higher things.

Now, as Prime Salvo Andric's principal adviser, his hard work was finally being rewarded. At last there was a Prime who was open to new ideas. Sukui had bided his time as adviser to three earlier Primes, all of whom had been hostile to innovation, but Salvo Andric professed a vigorous enthusiasm for his people; he often told Sukui that the citizens must benefit first from any advances made under his Primacy. Initially Sukui had been tentative about introducing the technologies about which he had read so much but Salvo had welcomed his innovations and then demanded more. After seven years Salvo Andric was the most popular Prime in Sukui's memory, and the adviser took great pride in his own small part in the triumph of rationality over the earlier ignorance of his nation's leaders.

With Andric's Primacy thoroughly established, Sukui's role had broadened. Now, as well as being Andric's principal adviser, he had sole responsibility for Alabama City's Science Project, directing research, advising the workers, scouting for new talent to revitalise the scheme. The project was the reason for his current barge trip across Mirror Bay. The first colonies established on Expatria had all been situated either on the island of Clermont or to the north, in regions now governed by the Hanrahan clan. Consequently, the greatest hoards of artefacts were located in these regions and Sukui had to organize frequent trading trips, often going himself in order to ensure that prize items were not missed by his juniors.

The terrans had built their technologies to last; early records indicated that this was deliberate, so there would be ample time to set up industries and also, they said in parentheses, in case of tragedy, so that the survivors would not necessarily revert to savagery. Sukui could see that happening to the north, with the fundamentalist cults and their frequent tirades against knowledge; years earlier it had been happening in his own land but Prime Salvo had put a halt to that.

Sukui closed his diary. He had been writing at greater length than intended. He had meant only to record the chaotic motions of the waves, no more. Adjusting the clip of his diamond-shaped skullcap and then straightening the waistline of his grey robe – he had learnt early in his career the importance of appearance – he climbed the steps from the hold and joined the skipper at the helm of the barge.

Clermont was looming large now, far closer than the mainland. Sukui estimated, from experience, that they would be tying up at the docks within twenty-five minutes, give or take three.

The port of Orlyons was a cosmopolitan cluster of buildings, squeezed into a gorge between granitic outcrops. The place was unruly like the sea, but beneath the anarchic exuberance Sukui recognized a framework of order. Of all the places he had visited there was nowhere quite like Orlyons; he often felt that he was close to defining the town's wildness, categorising it, but somehow another quirk would arise and he would start all over again. His diaries were crammed with observations and interpretations of the rabble that was Orlyons.

A yell came from out to sea and Sukui turned to look. Fifty metres beyond the barge there was a tall-sailed catamaran skimming across the waves. The boat was an impressive design, its twin hulls polished and tapering to knife-edge prows. It was a vessel constructed expressly for speed. The boatbuilder was a skilled individual.

'The barge's skipper and five crewmen were lining the seaward railing, along with Sukui's two juniors, viewing the spectacle. As the catamaran slipped away the skipper returned to the barge's untended helm. 'The twin-hull is an efficient design,' said Sukui. 'Tell me, who is its creator?'

'Ah, Sukui-san,' said the skipper. Sukui liked the -*san* to be appended to his name; it added an unthinking respect, a subliminal acknowledgement of his status. 'The cat is Matt Hanrahan's. That's his fun-boat, he says he wants to go faster than the cutter-birds one day. Ha! That one's the Matt III, the first two fell apart. Ha ha!' The skipper had been drinking, but Sukui knew from experience that he handled the boat better when in such a condition.

Sukui walked back to his sheltered seat. So this was Mathias Hanrahan. Sukui knew the stories: that Hanrahan had killed his father and then been driven from the throne or, as others said, that he had fled *from* his father's killer. That had happened more than three years earlier. Sukui had heard much of Hanrahan's achievements since he had fled to Orlyons; much of it was no more than rumour, but he had clearly made a success of his life in exile if he could wreck two catamarans and still afford a third.

Sukui made a note in his diary and then settled back to pass the fifteen minutes – give or take a minute – until they would tie up at the Orlyons docks.

The streets of Orlyons were narrow and dense with people and animals. Sukui edged through the crowds, walking in the gutter where the flow was less urgent. He had left the barge as soon as it had docked. His juniors were capable of supervising the disembarkation of the delegation's provisions and trading stock.

Orlyons was a good place to trade. The supply of artefacts was steady and varied and the vendors were unaffected by northern fundamentalism. On this trip, Sukui's delegation had brought the usual exotic foodstuffs from the cooler south and a plentiful supply of money, but this time they had brought weaponry, too. Sukui felt uneasy about trading in arms – they so easily gave power to extremists – but the Orlyons collective council were in favour of the trade and this was one area in which Sukui had no influence over his Prime. On several occasions Salvo Andric had even tried to persuade *Sukui* to carry a gun, but each time he had refused; he felt far safer unarmed.

The street opened out into a square and here Sukui had more room to move. The hotel was only minutes distant. His juniors would stay with the trading stock in a harbourside rooming house, but Sukui always stayed in comfort. It was a part of his role.

He booked in and placed his small bag on the bed. The room had a basin, so he stripped to the waist and sluiced himself with cold water from the faucet.

Outside, the sky was darkening. Soon it would be MidNight.

Years before, Sukui had discovered Orlyons's idiosyncratic view of the calendar. From his reading he had learnt that the human brain was adapted to a 24-hour cycle: awake for sixteen, asleep for the remaining eight. The histories said there had been trouble adapting to Expatria's 14-hour day: some of the first colonists had even tried to impose a 28-hour system, working through two days and a night and sleeping for the remaining night. But the pressures of light and dark had proven greater than the so-called internal clock and the norm of waking an hour before dawn and then retiring an hour or so after dusk had taken over. Orlyons, however, had kept to its own version of the 28-hour system. In Orlyons alternate nights were different: *Night* was for sleeping, usually dusk to dawn; *MidNight* was for partying. Most of the port's population followed this system and consequently the town contained a network of drinking dens, gambling parlours, discothèques and many more houses of high ill-repute.

Now Kasimir Sukui prided himself on being a man of rationality, a man of science. As such, he had to recognize that his intellect was carried in a vehicle that was entirely animal in origins. Seeing the logic of this observation, long ago he had accepted that, like all human beings, he had his vices. He had urges that, if unsatisfied, would impair his functioning. Being a rational man, he looked after himself, and there was no better place on all of Expatria to look after the occasional animal urge than the port of Orlyons. Glancing through his window at the darkening streets, he tried to decide where he would go first on this, his first MidNight for five months.

One of his vices was gambling – it was so easy for logic to triumph over the probabilities of most games of chance – but that could wait. He decided, first, to call on Mono. She was a hard worker, something Sukui respected in anyone, regardless of profession. Mono was perhaps his favourite of all Orlyons vices.

She was the first woman he had been with in near to three months.

Kasimir Sukui's breathing rapidly returned to normal; he always kept himself in good physical condition, it was the rational thing to do.

He had found her easily. The bartender at Salomo's, her usual rendezvous, had told him she was in her room in the Gentian Quarter. Sukui knew her room well. 'She is an acquaintance,' he had told the bartender. 'I will visit.'

She hadn't changed since his last stay at Orlyons. Her olive-brown complexion was pure as ever, her hair long and straight and a black that was blue when caught by the sun. Her face had lit up when she saw who was at the door. It had been a long time, but she had remembered how he liked her to treat him. Sex was a bodily function just like any other. Sukui did not like women who lost control in their passion, the ones who moaned and begged and clawed at a man's back. Mono was always quiet and dignified, only occasionally did she lose her poise and cry out. This time she had cried out, towards the end; Sukui took it as a compliment.

Lying slightly apart from Mono's tiny form, he studied the contours of her face. She looked composed in her sleep, content with the ways of her world. It made him feel good to think that he could make another person look so at peace. It made him feel whole again.

He had often considered the option of taking a permanent companion back to Alabama City with him. Perhaps it was the greying and thinning of his hair that made him think in these terms now. He had never shared a bed for more than simple gratification before and the thought of a face as contented as Mono's now was, beside him each morning, was a source of great temptation.

Mono twitched, her whole body jerking in her sleep. It was an animal movement and it reminded Sukui of the impracticalities that had always deterred him. On at least one earlier occasion he had almost asked her to return with him, but he had stopped himself. It could never work: a constant companion for a man so accustomed to his solitude. It was fine on occasion, something he needed. But she would be a distraction, he would be thinking of her when he should be working, he would be constantly tired from her attentions. He had always concluded that he would be losing far more than he gained.

But, lying by her side, sensing her stir and stretch, everything seemed different. Maybe the time had arrived.

She put a hand on his chest and kissed his shoulder. 'Sukui-san,' she murmured. 'It's been a long time. You know how to direct a woman's passions.'

Sukui felt a surge of emotions that he would normally have rejected, but now he sorted them, tried to itemise exactly how he felt. Mono often made him feel this way, helpless and glad about it. 'Mono, you are very accomplished.' He took a calming breath. 'Mono, would you come—'

She sat and then climbed off the thin mattress that was her bed. She didn't appear to have heard him, she didn't appear to recognize the effort he was having to make to squeeze the words out and he stopped helplessly. She wrapped herself in a purple kimono and tied it at the waist with a cream obi. His passion spent, Sukui could assess her beauty more objectively now and still he was impressed. She moved quickly around her room and then, seeing Sukui still lying on her mattress, she threw one of his shoes at him.

Dressing, he realized that it could never work. He admired her looks, her grace, and also her discipline and dedication to her work, but underneath it all there was the raw edge of the streets. There was a wildness that Sukui associated with the most basic elements of nature. Like the sea, Mono controlled herself but she could never be tamed; a man could sail across the sea but always in the knowledge that he might easily be swallowed into its depths.

Kasimir Sukui shuddered and pinned his skullcap into position, suddenly glad that he had stopped himself from inviting Mono back to Alabama City.

'Shall we go?'

Mono was by the door and Sukui nodded, suddenly aware that MidNight had been happening without him. 'Yes,' he said 'Let's go.'

# Chapter Six

Two hours into MidNight the streets were alive. It was a phenomenon Kasimir Sukui had documented repeatedly in his diaries. It was a synergy, a multiplication of parts. The crowds of the streets of Orlyons were like an animal, alive and eager. Hungry.

In the Gentian Quarter the crowd-animal was nervous, twitching and jinking at the slightest provocation. Mono tugged at Sukui's hand. Her grip was delicate and he felt that he might lose her, at any moment, to the crowd. She led him along a smooth pavement, across the Rue de la Patterdois, and through a jumble of stalls, set up to sell pleasures to the night. Passing through the Leaning Arch they skirted around a knife fight, ignoring a tout who offered them miserly odds on the outcome. 'Three-twenty for a cut throat,' he called, but Sukui was not interested, the variables were too great and the likelihood of a rigged contest was high.

Mono released his hand and disappeared.

Looking around, Sukui recognized a landmark: across the street was the drinking house known as Salomo's. He crossed over, pushed through the door and surveyed the packed room for his companion.

Mono stood in a doorway on the far side of the bar. She nodded and then let the door close. She was like that. If he had wanted her to hang on his arm in public she would have charged him more. He did not mind about that, he was not vain. He knew what she was like when they were alone and that was enough.

Sukui made his way across to the door. It was to be a closed school, but buying him in would be no problem for Mono. His throat felt dry already. The smoke in the bar was thick and a proportion of it was heavily narcotic. He entered the back-room and closed the door behind him, breathing deeply in the clearer air and wishing his head would stop swimming.

The room was more crowded than Sukui would have preferred and the game was already in progress. A space had been made at the table and a chair squeezed into it.

Sukui took his seat and studied the players.

There were four of them. One was old and balding; his face grey and swollen and netted with burst capillaries. This was Salomo – Sukui had played him before. His game was sloppy and he was easily distracted; he was there because of who he was.

Opposite Sukui was a younger man, curly black hair, stubble, the physique of a labourer. This one was laughing and merry and needed continual reminding of when it was his turn. Despite this, he had a good stack of coins in front of him; Sukui was reminded that the game involved luck as well as skill.

The third player was tall and her features were pointed and tightly controlled. Her eyes followed every move, every flash of expression on her opponents' faces. She had already acknowledged

Sukui's presence with a brief, appraising glance.

His fourth opponent was mature and strong-featured, a pragmatist, a grafter. This one would take no risks and would miss no openings. He would probably break even on most occasions.

Sukui opened his notebook and marked down his preliminary observations in the margin of the previous page, keeping his paper consumption to the minimum. Over the years he had learnt the value of first impressions in the statistical science of gambling. Technique was intimately tied to a player's approach to life and this was one of the first things that could be observed. Sukui closed his book and sat upright. He would join the game when the round was complete. He watched the play. He felt confident tonight.

There were seventeen other people gathered in the room. Sukui knew that he must keep his cards close to his chest; he had studied the tactics of deceit closely on his visits to Orlyons. He knew few of the faces, other than Mono's. She was like a firefly, full of energy, flitting from person to person about the room. She was entirely different in company – her wildness was more evident. Eventually she settled behind the young man, opposite Sukui. He was not surprised when she put a hand on the man's shoulder, he knew she maintained other relationships, both business and private. He had never pursued the matter, it was irrelevant. Still, he felt pleased that he had not allowed himself to ask her back to Alabama City. He saw it now as no more than a sexual response, an emotional erection. He returned his attention to the game. The round was over.

The players each nodded formally to Sukui and then Salomo threw the stones into the centre of the table. Each player followed in turn and Sukui threw the final combination. This part was purely luck and it went the way of Mono's manfriend. Salomo dealt him four cards, face up, face down, up, down. The combination bore potential. The man glanced at his concealed pair, tossed the face-up jake into the centre and then turned back to his noisy group of friends.

The cards went round until Sukui received his own, a modest configuration. He discarded a red nine, probabilities flashing across his mind. The stones went round again, the players shaped their hands and Sukui felt his own intensity grow as the game moved out of the realm of luck and into that of logic.

As the round progressed, Sukui made brief calculations in the margins of his notebook, noting the moves of his opponents on a fresh page. Salomo was the first to put money on the table, even though his hand was unlikely to come to anything. The pragmatist to Sukui's right followed with a matching bet, the safest move. Two rounds later, Salomo withdrew.

The sharp-faced woman played correctly, even cleverly, but her starting hand had handicapped her. She recovered her stake money on a side-bet with an onlooker and then modestly withdrew.

For a first game, the tension was high. Sukui revelled in it, sitting calmly and observing how it affected the people around him. He knew that some players believed the adrenalin sharpened their performance, but in his experience they were deluding themselves. Rationality was the key.

As the game progressed, Sukui became more aware of how it was being moulded by the absent-minded actions of the young man opposite. Casually he would throw away a card that was almost the one Sukui needed; sometimes he even placed bets without counting out how much money he was putting down. The pragmatist would always trail behind, copying and shadowing, never trying to seize control.

Sukui's own hand was maturing well. By his calculations he just had to stall the opposition for another two rounds, maybe three.

The pragmatist withdrew, his losses moderately heavy. Sukui caught his opponent's eye and discarded a red three and a black twelve. 'It is your move,' he said. 'Please, would you tell me your name? I am Sukui-san.'

His opponent laughed and drew a card from the pack. 'Sukui? I've heard the name. Me? I'm Matt Hanrahan.' He threw a pair of red aces on to the discard pile.

Sukui's surprise at his opponent's name was blown away by the sight of the two aces. They were just what he needed! But nobody would discard a pair at this stage . . . Was Hanrahan playing to his own devious rules? Sukui scanned his notes, tracking the game's progress. The aces would give him victory.

But this was *Hanrahan*. Why had he offered the pair to Sukui?

Sukui was not accustomed to such a situation. Logic told him to accept the pair and follow his calculations. But logic also told him that Hanrahan was intelligent, his game was good, and no-one could throw away a pair at a time like this!

Sukui drew a card from the pack. It was no good. He should have taken the aces. He felt humiliated.

Hanrahan was laughing with his friends, his back to the table. Sukui cleared his throat. Then he knocked on the table. 'Mister Hanrahan,' he said. 'I believe the game is still in progress.'

Hanrahan turned back to the table and glanced at his cards. 'Hey, did I do *that*?' He slapped himself on the forehead and laughed. Then he drew a blind card, sorted his hand and laid it out on the table. 'Mister Sukui,' he said quietly, 'I believe the game is no longer in progress.'

Kasimir Sukui remained calm as Hanrahan sorted the money before him. He scanned his notebook, spotted where he had begun to lose control. The money was immaterial, Sukui's benefactor was wealthy. 'We will play again?' asked Sukui. 'MidNight has three more hours to pass.'

They played again. Salomo withdrew early, along with the pragmatist, who managed to recoup some of his earlier losses in a side-bet. The night progressed and Hanrahan appeared to pay little attention, yet he always managed to slip through Sukui's net, using moves no serious player would ever use.

When the back-room at Salomo's finally emptied, the sky was lightening and the streets had returned to their normal, workaday bustle. Sukui felt drained. He had not lost so heavily in six years. He could not work out where he had gone wrong, why his system should fail him so drastically.

Standing outside the bar, he heard a voice he now knew and, without thinking, he hurried over and caught Hanrahan by the arm. Mathias was still laughing and, in the morning light, his face looked warm and open. He did not look at all like a man who could so casually humiliate Sukui and take all of his money.

'Please, Mathias,' said Sukui. 'Will you tell me how you did it? What system did you use?'

Hanrahan shrugged Sukui's hand from his arm. 'System? No, Kasimir, I just played the game. That's all. Listen, you play well, you're just a bit *stiff*, that's all. Are you stuck for money or something? This isn't your place, I know how it is. Here,' – he held out a handful of money – 'take it back. I don't play for the winnings.'

Sukui could take no more. He turned and strode away from the young Hanrahan, keeping his shoulders square and proud. How could he say he had 'just played the game'? It was a blatant lie. No-one could win like that without some sort of logical understanding of the game's dynamics. *No-one*. Sukui paused to make a note in his book. A rational man could learn from any situation and Kasimir Sukui knew that there were few as rational as himself.

Calmer, he headed for the docks. MidNight was over and now he must return to his duties.

There was a stall on the Rue de la Patterdois that Kasimir Sukui had known for a long time. It was invariably in a different place, sometimes even on a side street, but he could always locate it. The

73

proprietor, a bloated, red-faced woman by the name of Alya Kik, was Sukui's best contact in the port of Orlyons. If she had nothing of interest she knew it and did not waste his time in trying to sell him bric-à-brac; instead she would tell him where he *might* just find something he would wish to purchase. Even if she made a deal with him she would pass on this sort of information and Sukui treasured the relationship.

'Alya!' he called, spotting her among the stalls in the Playa de l'Or. 'Alya, you are trying to avoid me!' He had been walking with Sanjit Borodin and Egon Petrovsky, his two juniors, but now he gestured for them to stay in the background, ready to assist when details became tedious but out of his way all the same. That was how Sukui liked to work.

'Ah! Sukui-san, you old rogue. You've not been to Orlyons for a time, now. It's *you* who's doing the avoiding, you rogue.' The banter formed a framework to their communication. Sukui was never sure if he was putting it on for Alya, or she for him; either way, he was pleased to see her.

'What's this "Old Rogue" then? You're old enough to be my mother.' He laughed with the woman. 'To business, Alya. I have little in the way of time, on this occasion – my lord likes to keep his advisers by his side in periods such as these.'

'The conflict is serious, then?'

Alya was a tough and experienced trader; already she was probing for information, anything to boost her importance in her own circles. The border conflicts between clans supported by the Andricci and those supported by the Hanrahans were minor and seemingly interminable; Sukui did not think they would last. Fighting was primitive and, under his own guidance, Salvo Andric was leading Expatria away from such sources of waste. 'No, Alya,' said Sukui. 'My lord is merely prudent. Now, to business?'

Alya had little for Sukui and she knew it. He took some permi-bulbs and some documented micro-circuits off her and paid with cash. She looked like she needed it. 'You might see Lui Tsang, on your way,' said Alya, as Sukui turned to leave. 'By the Leaning Arch. Tell him I say hello.'

Sukui muttered his thanks and left. Lui Tsang. After a few paces, he paused and noted the name down in his diary, along with the details of his deal with Alya Kik.

He found Tsang's stall in Greene Gardens, a good distance from the Leaning Arch. Sukui knew from experience that location was a fluid concept in Orlyons.

'Alya Kik said you might have something to sell me,' said Sukui, looking over the stall's wares and frowning. 'I fear she may have been playing a minor joke at my expense.'

'Sukui-san, right?' The young trader was not fooled by Sukui's attitude. 'She said you were in town. I have these . . .' He gestured to a stack of circuit-discs.

'Plentiful.'

'These . . .' A selection of crudely ground lenses, clearly not the terran artefacts he was trying to pass them off as.

'Fake.'

'This . . .' An assortment of fibre optics set atop a large coil of heavy-duty power cable, something that interested Sukui.

'Commonplace.'

'These . . .' A good range of tools, including a soldering pen and a small TV unit that appeared intact.

'Hmmm. I would need to test it, before agreeing a price.' He knew it was not worth feigning indifference at these last offerings. 'But still I am disappointed. I had hoped . . .'

Tsang drew a box, about thirty centimetres by ten by ten, from under his stall. 'Sukui-san,' he said. 'I was keeping this, but . . . I know you are a special customer. All the merchandisers of Orlyons come awake when it is known you are in town. See here.' The box was made of black plastic and there were switches and dials along one of the longer sides. Tsang activated the machine and held his hand behind it.

And instantly another hand appeared above the device, hovering in the air. The new hand was naturally coloured but faint in the bright sunlight of Greene Gardens. 'It is better in the dark,' said Tsang. 'Then it glows like the hand of an angel.' The hand moved and then vanished in a line that advanced across it; Tsang was moving his hand out of range of the device's receiver and, for a moment, only his fingers hung in ghostly replica. Then they were gone. 'It is fully documented, of course. What is your offer?' asked the young trader.

'A Toshiba trifacsimile,' said Sukui. He had read the device's name on the front of the box. 'I can see why you like it, it is a pretty toy, although it has little practical use. But we have trifacsimiles in Alabama City – the Lord Salvo Andric's nephew has one in his playroom and even *he* tires of his.' Sukui felt momentarily sorry for Lui Tsang. The youth had clearly been convinced by his lies: if he knew the device's *name* then he *must* be telling the truth. Sukui wanted the trifacsimile, more for what he could learn from it than from any application it might have. He had come across references to these devices in the technical literatures back in Alabama City; having one to experiment with might be another step forward in uniting the theories of ancient technology that had become his life's work.

'Let me see. I will take everything.' Sukui knew from experience that job-lots came cheaper than buying items individually, and this way he did not have to reveal his real interest in the Toshiba unit. Sukui struck a favourable deal and then gestured for Sanjit Borodin to come forward and finalise the details.

The day's trading proved a moderate success. The stock of exchange goods and money was largely replaced by the delegation's acquisitions and Sukui was pleased with his work. As the streets darkened, traders closed their stalls and others opened new ones. Although tonight was not MidNight there was still a demand for some of the dealers in pleasure that Orlyons supported so lucratively.

'Hey, Sukui-san,' called a voice. 'Come, see what I can offer you.'

It was Chet Alpha, host of the travelling peep-show and General Purveyor of Pleasure (Most

Tastes, No Surcharge), as his little trailer's placard proclaimed.

'Fine quality, certified clean,' he said, hanging an arm across Sukui's shoulders. 'I checked 'em myself.' He laughed drunkenly and Sukui stepped clear of his sweating arm. 'Sukui-san, I know you're a man of taste. Only the best. Come and see.'

Sukui was tired and he did not like Alpha, especially when he was drunk. But he *did* have a certain reputation. 'I want nothing myself,' said Sukui. 'But maybe you could visit Alabama City. The Lord Andric might look upon you favourably. He is a patron of the arts, you know.'

'Hey, I'll do that. I've lost trade since I stopped working Newest Delhi, you know. That Prime Edward, he's not keen on the arts, you see. At least his *wife* isn't! No, I don't go there now. Too dangerous.'

Alpha straightened, and shook Sukui's hand. 'Yes, I'll come down to your Alabama City, sir. Maybe I'll even set up base down there, the way this place is going. It's that Hanrahan, the one who killed the Prime; now that *he's* here, things are no good. They're after him, you see. They were asking me about him and I told them, "Look," I told them. "He's nothing to do with me," I told them. "He can—"'

'*Who* is after Hanrahan?'

'I recognized them from Newest Delhi,' said Alpha. '*Trade*. You know. They were in the Guard then. I think they still are. Only, yesterday . . . You know who I saw yesterday?'

'Who?'

78

'Name's Ngota,' said Alpha. 'Lucilla Ngota. I reckon things are going to turn bad, round here. Reckon it's time I moved the show. Alabama City, yeah!'

Sukui left Alpha to celebrate the prospect of moving base. He paused in the light of an open tavern window and made a few notes in his diary. Lucilla Ngota. He knew the name. He smiled; things were certainly becoming interesting in the port of Orlyons. He noted another comment in his diary and then walked on, through the darkening streets.

# *Chapter Seven*

Mathias had misjudged Kasimir Sukui's reaction to defeat. He'd offered him money – he knew what it was like to be penniless and foreign in the port of Orlyons – but that had been a bad move. He knew that he should have read the situation more accurately, but he was tired, it had been a long MidNight. Too much concentration always did this to Mathias, left him feeling fuzzy and slow. Sukui shouldn't have kept on playing as he had. Still, Mathias felt guilty; Mono was fond of the old scientist, he should have been easier on him.

What he had said was true, though. Sukui was too *stiff*. He'd spent the night writing notes and missing half of the action; Mathias had even thrown him a few chances – for Mono – but it had been no good. Sukui was a moderate player, he probably broke even more often than not but he would never be a grandmaster, like Ilya Borosche or Françime Boucher. Françime had taught Mathias most of what he knew; she had said he was a good learner, he had a *feel* for the game. Sukui did not have the feel.

Mathias turned away from Salomo's and headed for the room he kept by the docks. He didn't like confrontations, they unsettled him. He hunched his shoulders and walked.

'Winning again, eh, Matt?' It was Vera-Lynne Perse.

Mathias turned. 'Please, Vera-Lynne. I'm tired. You know my answer and I still think you have a nice face, OK?'

'You're cute too, Mathias. Or too cute. No, I just saw you and we're walking in the same direction.' She fell into step by his side.

When Mathias had fled Newest Delhi the barge captain had clearly felt his obligation was over as soon as they docked in Orlyons. Mathias had known no-one until he met Vera-Lynne.

His first night in Orlyons had been a Mid-Night, something he had never heard of before. That night, he had wandered through the maze of streets, confused yet excited by the currents of energy that flowed through the town. There had been people everywhere, drunk and high and laughing and shouting, every single one of them a part of this thing called Mid-Night. Mathias's spirits had lifted themselves and eventually he'd stopped by a huge street fire and felt that maybe he was a small part of what was happening.

Vera-Lynne Perse had found him by that street fire. She had warmed her hands on his chest and then engulfed him in a piercing kiss. He had never been so close to a woman before and he had been stunned, too slow to react. Then she had paused and drawn her face away from his. 'Ooh!' she had squeaked. 'I thought you were . . .' Then she had kissed him again. She had taught him a great deal in the ensuing weeks. He had learnt the ways of the world from Vera-Lynne, and also the ways of some of its inhabitants.

Since those first weeks they had drifted. They had learnt more about each other and more about themselves and finally Mathias had moved into his small room in Westward Street. 'It's closer to the fishing,' he had told her. She had agreed that it was the best thing. For his fishing, of course.

The woman beside him, as they walked through Orlyons, had changed. She was more controlled now, less given to partying. She had become involved with politics, what she called the musical underground. 'We're free to play our instruments,' she would say, 'but only in the streets.' 'We play our tunes,' she would say, 'but only on this island of Clermont.' 'We sing our songs,' she would say, 'but we don't have a voice.' The underground wanted to play wherever there was an audience, but wherever they played they stirred up trouble. The bars and clubs simply didn't want them. The underground wanted to get on to Clermont's collective council, too, they wanted street politics to run all of the island, not just the port of Orlyons.

Vera-Lynne Perse wanted to change the world, and instantly, but Mathias had never been quite sure *how*. He doubted whether Vera-Lynne did either; she was just kissing a stranger at MidNight and hoping she could muddle her way through, as she always had.

'You won at the cards, did you?'

She had tried this angle before. Next she would mention Françime.

'You were taught by the best,' she continued. 'Françime Boucher was unbeatable at one time. I opposed her only once. She took everything. One learns, like that.'

'No, Vera-Lynne. Not me.'

She looked at him with her hurt expression. Once, he had found that attractive – she wanted only to be 'won over' – but now his response was a mere echo of what he had once felt.

'Look, Vera, I *know* Françime is on the collective council. I know she has sympathies with people like us, from when she *was* one of us. And yes, I know I still see her occasionally. But she reached where she is by ignoring outside pressures, by putting *herself* forwards. I can't influence her, Vera. You should know that.' He shrugged. 'And anyway, I've left all that behind. I don't want to get involved, it doesn't do any good. That's one thing Orlyons has taught me: whatever the people at the top may think, they don't run things, life goes on whatever they decide. You're wasting your time, Vera-Lynne. Why don't you just enjoy life? I didn't see you at MidNight.'

'You could at least *try*,' said Vera-Lynne. 'Everybody should have the chance to hear the new music. It feeds the soul. You do have influence, Matt, you just don't want to use it. You were scared of it in Newest Delhi – I've heard your stories, Matt, I can make my own interpretations – and now you're scared of it in Orlyons. You haven't changed one bit, Matt. Not where it matters. You're still the same irresponsible *boy* you were.'

Vera-Lynne hurried away.

Mathias didn't understand. She had no reason to let go at him like that. She must know that he could do nothing; what made her think he had any influence in Orlyons? That sort of thing was far behind him, now.

He didn't know what to think. He decided to look for Mono; at least *she* would not confront him.

'Hey, Slide!' He had spotted a friend standing in the mouth of a narrow alley. Slide was the best trombonist on the island, good with the mouth-organ, too. 'Have you seen Mono? I'm looking for her.'

Slide shook his head. 'Guess she's somewhere in Gentian Quarter, hawking vee, I guess.' Slide was spaced out; MidNight had clearly been a good one for him. Mathias set off for the Gentian Quarter, hoping Mono hadn't found a client yet. He wanted to talk.

Mathias had met Mono soon after his arrival in Orlyons. When Vera-Lynne had still been into partying, Mono had been one of the group she mixed with. The two women were musicians and when they weren't jamming or partying they were arguing about the blues and the new music and why the clubs wouldn't let them play.

Mono had always blamed the underground. Songs like *Paragon of the Dead* and *Killing Mothers is Fun* (Parts I and III) were what put people off; singers saying 'If you believe in yourself wreck something' were the problem. Now, even traditional music was banished to the streets. Vera-Lynne always said she was missing the point, but she never seemed to say what the point was. Mono just wanted to play her stately old Gibson Semi-A, and sing a few soulful phrases. Vera-Lynne wanted to fight, her saxophone was a weapon and she screamed through it at anyone who would listen.

Mono was a real artiste, she had a natural gift for her music, she could make that old Gibson sing, she could make it weep, she could make it tell any story she wanted. She would spend every spare moment crouched over her guitar, working at an awkward phrase, testing new combinations, rearranging the old. Always, she was extending her range, broadening her grasp. One evening in her room in the Gentian Quarter, when Mathias was almost drunk and Mono was bending the strings wildly, trying to perfect a difficult interchange, Mathias had told her he could never work at something like that, he just couldn't. Mono had taken a swig from his mug of vodka-dry and said, 'No, you couldn't, could you?' Mathias had gone back to his drink and Mono to her practising.

Vera-Lynne had pushed them together. Not long after Mathias had found his room by the docks, she had accused him of becoming a recluse. 'You're too good to waste,' she had told him.

Mono had turned up at his room that night. 'Can I come in?' she had asked. Mathias knew her from Vera-Lynne's parties but he had been surprised to see her there. He let her in and pretty soon she went to work on him. Then she stopped. 'It's no good,' she said. Then she explained that Vera-Lynne had paid her the union rate – Mathias knew Mono's line of work: she needed to support her music – and asked her to seduce Mathias. Mono was upset but

Mathias found it hilarious and resolved to hire a call-boy for Vera-Lynne the very next day.

When Mono had stopped crying on his chest Mathias had asked her why she hadn't carried on. Wasn't it her job?

'I will, if you want,' she had said. 'But you're a friend, it's . . . different. It shouldn't be like that. If we fucked you'd just be like all the others. Or maybe not, maybe you'd be *more* than all the others. Then where would I be?' She seemed desperate. 'Will you give me some space? I like you too much, I don't want to complicate things.'

Of course he had given her the space. They had grown closer, but never in a physical sense. Under Mono's restrictions, Mathias felt different to all the others. He didn't resent her clients, not even the ones like Sukui, whom Mono tried especially hard for. He had known of Sukui long before the card game; Mono said he was like her father had been, starched and withdrawn but, beneath it all, vulnerable.

Mono had taught Mathias to play the slap drums and soon he had constructed his own set of over-sized bongos from a pair of gin-shells and some pigskin from a stall on the Patterdois. She told him his rhythm was good but his concentration poor, he would have to work at it. He never did, but he was good enough to back Mono's loose af-filiation of buskers, the Monotones.

Passing through Greene Gardens, Mathias heard the familiar sound. Flute, sax and, as he drew closer, the gentle whisper of Mono's guitar. 'Mama gonna sell my soul,' she sang, breaking in on a saxophone improvisation and sounding almost as if it was an accident; Mathias knew how long they had practised the timing of that passage. 'But my papa done sold it before.' They were well into the third movement of the song, one of the longest in the current set. 'Mama gon' sell my so-oul.' There was a crowd of twenty or so passers-by; others looked but didn't pause. They were enjoying it, Mathias could tell by their faces and by the pile of coins and fruit in the Monotones' collecting hat.

Mono spotted Mathias and smiled. This was the music, this was what life was about. Mathias settled back to listen, the morning's confrontations behind him.

When the song finally wound down, Mathias kept his eyes closed a moment or two longer, just to let the buzz run itself down in his head, the music was that good. 'Matt, Matt!' Mono was kissing his eyelids, tugging at his folded hands. 'Matt, we've got a gig. Salomo says we can play next MidNight in his club. He says he knows we're worth it, he says he's doing it just so he doesn't have to come out on the streets to hear us. Matt, we've got ourselves a gig!'

There was no containing Mono when she was this excited. She pulled Mathias to his feet and led him running across to Milly and Katsushita, flute and sax, and said, 'I've told him, Milly, Kats. I've told him and he says . . .' she paused and looked at Mathias, then her face broke and she laughed with him.

'He hasn't said a word because you haven't shut up since Sal said "Yes,"' finished Milly. 'You free for the rhythm section, Matt? We want a solid sound – Mono'll need holding back if she's any like this.'

'Yeah, right.' Mathias was surprised to be asked; he hadn't thought he was that good, and anyway his mind had been off in another direction. 'Mono,' he said. 'I've been thinking over what you said about the Semi-A, about it needing more guts. I don't want to mess with the body, it's too good.' Neither did Mono, but she wanted more sound from her guitar, it was too often drowned out by the 'tones and Mono fronted the band because she *wanted* to front the band; she didn't want drowning out. 'There's a guy with some books I checked up, down on San Clemente. I found out some interesting stuff and I think we can rig your guitar with some kind of electronic amplification. I've . . . experimented with something similiar before and I've tracked down the parts through Alya Kik. I think it's what you're looking for.'

Mono's face was all the answer he needed. 'We'll try it,' she said. 'Yes, we'll try it.' Then her expression changed. 'Hey, Matt. There was somebody looking for you. Asking questions. Slide said they had northern accents and they called you Mathias, not just Matt. He said they were probably friends' – Mono's expression faltered – 'but you'd better go easy, Matt: they might not be.'

On his arrival in Orlyons, Mathias had found that he had to feed himself for the first time in his life. He had no masked servants to tend to him, no kitchens of top-class chefs to feed him, no Home Secretary to

88

organize his domestic routine. He had only himself.

He was smart, though, he could mend things and make things and sell them from stalls, he could fake terran artefacts along with the best of them; with Vera-Lynne's help he had established himself easily. It was his days in the Mondata fishing boats that proved most useful, however. In Orlyons there was a steady demand for anyone who could handle a boat or a line or, best of all, the trawlers' vast purse-seine nets. Mathias could do all three and had never been short of work.

That afternoon, after Mono told him of the Mono-tones' impending gig, Mathias skippered one of the big cats out of Orlyons for a night's fishing. The sea was calm, as ever, but the undercurrent had backed and was bringing cold waters up along the coast from the south. The fish were less abundant, but the cooler waters favoured the terran introductions and it was these that were the most valuable.

Repeatedly, they lay the purse-seine in a wide circle, winched its bottom closed and then hauled it up between the cat's twin hulls; since Mathias had introduced catamarans to the local fisherpeople there had been a large reduction in the capsizes that had been common before. That afternoon the catch was moderate, lots of blue bass – Idi would have been proud – lots of doggies and a few mawfish. Then, as night drew in around the boat, Mathias set his halogen lanterns over the water and wired them into the cat's power-cells, charged during the day by the motion of the waves. The catch was good, that night. The profit would be high, after the boat-owner and docking dues had been paid.

Sitting with his feet over the edge of the port hull, Mathias watched the sun climb slowly from the sea. It was morning and they were not long from docking at Orlyons. Mathias tried to estimate how long it would take them but gave up; it was too much work. Staring at the waves, he wondered if he would ever see his old friends again. At one time it had mattered to him, they were all he had, but the years had faded his memories. He had a new life now.

Mono had been worried by the stories of people asking around Orlyons about him. She thought they might be agents of the Hanrahan clan, out to seize him and take him back. At one time he would have agreed, but not now.

Back when Mathias had been under close arrest, Idi had been right. The new authorities did not know how to handle the situation. Edward had known that he couldn't allow a trial – they had no evidence – and he couldn't simply keep Mathias locked away while he stole the Primacy.

So he had been allowed to escape.

Sala, in her efforts to keep Newest Delhi from falling into chaos, had gone along; maybe it had even been her idea – it would smooth the transition and, at the same time, ensure that Mathias could escape to some sort of freedom.

From the security of Orlyons, Mathias could see how neat the plot to let him flee had been. To any outsider, it would be apparent that he was the guilty party. Why else would he run? At the time, there had been no other option, but now, even Mathias saw that it had cast him in an unfair light. He could never return to Newest Delhi.

Presently, he could make out the docks. He stood and stretched. Other skippers would be hurrying about at this stage, but Mathias was not like that. His crew was experienced – the best fisherpeople in Orlyons queued up to work under Mathias – and he preferred to let them do their own thing. He had never had any problems working this way, so he joined the crew, sorting the ice-boxes ready for unloading.

Sukui was on the docks, watching Mathias unload his boat and sign chitties for a number of traders. Mathias did what he could to occupy some more time but Sukui waited patiently, writing the occasional note in his small book.

'Sukui-san,' said Mathias, finally, clambering out of the cat. 'I hope your visit has been successful.'

Sukui nodded slowly. 'I am told that you designed these twin-hulled vessels. Your talents have been noted.'

Mathias didn't know quite what to make of Sukui's genial approach. 'Thanks,' he said. 'They're a lot more stable than the old ones. You need that when you have a catch like this.' He gestured at the remaining crates of iced fish waiting to be wheeled away from the docks. 'The sea was generous this time.'

'You have an affinity with the sea.' Sukui nodded and visibly stopped himself from opening his diary to make a note. 'That is not a characteristic we share.'

'The sea's always helped me think.' They began to walk. 'I used to spend a lot of time by the sea, when I was in Newest Delhi. If I ever wanted to

91

get away I just made for the cliffs.' He sighed. 'That's a long way back, now.'

Sukui gave Mathias a quizzical look.

'I know,' said Mathias. 'Everybody who knows who I am eventually asks me the same question. No, I didn't kill my father. The Primacy didn't matter that much to me. I . . .' he faltered. 'The stories aren't true.'

'In Alabama City we have a Project,' said Sukui. 'There are many people of a certain type. We are scientists. We have the favour of the Lord Salvo Andric, Prime of Alabama City. We work in many fields but our main goal is to restore understanding of the ancient technologies.' He stopped and smiled at Mathias. 'Let me be succinct, Hanrahan. You are lazy and unscrupulous – I have investigated you thoroughly – and your history is tainted with dishonesty' – he raised his hands to silence Mathias – 'but you also have a vestigial talent. At some level you are gifted. There is a place for you in Alabama City. You must think about it. Talent must not go to waste.'

Mathias was surprised by the offer. Sukui didn't like him, and it was clear that he did not trust him either. 'No,' he said, grinning, happy to overlook Sukui's insults. 'You're too generous.'

'Think about it,' said Sukui. 'You may wish to reconsider.' The scientist started to walk away.

At least Mathias had an explanation for why someone had been asking about him: it was Sukui, as crude with people as he was with the cards.

Then the scientist stopped and turned to Mathias. 'I am growing old,' he said, 'I almost forgot: there is someone looking for you. She is, apparently, very keen that she should meet you again. She said something about a *debt*?'

'Who?' asked Mathias, suddenly wishing he had not asked.

'Her name was . . . it began with an L.' Sukui opened his diary and scanned a few pages. 'Ah,' he said, 'this is it: Lucilla Ngota. Apparently she is quite eager to renew your acquaintance.'

Mathias spent the hour before MidNight wiring Mono's Gibson Semi-A into a makeshift PA system at Salomo's.

He tried to put thoughts of Lucilla Ngota out of his head.

She was the wild card he had not even considered. He remembered her reaction to March's death, the look of hatred in her eyes.

And now she had found him in Orlyons. He tried not to think of it.

The materials weren't as good as those he had used in the market-place at Newest Delhi, but they were the best Alya Kik had been able to locate. The amplifier and speaker were a single unit; from the tuning dial Mathias guessed it had been some kind of radio apparatus at one time. Now it was powered by a newly charged cell that Salomo had lent to the Monotones for the night.

Mathias's wiring was crude. He had no soldering pen, so the connections were just twisted together, but it worked, after a fashion. The speaker's size limited and distorted the range and tones and there were a lot of buzzes from the bad connections; it wasn't very loud, either, but Mathias guessed that it would give the guitar the sort of guts Mono was looking for.

Mono came in and kissed Mathias. She was dressed the same as usual, leggings and a short kimono. The 'tones were about music, not looks, she always said. 'Ready to try?' he asked.

Mono nodded, then picked up her guitar and looped the strap casually around her neck.

'Mind the cable,' said Mathias, but Mono wasn't listening.

The Semi-A had hummed when she lifted it, and she studied it curiously. She formed a chord and strummed once with the back of a fingernail. The chord was fuzzy and distorted but she smiled and played the chord again, adding a sixth. 'Yeah,' she said, and Mathias knew she was pleased.

As Mono explored the new dynamics of her old Semi-A, Mathias began to see what she was doing, how she was using the distortion to add to the sound. It drew the notes out, made the guitar really wail. It gave a chunkiness to the power chords, too, filling gaps in Mono's playing he had never even noticed before.

Gradually the rest of the Monotones turned up. Unpacking their instruments, they stared at Mono as she practised, then they joined in, adding to the wall of sound. It was a good turnout for the 'tones, Mathias counted nine of them, plus himself. They had a good puffer's section, fronted by Slide and Milly. Belugi was there, hands too fast to follow across the keys of his piano-accordion, and last of all there was Mabella with her banjo, pulling it from its plastic bag and joining in to a pulled-about twelve-bar blues.

Aisha Lucas was slapping away at her free-standing drums, trying to hold the whole thing together, and she shouted across to Mathias, 'You merely spectatin'?' Mathias was so used to being the onlooker that he had forgotten to join in. He scouted around for his drums, found them, picked up the beat.

'What's the row?' yelled Salomo, a short time later. 'Will you wait till we're at least open, huh? I want them at least to buy their drinks before you drive them out!' Someone threw an orange at him but the Monotones wound down. The sound check was complete.

The streets outside were already alive with the energy of MidNight. The group waited in the bar at first, watching the people passing by. Then Salomo opened up and told them to move out back so the paying customers didn't have to look at their ugly faces. Not for a while, anyway.

Mathias was glad to be out of the way. He stood in the doorway of the room where Salomo held his card schools and watched the faces of the people who were rapidly filling the bar. He recognized no-one from his past, only faces familiar from Orlyons. But then he wouldn't *expect* Lucilla to bring along anyone he might recognize. He considered pulling out of the gig, but the bug had reached him: something special was happening tonight – he had heard the beginnings of it in the warm-up – and he wanted to be involved, he wanted to be a part of Mono's triumph.

Salomo headed for the back-room and Mathias stepped clear. The big man's head poked through the doorway and he said, 'If you're going to do it, then you might as well be doing it now.'

The Monotones stirred, then Mono took the lead and headed for the small stage where their instruments awaited them. 'OK,' she called to the packed club. 'We're gonna play some music.' She hit a chord straight away and those who had reached their instruments joined in on a loose blues medley.

At first Mathias didn't like the response. The talking grew louder and there were a few hecklers at the back. But Mono started to make her guitar do unbelievable things and pretty soon the feeling that this was a one-off event had spread around drinkers and musicians alike. Steadily, the background noise died down and the music took its place.

Sitting with his gin-shell drums in his lap, Mathias felt both participant and spectator. He knew he was contributing to the event but he was on the outside, too, watching it happen. He wondered if the others felt like that, watching Mono hit that guitar, hearing that amplified Semi-A scream and so-gently-murmur its message to the world.

They finished the set on 'Mama Gonna Sell My Soul', and that guitar was crying, weeping tears of sound to contrast the grit in Mono's voice. The room was silent when the last chord finally died. The crowd caught its breath and murmured approval, then it roared and bayed and Mathias was thankful they had set up close to the back-room door and sanctity.

Mono was buzzing when they dragged her through that door. 'This is it!' she cried. 'This is *it*!' Through the closed door the crowd was chanting for more.

Salomo appeared for a time. 'Give us a few minutes for them to buy their drinks, at least, will you? Then keep it *short*. Those fuckers didn't buy a *thing* while you made that row. Not a god-damned thing.' Salomo was smiling like Mathias had never seen him smile before. 'God-*damn*,' he muttered, as he closed the door and returned to the bar.

They gave Salomo his selling time, then they filtered back into the main room. Mono and Mathias were last out. As they reached the doorway Vera-Lynne Perse appeared before them, a stranger by her side. 'Hi,' she said. 'They liked it, traditionalists that they are.'

Mathias pushed Mono forward and said, 'Go on, Mono, they want you. I'll be up soon.' To his relief, she went. He didn't want her to be a part of this.

The stranger stepped into the back-room and Vera-Lynne followed. 'Matt,' she said. Her voice was faltering. She appeared to have noticed that something was amiss. 'This man . . . he said he was an old friend of yours.'

The man was wearing a thick leather coat, his hands buried deep in its pockets. 'Miz Ngota sends her regards,' he said, and suddenly Mathias placed him: an officer with the Guard, Andras MacLeugh. 'And she asked me to give you this.'

His hand jerked out of his coat and Mathias saw a flash of metal, a knife.

MacLeugh was close, but Mathias had been ready for him. As the knife swung up towards his belly, he caught MacLeugh's wrist and spun him with his own momentum. He cracked the man's hand against the open door and the knife flew into the crowded bar. MacLeugh countered with a head-butt to the body, winding Mathias, pushing him back into the room and then Vera-Lynne finally screamed.

Staggering to his feet, breathing deeply, Mathias barged his opponent, the force of his charge carrying them both past the flapping Vera-Lynne and into the main room of Salomo's club.

Mathias broke free and immediately he lost MacLeugh in the crowd. People were yelling and shouting, but Mathias just kept his head down, forcing his way to the door and out into the bustling street. As he ran, listening for sounds of pursuit, he tried to make a plan, but instead, all he could do was ask himself why a member of the Primal Guard had tried to kill him. Until then, he had assumed that it was only Lucilla, that it was only a matter of revenge. Now an alternative loomed: secure, at last, in the Primacy, Edward had decided that it was time Mathias was silenced.

He slowed to a trot and then a fast walk. They might have Mono's room under surveillance so he couldn't go there. But she was his only chance. He would just have to stay low and try to find her.

He jerked around at a sudden sound, but it was only a gang of adolescents, chasing through the streets. Lie low, lie low, was all he could think as he headed for Greene Gardens, hoping desperately that Mono would be the first to find him.

# Chapter Eight

Greene Gardens formed the only open space in a town with little room for open space. The Gardens were a series of oddly shaped areas, connected by a stream and its overgrown banks. They were on the north side of Orlyons, where the densely packed streets gave way to the rising side of the gorge. Here, great crags of blue and grey intruded into the edge of the town, dragging with them a few pieces of green: some trees and a few mown areas of grass wherever the land achieved a precarious horizontal.

At MidNight, Greene Gardens was the haunt of lovers and drunks, enchanted by the sounds of the stream and the soft scents of wilderness. At other times it was the haunt of merchants arranging deals, traders selling wares too risqué or hot to expose on the streets, whores looking to sell, the wealthy looking for ways to spend.

But despite the ever-present commerce, Greene Gardens was essentially wild, virgin territory enclosed by the growing port of Orlyons.

Away from the pathways and lawns, there were dark places, corners known only to animals and fugitives.

Mathias changed position, **again**. Stiffness had set in as he waited out the few remaining hours of

MidNight, shivering in the cooling wind and trying to shelter from the repeated showers.

He had a good view from where he crouched. He was in the undergrowth that grew up the side of one of the larger crags, well concealed but with a clear outlook over a wide mown area and a pathway that led out of the Gardens and into the part of the Gentian Quarter where Mono lived.

Greene Gardens was almost on Mono's route back from Salomo's and Mathias knew that she loved the place. 'I like the scents,' she had once told him, 'they turn me on.' Her cheeks had dimpled and she had laughed when she saw Mathias's face. 'No, not like that. They turn me on in *here*.' She had smacked herself on the chest, over the heart. Mathias had said something about that being as good as place as any *he* could think of and the moment had passed, but it came back to him now, the mood, the happiness. He could smell the same scents now, Greene Gardens fresh from the MidNight showers. Mathias knew in his heart that Mono would be drawn to the Gardens that day; she could do nothing else.

Someone was walking along the footpath; the Gardens had been quiet that morning and this was the first person Mathias had seen. He peered at the figure but it was not Mono. It was a tall youth, oriental, a wisp of a moustache over his wide, sensual mouth.

'Lui!' hissed Mathias. It was Lui Tsang, a trader with a special talent for electronics.

Lui looked around and Mathias noticed that his face was badly bruised and swollen on one side.

After a final reconnaissance, Mathias stepped out from the bushes. 'What have you been doing?' he asked. 'And why wasn't *I* invited?'

Lui laughed and looked around cautiously. 'They said you were dead,' he said. 'Come on. If it's good enough for you then it's good enough for any of us.' He stepped into the undergrowth. 'The word is out, Mathias. After last night. They're out to get you and my guess is they want to get you quick before they draw any more attention to themselves.'

'Lui, do you know *who* they are? One of them tried to knife me last night. Andras MacLeugh. He used to be in the Primal Guard and probably still is. Listen, Lui, I have to know why Lucilla has the Guard with her, I have to know if it's Edward after me or just her. Can you find out?'

'Hmm.' Lui tugged at his moustache. 'The word in Orlyons is that they are militia, posing as cultists. After last night's mess they leaked that they were from Ngota Clan and they had sworn revenge on you.'

'*No*,' said Mathias 'That's not right. MacLeugh isn't Ngota Clan. He's from north of Abidjan!' So it had to be Edward. He had finally decided that his stolen Primacy would be more secure with Mathias dead.

'What can I do, Lui?'

Lui shrugged. 'I don't know, Matt. I guess all you can do is, next time, don't get born into a royal family. Get born in the gutter like the rest of us. When no-one can tell you from shit in the street then they have no reason to kill you.'

'You know a scientist called Sukui?'

'I've sold him junk.' Lui smiled awkwardly.

'He said I could go with him to Alabama City, that there was a place for me with his Project. Doing what, I don't know, but it's a place.'

'Then what are you doing sitting here? Jesus, Matt, you get a chance to get out of all this and you hide out in the bushes. Is that' – he pointed at Mathias's head – 'bone right through, or only most of the way?'

Mathias shrugged and stared at the strands of lichen that were hanging from the bushes. He knew what he should do, but that would be running away again.

When it was run or be killed, though, what choice *was* there?

Scared as he was of staying in Orlyons, he didn't like the prospect of going with Sukui much better. He had to talk to Mono, she was all he had left. 'You never *did* tell me where you collected those bruises, Lui.'

Lui looked at him strangely. 'Where have you *been*, Matt? I was at Salomo's, at the gig. All I knew was the 'tones going up for an encore then a knife came flying through the air. People started screaming and then *you* came charging through. And this other guy. Then I got hit and someone else got hit, and some furniture got broken and somehow I came out of it alive.'

'Is Mono OK?'

'Oh sure,' said Lui. 'I don't know how, but they say no-one had more than a few broken bones. I saw Mono afterwards and she was OK. Physically, anyhow. Listen, Matt, one piece of advice: don't ask Salomo for any help. He's liable to tear you apart, from how he was last night.'

Mathias sat down heavily. 'Thanks for telling me, Lui. I'll sort things out.'

Lui stepped back, uncomfortably. 'I've got to go,' he said. Then he turned and headed out of Greene Gardens. Mathias just sat there; it was a long time before he even bothered to conceal himself again.

He must have dozed, because when he opened his eyes she was sitting there by the stream. She was only a distant figure but he knew it was Mono. She had her head in her hands, her black hair spread over her arms and legs as she slumped forwards over the water. Mathias knew from her pose that she was adding, minutely, to the flow and saltiness of the stream.

He had never seen her crying before.

There were others on the mown area nearby but Mono was apart from them. Mathias could reach her easily without coming into the open but he held back, not wanting to break her solitude. He had done her enough harm already, maybe he should just turn and leave.

But that would be running away.

He waited while a trader he vaguely knew passed along the pathway, hand linked through the arm of a glasshouse farmer. 'I know someone who could throw stones,' he was saying; the farmer laughed half-heartedly, it was clearly a familiar joke.

Closer up, Mono looked terrible. Her knuckles were white where she pressed her hands into her face. The stream gurgled past, not caring the least if it sounded cheerful against Mono's quiet sobbing.

He crouched by her side, said, 'Mono, I'm sorry.'

She lifted her head, looked around, a dazed expression on her shadowed, creased face. Then she sprang at him, crying, 'Matt! Matt! *Matt!*' She hit him in the chest and he fell backwards, Mono in his arms, clutching at him, begging him to be real, to be alive, to be *Matt*.

He tried to hush her, and suddenly she was quiet, not calling his name, just kissing him and holding him to the ground. 'Mono,' he said. 'I didn't know what would happen at Salomo's. I don't know how . . . but I feel responsible. I wrecked it, Mono, I spoilt it for you . . .' He carried on, not knowing what he was saying but saying it nonetheless. He didn't know what else to do.

Eventually Mono recovered. She leaned away from his face, sitting astride him, still pinning him to the ground. 'Matt,' she said. 'You talk shit. You're *alive*. I didn't see what was happening – all I could do was duck out. They said there was a guy after you with a knife. Slide said you'd never have got out. Matt, *I thought you were dead*.'

'But . . . the gig.'

'It was no good, Matt. The music wasn't right.' He could see in her eyes that she was lying, maybe lying to herself rather than to him. 'The music was shit. Who cares if Salomo doesn't want us back. If I want to play again I'll play Greene Gardens like everybody else.'

'Of course you have to play, Mono. What about the Semi-A?'

'It got broke.' Mono slumped against Mathias and began to cry again. 'We were good, weren't we, Matt? They liked us . . . before . . .'

'Yeah.' He stroked her hair and waited for her to stop.

'What are you going to do, Matt? You're not safe in Orlyons.'

Mathias thought of Sukui's offer. Maybe Mono could come along – Sukui was one of her regulars, maybe she could whore her way to Alabama City and, once there, they could start again. Or maybe they could move around Clermont, find a fishing village somewhere and hope they weren't found.

It was a decision Mathias didn't want to take.

'Come on,' he said. 'I'm going to lie low for a while, think things through.' He stood and pulled Mono to her feet. If he lay low for long enough Sukui would have left and there would be no decision to make. He was honest enough to recognize that maybe that was what he was doing.

Mathias sat in the mouth of his cave, listening to the gentle susurrus of the sea. Earlier, he had left Greene Gardens with Mono, his head tied in a tight bandanna, Sikhist style. He had walked boldly through the streets, insisting that Mono walk ahead, clear of any trouble that might arise. No-one had challenged them. If the search persisted then they were probably seeking him out in any of the bolt-holes a fugitive could find throughout Orlyons; they wouldn't expect him to be striding openly through the town, out past the merchants' houses that had been built into the gorge-sides when the first trade boom had struck the port.

The northern cliffs were riddled with caves, some no more than hollows in the rock, others deep and unexplored. Mathias's cave was a deep one, although he had penetrated no more than the first fifty metres or so, back to where the light was mid-grey and his eyes were unable to focus.

He sat in the lotus position, letting the world pass him by and, at the same time, trying to grow closer to his surroundings, trying to feel like a part of Expatria, not just someone dumped there by alien ancestors.

It didn't work. He knew that he didn't fit.

Mono had returned to him with food and an opal pendant which she placed around his neck and told him to keep. 'Whatever happens,' she had said, 'this is for you. My eleven-greats grandmother bought it in Jakarta, before she joined the Ark Ship. So the story goes.'

Mono had stayed for a short time and then left to see what was happening in Orlyons. 'Come back soon,' Mathias had said; then, as her figure diminished in size and finally lost itself on the rocky beach, he had repeated it softly: 'Come back soon, Mono.'

So Mathias Hanrahan sat, listening to the waves and trying, again, to stop the thoughts that were running through his mind. Things were clearer now, but it was still too much for him to handle on his own. He watched a cutter clipping the wave-tops with its wings and then dodging a gull that stooped at it, trying to make it regurgitate its most recent meal.

'It would have been a simple matter to kill you, Mister Hanrahan.' Mathias flinched. 'You are somewhat inattentive for one in such a predicament.' It was Sukui, standing to one side, hands folded in front of him, showing that he was unarmed.

'Sukui-san,' said Mathias. 'I didn't hear you approach.'

'As I initially observed.' Mathias gestured for him to sit, but the scientist remained standing. 'Silence is a simple manner, if the codes are logically followed. It is no feat.' Finally, Sukui sat and stared out to sea.

'The old books talk of waves higher than I've ever seen,' said Mathias, in an effort to keep the conversation neutral. 'Do you have an explanation?'

'The old books talk of many things,' said Sukui. 'They talk of animals the size of large buildings and particles smaller than specks of sand. They talk of weapons that destroy entire cities with their blasts and of nations that exist only as electrical patterns in global communications networks. My colleagues in Alabama City know that all these things are possible.

'You ask about the sea. Our planet is smaller than Earth, and it turns more rapidly; a logical hypothesis is that our planet turns so fast that there is little time for one side of the sphere to heat up before it is turned away from the sun and cooling again. Old books say that it is such differences in heat distribution that drive the weather systems and they that drive the waves. A hypothesis to consider in more detail, perhaps once you have proven yourself in Alabama City? If, of course, you act rationally and accompany me there.'

'How did you find me?'

Sukui smiled briefly, 'Another elementary piece of deduction. You are not fool enough to stay in Orlyons; I credit you with that much sense. On an earlier occasion you told me that you found the sea therapeutic. There is a certain prostitute in Orlyons who I understand is an acquaintance of yours. She was careful, but clearly she is not a deep thinker. You have no reason to worry: I was the only one to follow her, I am sure of that. Please, you are avoiding the issue.'

'If I went with you . . . would there be a place for a companion? I would—'

'No,' said Sukui. 'Your prostitute will be safe in Orlyons. You have no need to worry. You will not be a prisoner in Alabama City, there will be occasions when you can return.' Sukui stood and looked down at Mathias. 'You occupy much of my time. I must return.'

'Sukui-san. You win: I'll come. Will you tell Mono for me? Tell her I'll be back for her.'

'It is not a matter of victory,' said Sukui. 'I only serve the Lord Andric. You must stay here for now. I will make the necessary arrangements.'

'What about Lucilla?'

Sukui smiled and backed away. 'Forget about your past, Mister Hanrahan, and it will forget about you. I will take care of your Miz Ngota.' Sukui turned and walked rapidly away, along the rocky shoreline and out of Mathias's sight.

# Chapter Nine

Drinking with Chet Alpha was not Kasimir Sukui's greatest pleasure. It was more a necessary evil.

Sukui pushed his distaste aside. He had bled his animal urges dry and now he was back in his prime again. Every move was calculated beforehand, every casual remark a planned speech. He took another mouthful of vodka and tossed the drained finger-glass back over his shoulder. 'You're a good man, Chet,' he said, careful to slur the occasional word. 'You're good in your job.'

On returning from Mathias's hideout, Sukui had gone to Alpha, the one person in Orlyons he knew who could not keep a secret. He had spent ten minutes with one of the girls as a prelude to inviting Alpha out for a drink. It was a formality more than anything; Sukui had not enjoyed the encounter.

Alpha called for more drinks.

Sukui had not visited this bar before. It was dark and musty, and the customers looked constantly to be on the edge of violence. The girl had said Alpha liked this kind of place. She had said he liked to imagine himself as being part of the crowd. She had said he was full of macho shit like that. Sukui had smiled and made a mental note, his diary being inaccessible at that moment.

'You're a good man yourself, Suks.' Alpha was at a stage Sukui had noted as quite common, in his experience. The compliments, the vulgar familiarities; it was time to manipulate the flow of drink in order to keep Alpha at this level of insobriety. 'There's people would say different about me, you see. They . . . *disapprove* of my line of business. They say as if the girls aren't queuing up to work for me, but they are. Hey, it's empty . . .'

'Your work?' prompted Sukui, taking Alpha's glass and, for a moment or two, making it appear that he was trying to attract the bartender's attention.

'Yes, I *do* work.' Alpha's moods were changing rapidly, like moths flitting around the light of Sukui's questions. 'The girls, they wouldn't say it, but I do. It's like . . . I see myself as their kind of *guardian*, you see? I look out for them, I put money their way, I put a roof over their heads. And what d'they do? Huh? It's "Chet, do this" and "Chet, will you do that". "Chet, you're working us too hard" and "Chet, don't forget to do *this*". You know th'other day? Larinda was even straightening my collar. Straightening my collar! Jeez-Buddha, they're like having six mothers buzzing round your ass like flies on shit. I tell you, anybody'd think *they* were running the show!' He laughed and Sukui joined him.

'The way I see it,' continued Alpha. 'It's something *spiritual*, it's a need from inside. I'm bringing people together, that's my role in life. Sometimes I think there's somebody out there guiding me, a Jesus-Buddha or an Allah or something – *I* don't know, He doesn't leave His name. I sometimes think

110

if we could all give, like the girls give, then maybe we'd all be, I don't know, *giving* I suppose.'

Sukui wanted to bring Alpha around to the subject of Mathias Hanrahan, but he could see that it might be difficult. As Alpha meandered onwards, Sukui began to wonder why he was taking so much trouble with Hanrahan. He certainly had a talent, but his temperament was suspect, to say the very least. He appeared to shy away from effort and he had a certain lack of application about him, an inability to concentrate or follow the lead of others. He had even killed his own father.

But there was something about him.

Sukui did not like being unable to categorise a person but, no matter how he tried, he could find no appropriate slot for Hanrahan. Maybe that was it. Sukui had been locating talented individuals for the Project for long enough. Despite his distaste, he knew that Hanrahan would be worth this investment of effort.

Sukui was honest enough to know that he, himself, was little above second-rate. He had worked hard, he had made a success of his life, he knew exactly what it took to emerge from the crowd; but at heart he knew that he could never fulfil such aspirations. Maybe that was how he could spot it in others, this elusive *talent*.

There was a clock behind the boarded-together bar. Time was running out. Sukui decided that he must be more blunt. He opened his mouth to speak.

'Hey, did you hear what went down at Salomo's, th'other MidNight?'

111

Sukui could not have crafted a better opening himself. 'Salomo's?' he said, trying to sound insincere.

'*You* know. That Hanrahan, the one who killed the Prime. I *told* you there was somebody out to get him, didn't I? Didn't I? They tried for him at Salomo's. They wrecked the place trying to get at him, but he got out, so they say.'

'Really,' said Sukui. He looked around and leaned closer to Chet Alpha. 'I hardly think this is the place we should be talking about such matters.'

'No?' Alpha looked around. 'You think they're here, too? Hmm.'

'Hanrahan's life is in our hands,' said Sukui. Alpha stared at his hands and said nothing. 'We must guard our words with the utmost caution.'

'Caution. Hmm.'

'Time draws on,' said Sukui. 'I have a meeting at the Woodrow Gate. A certain *fugitive*.' He smiled at the look of dim-witted comprehension that drifted slowly over Alpha's face.

'Woodrow Gate, you say?'

'Yes, in only an hour and a half. Chet, you're a good man. I would be most grateful if you would keep this quiet. These matters can be blown up beyond all proportion, you know.'

'Sure, sure. My lips are steeled.' Alpha stood. 'This is MidNight you know. I have to be working.' He waved at Sukui and left the bar.

Sukui looked around. His words had been noted by two of the drinkers nearby. He did not think they were with Ngota, but he felt confident, now, that his untruths would spread. He stepped clear of his stool and left the bar.

112

Mono's face dropped when she saw who it was at her door. 'Oh,' she said. 'Sukui-san. I'm sorry, I'm not . . .'

'No,' he said. 'Neither am I.' Mono stepped back and Sukui entered her room. This was the first time he had been here on anything other than business. He had almost decided not to call on her, but he had given Hanrahan his word.

Upon entering the building, his suspicions had been confirmed: Lucilla Ngota was having Mono watched. But Sukui did not care if they saw him visiting her, or if they made the connection between himself and Hanrahan. Soon he would be away from Orlyons and this sequence of events would be relegated to a few colourful passages in his diary.

He sat on Mono's mattress. She looked tired and her room was a mess. She was usually fastidious about appearance, it was a part of her job. The business with Hanrahan was clearly taking its toll. Sukui had not fully realized the extent of their relationship. He made another mental note against Hanrahan: emotional weakness.

'I have spoken with Mathias Hanrahan,' he said, observing the effect of his words on Mono's face. 'He asked me to visit you.' He consulted his diary. 'He said to tell you he was leaving. He said he would return for you. That was all.'

Mono nodded slowly. 'He has to,' she said. 'Don't tell me where – I don't want to know.'

Sukui stood. 'I must go. I have an appointment with Lucilla Ngota.' He smiled at Mono. 'I will return too,' he said. 'I will visit you.'

113

They left the building together. 'I have things to do,' Mono said.

Outside, she disappeared into one of the many alleyways of the Gentian Quarter. Sukui walked on alone. He had spoken with his juniors before calling on Mono. Everybody knew what to do.

He smiled and walked on, through the ever-shifting throng. There must be a pattern to people's movements, he realized, some sort of statistical law that governed their flow. But – he sighed – like that of the sea, the pattern was just beyond his grasp and he had the irrational feeling that it would always remain so.

As he walked through the early MidNight crowds, Sukui kept feeling that he was being followed. Occasionally he paused, but he refrained from looking around. If his pursuers knew he was aware then they would only be more diligent, less easy to spot when the need arose.

Just before the appointed time, Sukui arrived at Woodrow Gate. The gate was a curious structure, a tall, wrought-iron folly of a thing, mounted on a single brickwork pillar. It marked one of the many ways into the series of connected pockets of parkland known as Greene Gardens. The Gardens were largely unsuitable for building on, so they had been given a name and treated as if they had always been meant to be, not the accidents of geology that they were.

Sanjit Borodin was standing by the gate, talking to two large men, each clad in leather and wearing knives in their belts. Sukui shook his head as he approached his junior. 'Are these all?' he hissed.

'When I say "men" I do not mean only *two*.' He did not feel angry – always the stoic, he was already reconsidering the scenarios, working out the probabilities – but he knew that a display of anger might have some effect on Borodin. He always tried to remember that his role was to educate the juniors; they were not merely his assistants.

Borodin bowed his head and accepted Sukui's words.

Sukui walked a short distance into Greene Gardens, away from the crowds that streamed past outside Woodrow Gate. The men would be enough. Ngota was just an underling; she would have to accept his words and pass them on to her master in Newest Delhi; for Sukui, that was the purpose of this subterfuge. There would be no call for violence.

Again, he sensed the presence of others. He wondered what Ngota would do. He had heard all about her and he was eager to see if she deserved her reputation. He controlled his breathing and worked through the probabilities in his mind. This was not a time to allow the emotions to surface, control was necessary.

Sukui looked at Dee, the more distant of Expatria's moons, hanging above the horizon. The time was right. He knew Ngota was watching him, waiting for him to move. Earlier, he had located the precise patch of vegetation behind which there was a good chance she was hiding.

He heard footsteps nearby and then he saw his other junior, Egon Petrovsky, approaching. He was wearing trousers and a jacket; Orlyons clothes, not his usual robe and skullcap.

Sukui spoke loudly: 'Ah, so you have decided to come.'

There was a sound from the bushes and suddenly a number of figures stepped into the open. A quick count: twelve. More than Sukui had expected. Dressed in inconspicuous town clothing, standing with knees bent, ready for action.

Closest to Sukui was a tall, dark-skinned woman. Her face was broad and her eyes wide. She was staring past Sukui at Petrovsky. The junior was still a number of paces away and Sukui doubted the woman could make out his features in the dim light that spilled over from the Gentian Quarter.

Sukui nodded. 'Miz Ngota? I was told you were in Orlyons.'

Ngota finally looked at Sukui. 'I have business to complete,' she said.

'So I hear. I am afraid I have business of a similar nature. A fugitive.' He turned to the approaching figure of his junior. 'Ah, Petrovsky. I am glad you chose to return.' He studied Ngota's face as Petrovsky drew near. 'He was tempted by the lights of Orlyons,' explained Sukui, 'but he has chosen to return.' He smiled.

Ngota knew she had been fooled.

But Ngota's troops were still poised for action and Sukui was suddenly reminded of his own lack of support. The odds were in his favour, but only narrowly now. 'I would like to remind you that this kind of covert activity is not within the current Primal statutes,' he said. 'Clermont must retain its neutral status. Any such incursions into *Andricci* territory, however, will not be overlooked. You will convey this to your Prime. You must also inform the Prime Hanrahan that his half-sibling is now beyond his reach. Mathias Hanrahan is out of bounds.'

Ngota gestured to her men and they began to move slowly forward. 'I must remind you of our position,' he said. 'Prime Salvo Andric expects me to return. He would be most unhappy if you did not accept the situation.'

Lucilla was looking at him. He had never before been looked at in such a manner. The animosity of her expression was a fascinating phenomenon; in Lucilla Ngota aggression had been refined to a form of art.

It was almost hypnotic.

Sukui had not expected anything like this. He had not expected such an emotional response. She should have accepted that she had been outwitted; she would gain nothing by turning on *him*.

Sukui stepped uneasily backwards, something shifting inside him. He could not take his eyes from Ngota's. A cold sweat prickled his face. 'I warn you,' he said. 'You are acting irrationally.'

Ngota did not appear to hear, she had stopped and was now staring right through him. He wondered why she was hesitating for so long, drawing out his fear.

'I'd say you were acting *very* irrationally.' The voice from behind startled Sukui. He turned.

The man who had spoken was huge and dark. His hair was stacked high and haloed by the light from the Gentian Quarter. He was wearing a long coat with 'SLIDE' scrawled all over it. There were others, too. Salomo, aproned and carrying

117

a table-leg; Mono, standing by Slide, carrying a stick and looking tiny among the mass. Sukui recognized some of the others, many of them from the streets: musicians and entertainers, traders and hawkers and anonymous faces that could have belonged to anyone. There were too many to count, and for once he did not even try.

'Word was, Matt might need help,' said Slide.

'Hanrahan has gone already,' said Sukui. 'He is safe.'

Sukui turned but Ngota had vanished. In the end she had acted, as he knew she must, in a rational manner. The odds had finally gone against her.

## Chapter Ten

Alabama City was an amber smear on the otherwise dark horizon. Mathias stared at the faint, unnatural glow. 'How do they . . .?'

'The city is lit by electric power,' said Sukui. 'Each block has a bio-converter which is used as a supplement to the solar collector-storage units. The main cause of light spillage is the street illumination around the Capitol. The Lord Andric plans to install more such lighting throughout the city. This was one of the Project's earliest successes.'

'Tell me, Sukui-san. What's my part in your Project? What does it *do*?'

Sukui shifted in his wooden seat. 'You would be wise to remember that it is not *my* Project. It is but a small part of the Lord Andric's grand design.

' "Project" is a misleading label. It is a co-operative of scientifically disciplined workers. We strive to develop a better understanding of our world. There is a team searching the archives and piecing together a detailed history. There are a number of teams restoring the technologies. There is a natural sciences team studying Expatria, and another studying the patterns of our society. Look around, Hanrahan: the world is ordered. Everything has a pattern; our function is to find such patterns and study their application. That is the divine purpose of our kind.'

119

'So why am I here?'

'You show promise. We find it easier to train people who have already attained a certain understanding of science.'

He had said as much before. 'And ...?' prompted Mathias.

Sukui stared at him in the darkness, and then continued. 'You are trouble, Hanrahan. Wherever you pass you leave a wake of destruction. It is as much a pattern of life as the ripples left on a sandy beach by the sea. You must be aware of the disputes between the Hanrahan and Andricci borderlands. Orlyons, being situated on an island, is neutral.' Sukui stood and walked over to lean on the edge of the barge, staring out at the sea; it looked as if he was counting the waves. 'Your presence was upsetting the equilibrium. You had to be removed. Prime Hanrahan wanted to remove you, and he was prepared to upset the status quo to do so. I identified what was happening and removed you first. I have despatched Lucilla Ngota with a message, reminding her Prime of Orlyons's special status. She is a determined woman; you have been lucky.'

Sukui returned to his seat and closed his eyes. Sitting upright, he was instantly asleep; earlier, when Sukui had slept in this manner, Mathias had not believed it possible but now he thought that, for Sukui at least, it was probably the most natural position.

They disembarked as the sky started to lighten, MidNight drawing to an end. There could be no MidNight in Alabama City for already the people were hurrying, serious-faced, through the wide thoroughfares. The buildings were tall and square, some looming over the streets, others set back, surrounded by high stone walls. Powerful, twin-headed lights on tall pillars lit the city – they were clearly near to the Capitol.

Away from the docks, the street-lighting disappeared and the buildings became more dense, the roads more narrow. The people, too, were more tightly packed, and they were less grim-faced about their business. Sukui led Mathias along a street lined with Harrod stores and Wimpy-Washes, Hitachi cafeterias and Happy Hobo Clubs. 'I thought entertainments were limited by Primal edict,' said Mathias, hurrying after Sukui.

'Entertainments?' said Sukui, looking around innocently. 'These are places of work, not funhouses.' They passed a tall placard that told them of Gino's Pretty Boy Dance Pack (supported by Bernie and the Blue Rodettes), playing twice nightly. 'The Prime approves wholeheartedly of the people's devotion to their work.'

They walked on, Mathias beginning to get a feel for the city. He had not thought much about his future since accepting Sukui's offer of refuge. He had been too worried by what was happening, too confused by thoughts of Mono and how she would react. Now, walking through Alabama City, he began to think about what was ahead of him; the alien environment of the city had finally made him realize that he was making another entirely new start.

The city did not appear as dull a place as Mathias had expected and, more than anything, Sukui's talk of the Project had ignited something in him. All his life he had been made to suffer because, where others rejected or at best ignorantly accepted, he had wanted to know how things worked, how they fitted into the world, how they could be improved. Now, at last, he had the opportunity to live among like-minded individuals, people who wanted to re-discover the ancient technologies. As he walked through the streets, tagging after Kasimir Sukui, Mathias's head began to whirl. There was so much to take in. He hoped they would let him settle for a day or two, before expecting anything major from him.

He soon grew accustomed to the long working day. He would begin two hours before dawn and he was rarely finished before twelve-thirty; then he had three hours before his next shift was due to start. He quickly learnt to make the most of those three hours. Within days he could sleep as soon as his body hit the thin mattress they gave him as a bed. Between sleep and work there was no time for anything else.

He would not have minded so much if his job had been interesting. He spent each eleven-hour shift in a basement laboratory in the Soho district where he also had his quarters. When Sukui had described the Project, Mathias had envisaged a purpose-built research centre, perhaps on the outskirts of Alabama City; the idea came from a terran book he had once read. Instead, the Project was spread throughout the city, squeezed into any spare space, hidden away in basements and tenements and the back-rooms of great square buildings. Alabama was clearly not as progressive as Sukui had implied.

Mathias need not have worried about the Project pushing him too far too soon. His work in the basement laboratory was demanding only in a physical sense. He carried boxes, he swept floors, he fetched drinks for his superiors. For several hours a day he did actually get to do science: classifying, counting, measuring. Mathias had never known boredom like it.

It was a life sciences lab. His room-mate, Siggy Axelmeyer, had explained the work to him. 'There's quantities of seeds left from the first colony,' he had said. 'They're centuries old but they're still viable – we think they were treated with some kind of preservative. Some are labelled, but they still need to be grown and analysed; others are only seeds and we have to see what they produce. It's a major task, there's still decades of labour to see it out.' Siggy had smiled and slapped Mathias on the shoulder. 'Work to do,' he had finished up.

He had tried, but finally he decided that there was nothing for it: he was at war with the system.

He began his own regime of MidNights: sleeping alternate nights and catching occasional naps at the lab; during the time he freed in this manner he became acquainted with the night-life of Alabama City. He was fortunate that both his quarters and the laboratory were situated in Soho, a district that made him think fondly of the Gentian Quarter. Some of the clubs were licensed and they proclaimed the fact in huge letters over their doors; the majority were illicit, they were places of work, not entertainment, and the customers went merely to create demand for the work that was being done. In theory, at least. In reality, it was a farce, one which irritated Mathias for some reason he could not fathom. He longed for the freedom simply to make music for the love of it, to play it on street corners, to do it in the open and not hiding behind the façade that was Soho.

One night, Mathias returned to his quarters and found Siggy still awake, sitting against the wall and reading a book by candle-light. 'Still up?' he said, by way of greeting.

Siggy looked up and grunted. There was something unsettling about Axelmeyer, a look in his eyes. He would be more bearable if he wasn't so bound up in his own serious world. Suddenly angry, Mathias said, 'Listen, Siggy. Why are you so *controlled*? It's like you're trying to fill Sukui's shadow or something.'

It broke through Axelmeyer's barriers. His face sagged and his big body slumped. He said, 'I have to, Mathias. Let me explain; I guess nobody tells you anything around here, am I right? You probably don't even realize I'm Salvo Andric's cousin. No? I live like this' – he gestured around himself at their shared room – 'because Salvo's made it clear our blood isn't close enough for me to succeed any other way. You may not believe it but I used to be wild, Mathias. I mean really *wild*. I used to go around town wrecking places and there was nothing anyone could do. Except Salvo. He made me do this, he said Sukui would be a good influence. He

124

told me I needed taming.' Siggy shook his head sadly. 'Now I can see the only way back up is by out-learning everyone else. I have self-control and one day I'm going to be back at the top and *then* I'll show Salvo what it's like.' Siggy's eyes had finally come alive; the control that Sukui had instilled was wavering, just a little.

Mathias was appalled by his tale. So this was what Sukui's scientific training did to people! He saw himself in a few years' – months'? – time, coldly rational, his spirit confined, restricted. Slightly drunk from his night's entertainments, he remembered his earlier vow: he was at w' with the system. 'You mustn't let them tak it all away, Siggy,' he said. 'Sukui'll destroy you.'

He drew a cold metal object from his pocket.

He squinted and remembered what it was. He had won a mouth-organ in a side-bet at the Happy Hobo Eaterette. He put it to his mouth and blew, tonguing a few unsteady notes, then he found a tune he knew from Orlyons.

After a minute or two he saw Siggy looking curiously at the instrument. 'Want to play?' Mathias asked. 'You just find a note for yourself and work out what's happening, there's no other way.' It was Slide who had introduced Mathias to the mouth-organ. He had said it was the purest musical instrument ever invented. Nobody could teach you to play, you had to feel your way around; you couldn't watch what you were doing and learn in any rational way. Harmonica music came straight from the heart. Mathias had never been very good

– he had not practised enough – but he knew that Slide had been telling the truth.

It made a curious kind of sense to him, watching Siggy Axelmeyer find his first few notes. A bit of music from the heart was the ideal counter to Sukui's indoctrination. Maybe Siggy was salvageable.

Mathias smiled. He recognized the tune Siggy had just played – 'Mama Gonna Sell My Soul' – the timing different, the emphasis more upbeat, more aggressive, but still recognisable. Siggy was doing well, he was a natural. Mathias fell asleep to the sound of his room-mate's music.

Mathias opened the door and entered the lab. There were trays of seedlings everywhere. The phrase 'decades of labour' kept leaping into the front of his mind. The work would take even longer when someone found more stores of ancient seeds. Decades of labour.

Even when he was involved in the science of the laboratory, Mathias's work was menial. He gave the seedlings measured amounts of water, noted down their rates of growth, drew them, described them, fed them to test animals. He never got to see the results of his work. His figures and measurements were taken away and analysed by Siggy or one of the more experienced scientists.

He was first at the laboratory, as usual. That meant he could get the messy tasks like watering out of the way before the others arrived. That was how his superiors liked it.

He went to the basin and a slight movement caught his attention. Standing in one corner of the laboratory, studying a chart, was Kasimir Sukui. '*Salix caprea*,' he said, glancing up at Mathias. 'A small tree. It should be decorative in the Capitol's arboretum. You are late. You have kept me waiting.'

Sukui was an occasional visitor to the laboratory – as Mathias guessed he was to most Project facilities – but it was unusual to see him so early.

'Sukui,' said Mathias. 'I'd hoped you might call by. I want to know why you're treating me like this: giving me work more suited to a servant. You said I'd be a part of the Project, that I'd be doing science.'

Sukui was smiling and bowing his head. It was one of his more annoying habits, it made it so difficult to be angry at him. After a pause he said, 'You wish to return to Orlyons? Or Newest Delhi, perhaps? It can be arranged.'

Mathias considered saying yes to Orlyons, if only to test Sukui. The latest news, according to talk in the laboratory, was that Orlyons had become the centre of conflict between Andric and the north; refugees were arriving by the boat-load in Andricci territory. Mathias was worried about Mono. In his heart, he knew she could look after herself better than most, but he would like to have known for sure.

'You're avoiding the topic,' said Mathias, keeping rein on his feelings.

'The topic. Ah, yes. You feel the work is beneath you? Perhaps that a man of your breeding should start from a privileged position? I started as a servant,' said Sukui. 'I worked my way up.

127

Now I know what service is like at every level within the Primal household. I have benefited from the experience. Hanrahan, I have told you that I consider you to be trouble. I have not revised that view. You are impetuous, you have not known hard, menial labour until recently.'

Sukui paused, considering his words. 'You have a talent but you do not have the attitude. Science is the triumph of logic over emotion; it is the rational exploration of the world. All else must be sublimated. You cannot simply leap in and *do* science, as you put it. When you understand that fact, then you will be ready for the next stage. You will work here until you achieve the requisite discipline.'

'But what about the intelligent guess, the intuitive leap?' said Mathias, feeling frustrated by Sukui's speech. 'What about the great scientists of the past? Verne? Darwin? Redway? They followed hunches . . .' He was clutching at straws, not sure what he thought any more. Sukui often had that effect on him.

'You claim such greatness?' asked Sukui, his head bowed, smiling gently. 'Science for the mortal is the rigorous pursuit of logic; there is no room for the unquantifiable or the emotive.'

The laboratory door opened and closed and Sukui stepped past Mathias. 'Jan,' he said to Kawabata, the laboratory supervisor. 'Hanrahan is relieved for four hours. Prime Salvo has requested to view him.' He turned back to Mathias. 'Come along. You have kept me overlong – we have little time. The Lord Andric waits for nobody.'

★

The Andricci Capitol was an extravagant building, to say the least. Even in broad daylight electric beacons lit what would otherwise be shady recesses, casting shadows at unnatural angles, burning blobs in Mathias's eyes. Every surface was painted in a jumble of colours that could never have been chosen as part of an overall scheme. Gold clashed with reds and pinks, lime greens with blues and jet black. Everywhere in the Capitol was filled with noise – laughter, shouting, sounds of ancient music; rich scents filled the air, too, so that every room, every corridor, was a bombardment of sensation.

It had still been dark when they arrived and Mathias had wondered why the Prime should wish to see him so early. Sukui had led him in past two precisely saluting guards at a side entrance and then they had spent nearly two hours in preparation. Sukui considered every detail of Mathias's appearance – robes and skullcap of the right shade, a manicure, a hair trim and a fresh shave, new sandals – and, while preparing Mathias's appearance, he had also schooled him in etiquette. 'Never meet the Lord's gaze, unless he speaks to you,' he had said. 'Keep speech to a minimum and, again, only when unavoidable. Stand proud – the Lord Salvo hates weakness – but never too proud. You must present no challenge. The audience will last only a few minutes. Then you must return to the laboratory.'

Sukui was clearly nervous, from his fussing over detail to the rapid, short steps he took as he led the freshly groomed Mathias into the depths of the Andricci palace. 'Remember your lessons, Hanrahan,' he whispered. 'The Lord Salvo is a fair man, but you must know your place. You are *nothing*. Remember that.'

They entered a long corridor lined with marble pillars. The sounds and gaudiness increased markedly and Mathias guessed they were close to Andric.

Guards stood at one end of the corridor and Sukui swept past them, suddenly a new man, confident and in control. They barely glanced at Mathias but he knew that his features were now fixed in their minds.

The room they entered was tall and wide. A long table occupied the centre, piled high with food of various sorts. Seated around the feast, laughing and talking, were a number of young men and women, all finely dressed and beautiful, with that air of nobility Mathias knew so well. A few years earlier he would have fitted in easily.

A quartet of musicians occupied a recess at the far side of the room. Three were sitting, plainly clothed and staring at the ground. The fourth was standing, foot on a chair, plucking discordantly at a big-bodied guitar and laughing louder than anybody else. Mathias guessed who he was as he handed the guitar back to its grateful owner and turned to face the newcomers. The Prime was a huge man, red beard flowing down over his chest, face ruddy and shining.

'My Lord Salvo,' said Sukui, bowing his head and sounding strong. 'I have brought you Mathias Hanrahan, as your equerry requested.' Sukui stepped back.

Mathias bowed his head and said, 'My Lord,' as instructed. So this was the all-seeing and caring

Lord Salvo that Sukui kept on about. He didn't quite fit. Mathias had expected a small man, sharp-eyed and gentle, with an air of command but also of understanding.

Andric laughed. Mathias had never heard such a powerful, booming voice. 'So the runaway prince has honoured me with a visit, hah? Come and eat at my table. Sukui, you too.' Mathias sat next to a milky-faced woman who carefully edged away from him. Sukui sat opposite, looking perplexed; his 'few-minute audience' was clearly not going as he had foreseen.

'Go on! Eat, for gods' sakes.' Andric sat down next to Mathias and took a handful of cashew nuts. 'Do you know what I was told yesterday, by my cousin, Siggy Axelmeyer?' He was staring at Mathias. 'He said that Edward Hanrahan's half-brother is in Alabama City. "*Alabama City*?" I said. Siggy told me that the deposed Prime of Newest Delhi shared his room in Soho, he said that he worked in one of my own laboratories! And do you know what he told me, too?' Andric leaned forward, drawing Mathias and Sukui towards him with a wave of one large hand. 'He told me that my trusted adviser, Kasimir Sukui, had brought Mathias Hanrahan here and had *neglected* to inform me. Hah! Preposterous. That's what I told him. Preposterous.' Andric turned to glare at Sukui, bringing his face to within centimetres of his adviser's. 'I told him that Kasimir Sukui would be mistaken to do such a thing. If he was not Kasimir Sukui, he would be punished severely for such an error.'

131

Sukui was white. His gaze fell away from the Prime's and he bowed his head. 'Should I leave now?' he asked.

Andric laughed, and he was joined hesitantly by the people around the table. 'Leave? No, you are my most trusted adviser and I am, as you so often tell me, a generous man.' He turned back to Mathias. 'Tell me, Mathias, what do you think of my city? Glorious, hah? Majestic, hah? You like it lots, I can tell.'

All Mathias had to do was nod.

'Siggy says you are bright, he likes you.' The Prime took another handful of nuts and swallowed them whole. 'I like you, too, Mathias. I have the feeling you may have a great future in my service. Tell me: what is the field that interests you the most? My Project covers them all. Come on, what is it?'

'In the past my works have tended towards electronics and the investigation of ancient artefacts,' said Mathias. 'My interests are broad, but that is where my main strength lies.'

'So be it,' said Andric. 'You hear, Kasimir? Move him immediately or I may not be so forgiving. In fact, Kasimir, I will give you another role. I'm going to appoint you young Hanrahan's guardian. You will look after him, nurture him, guide his progress. In fact, you can take him on your next trip. Orlyons, isn't it?' He turned back to Mathias. 'He goes to these places under the pretext of research, but really he goes for the whores. Hah! But this time he has to work. Things are unsettled in Orlyons, as you undoubtedly know. But it is a good source of artefacts and of people. Like yourself, hah! Before

132

things get any worse, Kasimir must recover what he can and you Mathias, can help him. You can make sure the whores don't overcharge him, at least.'

*Orlyons*. Things could not have worked out better. Mathias nodded and said gravely, 'I will look after him, my lord.' Andric laughed louder than ever and Sukui sat quietly, still pale, still avoiding everybody's looks.

'I can see that we will get on well,' said the Prime. 'Just remember, Mathias. You lost your chance to be Prime long ago. Forget any such aspirations and things will be fine.' He leaned closer. 'But if I hear of any ambitions in that direction I will act. I am generous but I am also hard. Work for me, Hanrahan, and you will have a great future; work for your own ends and I will, reluctantly, destroy you.' Andric's eyes were burning through Mathias, the Prime's breath smelt of sulphur and garlic. 'Do you hear me, Mathias Hanrahan?'

Mathias nodded and the Prime of Alabama City laughed and took another handful of nuts. 'These are good,' he said. 'You should try some. You haven't even *touched* your food.'

# Chapter Eleven

Mathias Hanrahan realized how serious the situation was when he saw the size of the convoy headed for Orlyons. Despite the rumours and the inflow of refugees, he had thought that maybe it was all being exaggerated. The troubles were not that bad; he couldn't imagine Orlyons as a site of conflict.

He looked out from his position on the leading barge and saw the rest of the convoy of six, each with only a skeleton crew so there would be plenty of room for the return trip.

Sukui joined him at the prow. Mathias could see that the scientist was uneasy and he remembered the man's distrust of the sea. 'I find this business somewhat distasteful,' he said, and for a moment Mathias thought he was talking of the sea. 'Even though we go unarmed, it is an act of aggression. We are to remove anything of value before Orlyons becomes too dangerous. But, in so doing, we accelerate the town's decline.' Sukui smiled sadly and bowed his head. 'Still, it is my lord's decree.'

Mathias watched the waves, feeling uncomfortable. 'Tell me, Mathias. What do you know of this Lucilla Ngota?' Sukui was regaining his self-control; Mathias could almost see his brain ticking over. Lucilla had made an impression on Sukui when they had met in Orlyons; he seemed scared by her and now he wanted to find out more. He wanted to rationalise his enemy away, a form of thinking that Mathias had come to recognize in his mentor, although he did not yet know whether it was a weakness or a strength.

'Lucilla is from the valleys,' he said. 'She reached a high position in the Newest Delhi militia, before . . . She was close to March: that's why she came after me in Orlyons, or at least that's why Edward chose her.'

'The lord's intelligence says she is orchestrating the conflicts in the Massif Gris,' said Sukui.

The Massif Gris was a hard region: humankind could barely produce enough food to survive, that high in the mountains. The people were poor of body and even poorer of mind, their villages were riddled with fundamentalism of a most primitive form. 'They would respond well to her,' said Mathias. 'She's a doer, she's no bureaucrat. She can motivate that sort of people – I can see why Andric is worried.'

'The Prime? Oh no, he does not worry,' said Sukui. 'I am merely curious.' Then he turned and walked away.

Mathias studied the sea as it slipped away on either side of the barge. Most of the day would have passed by the time they reached Orlyons. He wondered if the coming night would be a MidNight or not: he had lost track, something he had vowed never to do.

Mathias had expected the arrival of the convoy to cause something of a stir in Orlyons harbour. People would gather around, they would stop their work to stare and maybe ask questions; word would spread rapidly. That was what he had expected.

But this was not the Orlyons he knew. Most of the fishing boats were tied up and idle; those that were missing had taken everything from their dockside lock-ups, their absence clearly a permanent move. There were people rushing about, just as normal, but their faces were grim and it was a long time before Mathias saw anyone he even vaguely recognized. He looked around for his old boarding house on Westward Street and then he saw why the place was so discordant with his memories: the building was gone, one wall a ragged barrier holding back the heaps of masonry that had once formed his home.

For a moment he felt horribly responsible, then he looked beyond the ruined boarding house and saw a whole row of what had once been shops and bars and workshops but were now reduced to rubble.

Mathias found Sukui giving instructions to the barge crews. He dismissed them and bowed his head to Mathias. 'You heard?' he said. 'They are to moor in Mirror Bay. They will return at sunset tomorrow and then we will depart. We will wait for no-one. Mathias, you have done well since the Prime put you in my care. I feel I can trust you. We must all go our separate ways – I have despatched the other juniors already. We have to recover all that we can. I have no time to watch over you but you would be wisest to do as I have said and return tomorrow. There is nothing for you here.'

Sukui headed past Mathias and into the town.

Mathias knew he could lose himself in Orlyons and nobody would care but, also, he knew that he would be waiting at sunset the following day. Sukui was right: since meeting with Andric, Mathias had found a new sense of responsibility. He was working in electronics now, restoring radios and a curious Toshiba trifacsimile and, in any spare time, he was deciphering technical texts and trying to guess the gaps. He could see progress being made; he couldn't give it up now and return to Orlyons.

He set off, heading for the Gentian Quarter. His instructions were simple: people and goods, quantity and quality. Newest Delhi and Orlyons had a virtual monopoly on ancient supplies and Andric wanted a stockpile while he still had the opportunity; in addition he wanted anyone who could follow a wiring diagram or read a textbook.

Mono knew little of the ancient ways – she could barely even read – but Mathias knew this was his opportunity. He had to find her.

The Gentian Quarter had somehow survived the troubles. Of course, there were buildings missing and others damaged – there were signs of destruction throughout Orlyons – but the people were still there, the people Mathias regarded as his family, a substitute for what Edward had stolen from him all those years ago.

'Hey, Alya!'

It took her a few moments to recognize him, then she was around her stall and hugging him. 'You look good, Matt, you look *good*!' Her cracked old face was shiny with tears but she kept hugging him and cackling away. 'Oh, Mono will be pleased. Wait till she sees you!'

A heavy weight drifted away from his heart. *Mono was all right*. He had not realized how much he was worrying until that weight lifted. 'Alya,' he said, holding her at arm's length. 'Tell me what's happening here. Everything's so different.'

'Ah!' She shook her head bitterly. 'They are little children with toy guns. They don't know what it *means* to kill a person. "Somebody's baby!" I tell them. "You bastards, you're killing babies."' She spat into the dusty road. 'But they don't listen. I'm an old woman and they're too busy bam-a-bamming at each other.'

'*Who*, Alya?'

'It's that Vera-Lynne Perse, she's one of them. I told her she was causing grief, see, but she didn't listen to an old woman. She bought guns and bombs and things from the bastards who done *you*, Matt, only she wanted to fight them off. Your Prime Edward, he has an army in most of Clermont, save here. They thought Vera-Lynne was on their side but she's using their guns to fight them and she's making them mad. I tell her, she's killing Orlyons, but she don't listen to—'

'An old woman, huh?' Mathias hugged her to stop her flow. He had heard enough. 'Listen, Alya. I don't have much time. I'm here to take as many of you away as I can. We have boats from Alabama City. They're leaving at sunset tomorrow. Alya, you're good with the artefacts, you can read – I can get you a place in Alabama, easy. We want artefacts, too. Anything you can get hold of: wiring, circuit boards, tools, books, *anything*. Alya, will you come along?'

Alya was looking at him strangely. 'Oh shit, Matt,' she said 'Of course I'm coming. I saw that Sukui, just before you came along. He has a softness for me, he asked me to come. He didn't mention *you*, though!'

Mathias left her cackling and tidying up her stall. The streets were coming alive for another Mid-Night. It *had* to be MidNight, he could feel it in the air.

Vera-Lynne Perse caught up with him on the Rue de la Patterdois. She fell into step by his side, the same sharp features, the same proud set of her shoulders.

'Nice to see you're spreading the freedom of Orlyons so successfully,' he said, thinking back to her earlier tirades. This part of the Patterdois was a crumbling mess, sections of buildings reduced to rubble, windows smashed, walls cracked and leaning eccentrically. One gap in the buildings had been shielded with a wide canopy bearing a huge red cross; in its shelter men and women queued to see a medic or a nurse. 'You're looking good.'

'I heard you were back,' she said. 'Slide said you'd come to join the fight. I didn't believe him. I see I was right.'

'Slide?'

'He joined us late, not till after your brother's militia invaded Clermont. He's just gone back out in the field. Keeping them at bay. Most of the

Underground are street people – they're shrewd tacticians, they know what a struggle is. Your brother's taken ninety per cent of the coastline but his militia don't dare stay inland when it gets dark. They didn't think we'd resist. Will you join us, Matt? It's tough keeping control – you could bring us all together. We'd save Orlyons.'

'Like you're saving it now?'

'It's easy to sound clever, Matt. Not so easy to face up to your beliefs and act.'

'I have done,' he said, thinking that perhaps it was close to the truth. 'And my beliefs don't involve getting shot in Orlyons.'

'I thought so,' said Vera-Lynne. 'I told Slide, but he said to try anyway.' Her walk was still proud as she turned to leave Mathias. 'Mono is in Greene Gardens, busking by Weeping Rock.' She smiled and shrugged. 'I guessed you might be looking for her.'

The voice was unmistakably Mono's. Mathias hurried along the path. As he drew closer he recognized the difference: she was singing unaccompanied, she had found no replacement for the old Semi-A.

It was dusk and the sky was burning red, but still a good crowd had stopped to listen; the struggle could wait just a little, the lady was singing. She was a tiny figure before the thirty or so listeners and the great, bulking form of Weeping Rock; it didn't seem possible that such a powerful voice could be hers.

He hung back at the edge of the crowd and let her song wind itself down, drifting away on the muggy evening breeze. At first she had sounded mournful, but then Mathias realized that he was misinterpreting her. Her song was wistful but relentlessly strong; behind the barely intelligible words was a gutsiness that she would ordinarily have put out through the Semi-A. It sounded eerie, that strength expressing itself through her singing, but Mathias realized that it had always been there.

When she looked up it was as if she had been expecting him. Maybe she had heard that he was in town, maybe not.

The music over, the crowd began to disperse, until only Mono and Mathias remained. 'I've come back,' he said. It sounded feeble but he couldn't take back his words.

Then she was in his arms, holding him tight and he forgot everything, focusing himself only on Mono. It seemed that nothing else could possibly matter. Not ever.

They passed a long time just walking, holding each other. Mathias told her all about Alabama City, about people she had never met and things she clearly did not understand; Mono told him about what had happened since he had left, only five months before. There was a lot that he didn't follow, a lot that he had already heard, but he soaked it all up, just for the sound of Mono's voice.

'Mono,' he finally said. 'Will you come back to Alabama City with me? Please?'

Her face grew serious and he knew her reply before she spoke. 'No, Matt. I can't.' She shrugged. 'Where would I sing?'

'I'd get you a Primal Licence – Andric would listen to me, he'd *have* to!'

'Matt, I'm an artist,' she said, quietly. 'I need to be able to do what I want *when* I want. An artist cannot work within the constraints of Primal whim and, yes, Matt, you've said most performers get around the system, but I'm an *artist*. I'm *proud* of that, I don't want to hide it.'

'But what freedom is there here?'

'I'm free to think, Matt. I might get shot but I have that freedom.'

'I'll stay with you, then.' He was throwing everything away and he knew it, but he didn't care any more.

'No, Matt. You've grown since you left Orlyons, you have a sense of direction that I've never known in you. You can't lose that. You have to go back.'

'Don't you want me to stay?' He was sounding pathetic but that was exactly how he felt.

'Yes, I do.' Mono shook her head. 'But you can't, and you know it.'

Even then, he vowed that he would stay, but while Mono worked a bar on the Patterdois he found himself talking with people, bargaining, persuading them to be at the docks with goods for the coming sunset. Just because he was deserting didn't mean he couldn't get people out to Alabama City, he tried to believe.

By sunset he was at the docks, amazed at the quantities of goods and people being loaded on to the barges. It seemed that most of Orlyons was being transplanted to Alabama City. Three gunshots sounded in the distance, as if to convince the refugees that they had made the correct decision.

Mathias shuddered as he stood with Sukui, watching the barges fill up.

'You are returning to Alabama City?' asked Sukui.

'Yes, I'm returning,' said Mathias. He had always known that he would.

They left as darkness descended and, above the steady beat of the manoeuvring motors and the winches pulling at the rigging, Mathias imagined that he heard a voice, a song carrying faintly over the waves. He couldn't be sure he had heard it; it was so faint it might just have been a memory.

Working on the Project was a welcome respite after the emotional upheaval of Orlyons. Mathias could lose himself.

He was part of a small team responsible for sorting through old electronic items, deciding what could be repaired and what was fit only for breaking up. It was not the most inspiring work, but at least it held his interest; things had been a lot better for him since the Prime's intervention.

A week after his return from Orlyons, Mathias approached the research team's hut, situated on Dixie Hill on the fringes of Alabama City. The hut was weathered and patched together, hardly the research centre he had once imagined; inside, it was cold and cramped, but at least it was somewhere for the team to work.

He looked around, squinting. He was not usually this mean-spirited early in the morning; in fact it was usually a good time for him, to the annoyance of Sanjit Borodin, the group's supervisor.

The problem was Siggy Axelmeyer.

Despite the transfer of work, Mathias still shared Siggy's room in Soho and last night, like so many nights lately, the Prime's studious cousin had come in drunk or drugged or just plain crazy. Mathias didn't care which.

One time Mathias had confronted him, stupidly. 'What about your work?' he had said. 'You were so ambitious.'

Siggy had told him to relax and have a beer. 'You're becoming boring, Mister Hanrahan,' he had said. 'Go on, have a beer.' They had laughed and said no more; it hadn't been important then.

Last night they had said nothing at first. Then Siggy started playing his mouth-organ. He had practised hard and now he was very good. Last night he played 'Mama Gonna Sell My Soul'. Over and over and over. It made Mathias think of Mono, only the coarse feelings Siggy put into the music cast up all the wrong memories. It made him think of all the men she had earned money from, the ones who had never mattered before; it made him wish they had finally made love, if only so he would know they *had*, so he wouldn't let it get at him like it did when Siggy Axelmeyer played the blues on his battered old mouth-organ.

'I'm trying to get some sleep,' he had said, late the previous night. 'Will you give it some rest?'

The candles were still burning and he could see Siggy's glazed eyes fix slowly on to his face. It made him wish he'd kept quiet. 'Music comes from the soul, Matt,' Siggy had said. 'You shut up my music and you shut *me* up, you close down my soul. You want to do that, huh?' Axelmeyer's look had turned fierce, then. Mathias had never really believed the stories of how wild he had been before joining the Project. He had wrecked houses, he said, he had beaten people for no reason; once, he'd said, he had nearly killed an old woman for not smiling at him. Last night, Mathias suddenly believed those stories. 'You're nice, Matt.' The look had melted away. 'You wouldn't do that to me.' The mouth-organ had returned to his puckered lips and the blues came rolling on out.

So Mathias had plenty of reason to feel rough this morning. He looked around and Lui Tsang was standing by him with a steaming cup of coffee, a welcome break from the troubles-inspired rationing.

'You look fucked,' he said.

Mathias grunted and accepted the drink. Lui was the most junior member of the team, having been there for barely a week. For the past three mornings he had come in earlier than anyone else, his only opportunity to explore the restored equipment that littered the small hut.

'Listen to this, Matt,' he said, guiding Mathias to a seat and then crouching to fiddle with a radio set-up the team had recently pieced together. Mathias noticed some new wires trailing from the set and out through the window. He said nothing; Lui would explain, no doubt.

'It's something I thought of in Orlyons,' said Lui. 'But the equipment was limited. I had a radio and a small dish, but it was unreliable even when it worked.' He turned on a switch and the hut filled with a fuzzy hissing and crackling. 'This radio is a good one,' he continued. 'And the dish I found is four times the diameter of my old one. I made it work this morning.'

'What have you made work, Lui? You're not being very direct.'

'Listen, Matt. You're hearing messages from the universe.' He adjusted some controls and, for a moment, Mathias imagined he could make some sort of sense of the noise. 'I've moved the dish around, but it's strongest from one region of the sky. Listen, Matt: I think we're hearing messages from Earth. *Listen*.'

Sukui was brief with Lui Tsang. 'Messages from Earth would be too weak for us to receive with such a simple configuration,' he said. 'You have shown initiative but your reasoning is lacking. The texts tell us of the difficulties of transmitting and receiving signals over such vast distances. The power spreads and dissipates.'

'But . . .' Lui looked dejected.

'And if a message *was* coming from Earth you would constantly need to realign the dish as Expatria rotated.'

Sukui had just put into words the thought that had been nagging away at Mathias. 'What do you make of it then, Sukui-san?' he asked. Lui had been desperate to make a good impression; now Mathias wanted to protect his old friend.

'When the Lords created the universe there was a great blossoming of energy. Ancient texts tell

146

us that all the energy contained within our universe was once compressed into a tiny region of space, and the rest was empty, waiting to be filled. From the outpourings of energy there still remains what the texts call a certain "Background Noise", in the guise of various forms of radiation. *That* is what you can hear, nothing more.'

Sukui was clearly feeling generous this morning. He turned back to Lui Tsang and said, 'You have shown initiative. This can serve as an introduction to the scientific method. You have just proven the truth of another aspect of the ancient texts; now, you must document it, measure it, find out all you can. Mathias, you must supervise the work. Report your results to me in two days.'

They worked through the following night, Lui filled with an intellectual fervour, Mathias kept somehow awake by his friend's enthusiasm.

'If it's Background Noise then why isn't it evenly spread across the sky? It has to be a signal.' Lui's frustration was evident by dawn.

'It can't be Earth, though,' said Mathias. 'We'd have to track it across the sky. The source is fixed relative to the planetary surface.'

'What if there are other settlements on Expatria?' asked Lui. 'People that didn't reject the old ways when *our* people did?'

It was their best idea. Mathias went back to his work: he had made a disc-recording of the noise and slowed it down. It faded and strengthened to no apparent logic but behind it all there was a definite pattern. If there was one thing that Sukui had lodged firmly in Mathias's mind it was the importance of pattern. It was a means of understanding, of explaining, it pointed to something more than the random play of chance.

When the time came, Mathias reported his measurements to Sukui and Lui remained silent; they both knew to keep their speculations quiet. 'See the pattern?' said Mathias, and it was clear that Sukui had.

'This warrants further analysis,' said Sukui. 'Tell me what you find.'

As it turned out, Sukui was present when the pattern was finally elucidated. It took them three days of dead ends and blind corners; on the third day the whole team was working on it, Sukui was so eager to understand the strange pattern.

Mathias found the answer, by chance as much as anything else. His mind numbed by the impossibility of it all, he was playing around with the trifacsimile, letting it cast his hand in different lights and watching the three-dimensional projection hang ghost-like in the air. And then the idea struck him – his disembodied finger was pointing directly at a restored cathode-ray tube; it was as if a ghost had given him the answer.

As he worked, he knew that this was it. It had to be! The signal was a digitised code, each bit of information controlling an individual picture element on the screen. He had taken that TV set apart himself, just to see how it worked. It took him nearly an hour to set it up, and by the time he'd finished everybody had stopped to watch. *They* knew this would be it, too. Even Sukui was standing back and waiting.

Finally, he was ready. He flicked the control switch and sat back, hoping fervently that there was some sort of standard specification common to both the source of the signal and the TV set before him. 'Don't expect too much,' he said, suddenly nervous.

The screen leapt into life, but it was only a fizzing greyness, the same tone he had seen on it before. He adjusted the tuning, even though the signal was coming direct from the disc and should need no tuning.

And the screen cleared, momentarily. It sparked grey again and then back to the clearer, slightly orangey tone, with a dark blob in the centre. The picture kept leaping and spluttering, fragmenting and then pulsing more clearly, but they could all see that the blob was a human face.

A thought occurred to Mathias and he leaned forward and adjusted another control. Sound filled the hut, much like the crackle that Sukui had labelled Background Noise. But over the top of the static were the nasal tones of a man's voice, coming in pulses of clarity, in step with the pulsing picture.

' . . . broadcasting to the people of Expatria from the Orbital Colonies . . . greetings from the followers of Ha'an and the people of . . . we are a people of peace . . .'

The message was from a colony in orbit around Expatria! It made perfect sense to Mathias, as if he had expected it all along, another hunch he had been unable to elucidate.

' . . . must repeat . . . of some urgency . . . know if there's anyone down there but . . . we will be a surprise to you . . .' Suddenly the voice grew clear. ' . . . had a message from Earth. They say they have despatched a new colony ship and it's headed here. We have to consider a joint response. I'll repeat: there's a ship coming from Earth.'

# PART THREE

## *The Emotional, the Rational*

## *Chapter Twelve*

As soon as Kasimir Sukui saw the distorted face on the TV screen, he guessed correctly the origin of the signals. In his youth, reading the archive material his parents had preserved, he had learnt what was known of the history of the Ark Ships. There had been four of them, sent one after the other by an organization of nations that had spanned the Earth. The Arks had carried representatives of each member of this unity of nations. The colonists and their descendants had grown accustomed to life in the Arks and, when the fourth generation finally arrived in the vicinity of Expatria, they had not wanted to leave the security of their homes. The planetary surface was alien to them, they were people of the interior. It was no great leap for a rational mind to see that, despite the collective decision to land, some colonists may have chosen to stay in the orbiting Arks. Mathias Hanrahan's grandfather had believed this to be so; he had recovered an old shuttle and tried to escape into orbit. The shuttle had failed, but Sukui had viewed intelligence reports on the matter. He had considered explaining the incident to Mathias, but the subject had never arisen.

The pictures on the screen confirmed that the split had occurred. The fact that the signals corresponded with the TV specifications indicated a common technological ancestry.

There were people living in orbital colonies.

The message sparked into greyness and Sukui cleared his throat. 'Play it back and attempt to refine the signal,' he said. Hanrahan had already started making adjustments and he grunted in acknowledgement.

The words of the message were still seeping through Sukui's consciousness. There were people living in orbit around Expatria. But also, there were more people coming from Earth and they had been in communication with the Orbital Colonies.

Events of the past few minutes would send shock waves throughout Expatria. The situation required careful handling.

The message played again. The face was clearer but still the image was poor. On a second listening, Sukui could make out more of the words, but the content of the message was unaltered.

When the image sparked away for the second time, Sukui rose and stood before the screen. 'Colleagues,' he said. 'We must talk.'

He looked around. Mathias Hanrahan and Lui Tsang sat immediately before him. The others sat back in a loose arc of chairs. Sanjit Borodin, Helena Lubycz, Sun-Ray Sidhu, Mags Sender. All looked serious, all looked excited, all looked eager. They had rapidly become one of his best research teams.

'We live in unsettled times,' said Sukui, 'and we bear a message of great impact. We must consider how best to inform the world.' He looked around, but nobody wanted to contribute. 'Rumours can be dangerous things, they are the fuel of conflict and disruption. Until this news is officially sanctioned we must each agree that it be kept secret. I am a man of influence, I am close to the Prime. Please, let me handle this in my own manner. I *ask* this of you, I cannot command you – knowledge can only be constrained voluntarily.' He looked around. 'Does anybody have anything to say?'

Nobody did. He asked each of them in turn to keep the secret and, from his experience in the Primal household, he felt that he could trust them.

Now, he had to consider how best to approach Prime Salvo with the matter. His words had not expressed the real cause of his concern: the one person most likely to be disturbed by the message was Salvo Andric. The Prime had so much to consider, Sukui was afraid his master might react hastily to the situation.

He would have to handle it very carefully indeed.

He headed for the door. 'I have matters to attend,' he said. 'We must devise a means of communication. Work on it and keep me informed of everything.'

Sukui stopped outside the door of Prime Salvo's High Office. It was three days since he had heard the message from the Orbital Colonies. He would like to have been more involved in the work – he longed to be out of the Capitol and busy in that hut – but he knew that was not possible. Regretfully, he acknowledged that he had become more statesman than scientist. Shaking his head sadly, he knocked on the door and then entered the office.

The Prime was staring out of a tall, leaded window. 'Kasimir, you were right as ever,' he said, without turning. An aide hurried into the room, and back out with a stack of files.

'Sir?' Sukui lowered himself into a seat and leaned back. He had slept little in the past few weeks. The pressures of state were increasing their burden.

'This summit.' The Prime turned and rested a shoulder against the window-frame. 'I received word this morning. Edward Hanrahan has agreed to meet. I told him I would blow his balls off if he refused; he said he would blow *mine* off but there was no harm in talking. We both know the situation is at a stalemate. We kill some of them, they kill some of us and nobody within kilometres of the borderlands can live in security. Did you know the farmers won't even plant crops in Xiong-si because they don't expect to be there to harvest? It's spread that far!'

Sukui was not accustomed to the Prime talking in such a negative manner. 'The summit?' he prompted. He had seen it as the most likely solution, a meeting of the two opposing Primes.

'It will be here in Alabama City in nine days' time. Full attendance: myself and you and a number of others. See to the details.'

'Do we know who they will send? Apart from Olfarssen-Hanrahan, of course.'

'No.'

Sukui felt a surge of disappointment and cursed himself for letting his feelings have so much influence. Will Lucilla Ngota be there? he had wanted to ask. Ever since he had confronted Ngota in the park, he had been plagued by her memory. She occurred in his dreams, that fierce look cutting him into tiny pieces. She occurred in his daytime thoughts, too, cropping up out of context when he was trying to concentrate on matters of more importance.

'You've not been sleeping.'

'Sir?'

'You were staring.'

Sukui mentally shook himself. He had to concentrate.

'What about matters closer to home, eh? What have you scientists been doing?'

Sukui barely blinked. In that instant he considered informing the Prime of their discovery and in that instant he dismissed the thought. There was too much happening; it would have to wait until after the summit. 'We piece together what we have found,' he said. 'It is a slow process.'

The Prime nodded, accepting Sukui's platitudes. 'Kasimir, tell me: how is my cousin Siggy doing? I have heard conflicting reports.'

So this was what was bothering the Prime. 'Reports about your cousin are bound to conflict, my lord. Siggy Axelmeyer is the site of intense conflict and it is all internal. Until recently he was a model student. He worked hard in the laboratories – I moved him around every so often, to broaden his experience – and he studied hard in his own time. I sometimes wonder when he ever found time to sleep. Your cousin, sir, is very intense. When he works he pours himself into his labours but, apparently, when he pursues other activities he is equally dedicated.'

'He wrecked the Happy Hobo Eaterette, last night. Single-handedly. They served him chilli-dogs when he asked for peperoni. He broke a few tables and then he threw the Happiest Hobo herself out through the front window. That was the biggest single pane of glass in the whole of Alabama City.'

Sukui had not heard of this latest incident. 'Sir, he *is* very intense.'

'Somehow he's heard of the summit. He came here and demanded that I change my mind, he insisted that we make guns and bombs, instead. He told me what a wonderful technological base we have, he said we could beat Newest Delhi easily if only we did as he said.' The Prime shrugged. 'I've had him locked up for a few hours. He has to learn.'

'Sir, why do you tell me this?' The Prime would not normally talk of such conflicts. It could be read as a sign of weakness.

'I tell you because Siggy mentioned a friend of his.' He spread his hands on his desk and leaned towards Sukui. 'He said this friend was the only person who really understood him . . .'

'Sir?'

'He said his friend was Mathias Hanrahan. Siggy – he doesn't amount to anything, he's just an angry juvenile. But Mathias Hanrahan is in the background, stirring up trouble. Maybe it's just coincidence – maybe *he's* simply "having a good time", as Siggy puts it. But I don't like it when there is trouble and Mathias Hanrahan is involved. I warned him, Kasimir: I will not tolerate interference. You must observe him and report to me. If he deviates by a fraction, then I will have him dealt with. These are dangerous times, Kasimir, we must be harsh.'

Sukui bowed his head. The Prime was mistaken: Mathias had matured into his role in the Project. He was not causing trouble. The final test of Sukui's trust had been in Orlyons, when Mathias had resisted the opportunity to flee and, instead, had returned to the docks at the appointed time. 'I will do as you say, my lord,' he said. It was no lie: he was watching Mathias already, waiting for results from the team on Dixie Hill. Sukui backed out of the High Office; he had much on his mind.

The signal was still being received ten days after it had been decoded. Sukui sat before the screen, staring at the fuzzy face and listening to the softly accented words. The team had refined the broadcast to a remarkable degree, but Sukui knew that the equipment was capable of yet better results.

Lui Tsang was fussing about, making adjustments that Sukui felt sure were unnecessary. The message had been repeated for so long, Sukui had begun to worry that they were too late. Maybe it was an ancient recording, repeated by the automatic systems of the Ark Ships. Maybe all that remained in orbit were four empty hulks and some computer circuitry.

Or perhaps they were only marginally late and terran ships were, at this moment, landing somewhere on Expatria.

Sukui stopped himself. Such wild speculation was not to be encouraged. He had to stay calm and sift the facts as they were found, he must *not* let his imagination fill the vast gaps in his knowledge with idle fantasies.

'We're ready, Sukui-san.' It was Tsang, pointing to a muffed panel he had called a 'microphone'. 'Give me the nod when you're ready, then speak into here.'

Sukui had directed the team's efforts into producing a voice-only method of communication. 'It will be quicker,' he had said. 'They will receive it just the same.' Also it would preserve anonymity: he did not like the idea of his image appearing on a screen thousands of kilometres distant before people he had never met. 'Proceed,' he said, and leaned closer to the microphone.

Tsang flicked a switch and nodded.

'People of the Orbital Colonies,' said Sukui, reciting his speech from memory. 'My name is Kasimir Sukui. I speak for the Lord Salvo Andric, Prime of Alabama City. We have received your message. The people of the Andricci provinces extend their comradeship. Please reply, then we will have preparatory discussions of the matters you have raised.'

Sukui nodded to Lui Tsang and the message was over. Then he glanced at Mathias and raised his eyebrows in question.

Mathias nodded and said, 'It's all on disc. We'll play it back until they respond.'

Sukui stood and walked over to the window. 'We cannot be sure they will respond,' he said.

'I know,' said Mathias. 'But at least we've tried.'

Sukui had sworn that he would not wait at the hut but, even so, he found himself doing just that.

He did not expect any response to be prompt but he remained, just in case.

He stared at the talking head on the TV screen. It was becoming annoying, the way the head bobbed about, the tone of its voice.

He left the hut and stood outside in the gathering twilight. In two days his time would be occupied solely by the peace summit. Now that it was coming to fruition he was beginning to have doubts about even that, but it was too late now, he would have to let events take their course and guide them if he could. He had to be rational.

He sat down with his back to the hut. He could feel tendrils of sleep tugging at the corners of his mind. He had not slept well for a number of weeks. Affairs of state had been too pressing. He drifted, slowly. Things would work out, although he had not yet computed the probability.

The ground was shaking and his arms were pulling away from his body but then he opened his eyes and it was Sun-Ray Sidhu, shaking him roughly by both shoulders and saying, 'Sukui-san! Quick.'

Sukui was instantly awake. He struggled to his feet and hurried into the hut. Everyone was gathered around the screen.

He pushed through and assumed his place by the microphone. The face on the screen appeared unchanged and, for a moment, Sukui wondered why he had been summoned.

Then he saw that the face *was* different. It was at a new angle, looking to one side, not out of the screen as it had before. The face was saying something that Sukui could not distinguish. He watched as the face's expression changed and then the head turned to the front and spoke, its voice muffled, saying, 'OK, ready to go.'

There was a pause and then the face said, 'Um, hi. We've just gotten your signal.' The man was looking down at what Sukui guessed was a written speech. 'Oh, Jesus,' said the man in his orbit. He screwed up a sheet of paper and tossed it away. 'You mean there's somebody *down* there? Hey, are you listening down there? Can you say anything? Is somebody there?'

Sukui activated his microphone. 'Of course there is someone here,' he said. 'Why else would we reply to your message?'

# Chapter Thirteen

Mathias had trouble believing that he was actually hearing a voice broadcast from orbit. He looked at Sukui but the old scientist's face was unreadable.

'Your message informed us of an approaching terran ship,' said Sukui. 'Please elucidate.'

'Jesus, you mean you're really down there? Real people? Nobody thought you would last.'

'You hear my voice,' said Sukui. 'I am here.'

'Jesus. Jes*us*.' Then the man seemed to get a grip on himself, and he said, 'What kind of comms rig-up are you running? Why the voice-only?'

Sukui seemed to be having trouble with the terminology. 'Please, you mentioned a ship?'

'OK, we'll tech-talk some time different. There's a ship coming, they say it's like a big ark only it's a lot faster. Near-cee, they said. Nobody took their broadcasts seriously, at first. Sure, they were strong but they were so weird we thought it was some kind of ents show. You know: *Babette's Family Blues*, or *Starscraper*. We get them all the time if we fine-tune one of the big dishes. No, maybe you don't know – can you get any of that shit down there? You should see some of the things they do!'

'The ship?' prompted Sukui, sounding frustrated. Mathias wanted to take over but he didn't dare; he had learned his place.

'Oh yeah. Well these broadcasts, they were from the "Holy Corporate Powers of GenGen". They said things like all the universe was created out of love and they want to renew the link of understanding between the peoples of Expatria and this corporation they call GenGen. They say they've brought a few folks along to help make this link. Jesus, it *stinks*.'

'What has been done about this, in the Orbital Colonies?'

'*Done?*' The face laughed. 'Most people here still think it's an ents show. There's even a junior GenGen FanClub back in Ark Red. I've checked it out, though, and it all fits. I set up a search through ArcNet and found that GenGen were one of the major backers of the first Ark Ships that brought *us* to Expatria. Of course it could still have been an ents show, despite the strength of the broadcast. But ArcNet had trouble interpreting the signals at first and I've back-tracked through the files and found out why.

'They're coming here, all right. And they're coming fast. Those transmissions were blue-shifted by more than eight hundred per cent. They're headed here at close to point ninety-eight of cee.'

'Do you know how close they are?' asked Mathias, leaning over Sukui's shoulder, his patience finally run dry.

'Well, hello, Voice Two. No, I don't know for sure. But the signals started up four terran years ago and ArcNet says the ship was already at velocity then. The latest signals we've had are stretching out – the blue-shift is reducing. The ship is decelerating.

My best guess is that we'll be seeing them among us in about two to four years, given the time it's taken for the signals to reach us. But I could easily be wrong: could be tomorrow, could be in twenty years.

'One thing's for sure, though: we've got to decide how we're going to handle them.'

That first conversation was brief. Sukui had said he would consider the options and renew contact at a later date.

Mathias was annoyed by Sukui's handling of the matter. They were talking with people who lived in orbit around Expatria, it was a historic event. But Sukui had been formal, he had given nothing away; he was 'considering options' when there was so much they could have discussed. Mathias didn't even have a name to put to the face on the TV screen. He wanted to know how they lived, how they supported themselves, how they organized themselves. He wanted to know everything but Sukui had suppressed curiosity in favour of his own brand of diplomacy.

That night, Mathias dozed in the hut. He told himself he wanted to be on hand if there was another message but the truth was that he didn't want to go back to his room. Siggy would be there, if he wasn't stirring up trouble somewhere in the city. Mathias didn't want the hassle, he had too much else on his mind.

The following morning everybody arrived as normal. Lui Tsang was first, as ever. 'Let's call them up,' he said, his enthusiasm rousing

165

Mathias instantly. 'See what they say without Sukui here to muck things up.'

It was tempting. Mathias looked at the fizzling TV screen, still tuned in, ready for the next broadcast. He stepped over and flicked the microphone switch downwards, into the on position.

Then he flicked it back up.

He had heard the sound of approaching voices. Sanjit Borodin and Helena Lubycz had turned up early, inspired by the events of the previous day.

'Think what we could find out if we called them up now,' said Lui Tsang, too new in Alabama for his enthusiasm to be tarnished by the discipline of the Project.

Borodin shook his head. 'No, Lui,' he said. 'This is too big for us. We need a higher authority.'

'Sukui?' said Lui.

'Sukui,' said Borodin. 'Unless, of course . . .'

'Unless?' said Mathias.

'If the Orbitals were to instigate the communication, then we would have to respond. It would be undiplomatic to wait for Sukui to be summoned before replying.'

Mathias was disappointed. Everything seemed to depend on Sukui. The discipline he had acquired was being tested severely and he was aware of this fact. Self-control was a good thing but he had seen the extremes it could reach. Maybe he should just . . .

More voices.

Mathias looked out of the window. Sun-Ray Sidhu was approaching, Sukui by his side. Mags Sender was following them up the path. Mathias had not expected to see Sukui on the day before the summit – he should have had too much to do.

'I cannot stay long,' said Sukui, as he strode in through the door. 'Is there any news?' He looked around expectantly.

'There's been no more contact,' said Mathias. 'Sukui-san, would it be possible for you to clear up an area of misunderstanding? How are we to proceed? Can we contact the Orbitals?'

'Certainly not,' said Sukui.

'Then what are we going to do if they contact *us*?'

'Communication should be restricted to higher levels at present,' said Sukui. 'We do not know what degree of trust there should be between the two parties. Are they telling us the truth?

'I will be busy elsewhere for the next three days. There is to be no contact. If they wish to speak, then you must inform them that it is impossible. Affairs of state prevent it. We will call them three days hence.' Sukui turned to the door. 'Mathias,' he said, over his shoulder.

Mathias followed him out. Out of earshot of the hut, Sukui turned and studied Mathias's face. 'The next three days are of vital importance,' he said. 'A number of issues are particularly sensitive at this time. Your half-brother arrives soon. He brings a number of high officials. I understand Lucilla Ngota is in charge of his personal guard. My advice to you, Mathias, is to become part of the background. Keep out of the city, sleep up here, live as though you do not exist.'

167

'Lucilla wouldn't do anything in Alabama City,' said Mathias. 'Edward has too much to lose – he wouldn't allow it.'

'Nevertheless,' said Sukui. 'For whatever reasons, you, Mathias Hanrahan, are a source of conflict. Your presence in the city would be counter-productive. Prime Salvo would not wish for *anything* to work against him at this juncture. And one final word of advice: stay away from Siggy Axelmeyer, at least until the summit has passed. You would not wish to be associated with anything that young fool gets up to. It would not be well regarded. Do you understand?'

Mathias understood, but he didn't like it. 'Have you told Andric of our work yet?' he asked, knowing the answer already.

'It is a difficult subject and these are sensitive times,' said Sukui. 'Patience is a necessity of modern life. You would do well to exercise some.' Sukui walked away.

Mathias had wanted to call the Orbitals. He had stormed back into the hut and sat before the microphone, letting his feelings simmer. But he had retained his self-control. If he was to rebel then it would be a considered rebellion, not an act of anger.

The team worked hard for most of that day. Lui Tsang and Mathias kept returning to the problem of how best to achieve full audio-visual contact with the Orbitals but they made little progress.

Mathias was adjusting the trifax when the face appeared on the TV screen. 'Hey, is anybody still down there?' said a familiar voice.

Sun-Ray, Helena and Mags had already left; they wanted to join the crowds that would attend Edward's arrival in Alabama City. Mathias looked across at Sanjit Borodin, but his superior studiously looked the other way. Lui Tsang nudged Mathias towards the microphone. 'Go on,' he hissed. 'You do it. I'd muck up worse than Sukui.'

Swallowing, Mathias leaned forward and turned the microphone on. 'Hello,' he said. 'Can you hear me?'

The face grinned and said, 'Hey, Voice Two again! Where's the old guy then?'

Gritting his teeth, Mathias said, 'Sukui-san asked me to inform you that he has urgent matters of state to attend to. He is unavailable for three days and will call you then.'

''S OK by me,' said the face. 'He was too stiff anyway.'

'He is my superior,' said Mathias. 'He said we were not to talk.'

'You let him tell you what to do? Or are you going to parley?'

Mathias glanced at Borodin's back. 'Oh shit,' he said. 'Let's talk. What should I call you?'

'They call me Decker, hereabouts. You?'

'Matt,' he said. 'So. Where do we start?'

# Chapter Fourteen

On the first day of the summit there was something new about Alabama City, an atmosphere of expectancy. The citizens tried to pursue their normal activities but the mood pervaded everything, oozing into every opening, forcing undercurrents through the entire city.

It was an atmosphere Mathias found unnerving. He knew from experience that such tension could take over and drive events, all that was needed was the right prompt.

Walking along Grand Rue Street, he realized that he had shut himself away from the mainstream of city life. Waves of *déjà vu* broke across him as he walked: the boarded-up shops, the impromptu food auctions, the faces that were so familiar. It was as if the port of Orlyons had been uprooted and woven into the fabric of Alabama City; he kept expecting to see rows of buildings devastated by the fighting, to find Slide in a doped-up heap in an alleyway or for Vera-Lynne Perse to fall into step by his side. To hear Mono and the 'tones, drifting softly above the crowd-babble.

He caught himself, shook his head sadly. This was Alabama, there were street-lights and posters of Salvo urging the populace – or those of the populace able to read – to accept the shortages with patriotic fervour.

He found an empty table in the Happy Hobo Eaterette and ordered a vodka-fizz, which they called 'coffee' to avoid the need for a Primal entertainments licence. The Happiest Hobo didn't appear to be aware of the shortages.

The previous day, Decker had told him a lot. He had told him about life in the Orbitals, about how the Arks had been added to over the generations until they had become incredible growths: modules and rubble-cladding and solar collectors and galleries and any sort of unit that could retain enough air for the life it held. Mathias could picture it clearly, a fantasia of technology. 'What do your superiors say about your contact with us?' Mathias had asked.

'Just when I was getting to like you, Matt, and you have to bring that up.' Decker had paused. 'I told you, we don't organize like you folks do. No-one out here can govern, if we disagree we just go our own ways. Space is big, Matt, you can't know how big until you're out here. But there *are* people who matter, people you have to convince if anything's ever going to be done.

'It's like I told it to Sukui: there's a lot of people out here who still don't believe in the terran ship – they're waiting for the next episode, or maybe wondering why there's no punchline. This is nothing official, Matt – it's just me and a few friends. We couldn't convince anybody out here about the ship, so we figured we at least had to see if there was anybody on Expatria who should know. Now we've got ourselves an extra task: if we can't persuade anybody there's a ship coming from

Earth, maybe we can at least convince them there are folks still alive on Expatria.'

The irony of the situation had made Mathias laugh; it still made him grin wryly even now, a day later. They both had the same problem: how to spread the word. 'There's one thing we both know,' Mathias had said. 'We have to try, we have to let people know somehow, we can't just let things stay as they are.'

'You're telling me what I already know,' Decker had said. 'I'll wish you some luck and hope I get some too.'

Mathias finished his 'coffee' and let the fizz die on his tongue before swallowing. The summit was being held in Merchant Chapel, a large trading complex just across Alcazar Square from the Capitol.

He left the Eaterette and headed for Merchant Chapel. The day's session should be near to completion and the participants would soon be filtering out of the Inner Chamber. Sala Pedralis would be there. He could talk to her, try to explain about the Orbitals and the approaching ship.

Even when Sukui finally revealed the news, Mathias could foresee a dangerous situation if Salvo Andric was the first person to be informed. Mathias had liked Andric when he met him, but he also distrusted him immeasurably. Sukui made the Prime out to be some kind of folk hero, the munificent leader, ruling only for the good of his people. Maybe there was some of that in Andric, but Mathias had seen a whole lot more, the greed, the hunger for power that he had even seen in his own father.

Sala was the person to tell. The most recent information Mathias had was that she had retained her high position in the Newest Delhi government; she was trusted by Edward in much the same way that Sukui was trusted by Andric.

Mathias shouldered his way past a tired-looking crowd of peace protesters and into Merchant Chapel. Traders' Gallery was wide and crowded, open on one side, running around the circumference of the entire building. Half-empty stalls were crammed into every possible space and the air was full of proclaiming voices and an occasional animal screech and the scents of spices and foodstuffs, so familiar from every market-place Mathias had ever known.

He approached the steps that led to the inner sanctum of offices and meeting rooms and on inwards, to the debating chamber that was his goal.

As the crush of bodies grew tighter, Mathias realized that there was something going on, a scuffle, some shouting, a heaving of the crowd. More cautiously, he continued.

Closer, he could distinguish some of the words. 'He's selling us off to the highest bidder!' cried a loud, booming voice. Siggy Axelmeyer. Mathias scanned the crowd for his room-mate's face. 'We should be fighting, not talking!'

He was there, ahead, struggling up the steps and half turning to face the crowd. 'Let's tell the Prime what we want!' he cried. A number of Axelmeyer's supporters jostled at the foot of the steps, but Mathias guessed the rest of the crowd were merely there because they were restless and hungry and that was the way crowds were. The gallery was a packed place – a surge from Axelmeyer and his friends could appear impressive in such confines.

'Mathias, you're here!' Axelmeyer had spotted him edging his way towards the front. 'Come on. Help him through there.'

Mathias felt hands propelling him to the foot of the steps and then Axelmeyer was embracing him and yelling at the crowd.

'Siggy,' said Mathias. 'I don't know what you're doing, but I just want to get through. I have to see someone.'

It was too late. The troopers on the doors into the sanctum had called for reinforcements and now they were advancing down the steps. 'You'll have to move along, now,' said a sergeant Mathias recognized. 'You're wasting your time.'

'Andrei,' Mathias said to the sergeant. 'Will you let me through? I'm not with this rabble. I have to see somebody.'

He was fortunate. While the rest of the troopers stayed to disperse the crowd, Sergeant Andrei Lokov led Mathias through to the small office that had been taken over by the army for the duration of the conference. 'Who is it you want to see?' he asked.

'Her name is Sala Pedralis. She's a senior adviser with the delegation from Newest Delhi. She was elected into the Primal family a number of years ago.' Mathias shrugged. 'She's an old friend.'

The sergeant ran a finger slowly down a list of names, mumbling, 'Ped-ra-lis, Pedr-al-is, Pedral-isss.' Then, 'No,' he said, finally. 'There's no Pedralis here. See for yourself.'

Mathias knew Lokov was a poor reader and he was not unduly worried. Sala *had* to be there, he couldn't believe she would have been left behind. Her sharp legal mind and her loyalty were something no ruler could neglect.

She wasn't on the list. He thought that maybe the list was incomplete but there were all the other names, right from Edward down to the lowliest servants. Sala had been left in Newest Delhi.

Mathias thanked Lokov and wandered back through the emptying Traders' Gallery. With no Sala his carefully considered rebellion had foundered at the first obstacle. He had been relying on her. He hadn't realized how much, until he could see that he would have to act alone.

Sun-Ray Sidhu was back at the research hut when Mathias walked in. 'I've been waiting, for you,' he said. 'Sanjit didn't want this place left alone.'

Mathias glanced at the screen but it was sparking grey nothings at him. 'Sunny,' he said, 'I've been thinking – d'you want something to drink? I'm dry.'

'Listen, Matt, is it vital? I have a . . . an appointment. I'd hate to keep her waiting.'

Mathias shook his head and Sun-Ray headed out of the hut. 'Hey,' he called after him. 'Any more contact?' Sun-Ray shook his head as he jogged away. 'No,' Mathias muttered to himself. He had hoped Lui would be there; the scene at Merchant Chapel had perturbed him and he wanted to talk to somebody. Sun-Ray had preferred the chance to get laid and Mathias smiled and shook his head – he could understand Sunny's choice.

He sat down in front of the screen and, almost without thinking, flicked the microphone switch into the on position. He cleared his throat. 'Anybody there?' he asked. 'Decker, are you there? It's Matt.' The screen remained grey.

He flicked the microphone off and ambled outside to sit by the open door. Had he really expected Decker to be there, just waiting for him to call?

It was early evening and the crawlers were out, dragging themselves blindly up the grassy slope. He picked one up and turned it over in his hand. It was a gnarled oval pod with three rows of tiny feet on the underside, still marching in an oddly hypnotic rhythm. He put it back down, facing the wrong way, and watched it set off down the slope. After a few metres its path began to curve in a wide arc that eventually took it back up the hill. In Newest Delhi, Mathias had studied the local species of crawler, bigger and greener, but otherwise much the same. Sala had shown him that they were actually the seeds of the boondog tree. Their primitive navigation system would guide them away from the parent tree until the stored energy ran out and there they would either rot or put down roots.

Mathias picked up another crawler and sent it back down the slope. He felt like *his* energy had finally run out and he wondered whether he would grow or rot. It was a depressing thought.

It was a mild evening and, as the sky darkened, Mathias caught himself snatching away from sleep.

'What the hell?' he mumbled, and let himself drift.

At first, he thought the voice was part of his dream. 'Hey, Matt,' it said. 'Don't you guys sleep?' He moved, felt the stiffness send pains through his body, wished he hadn't. Decker. It was Decker's voice. He had to wake up.

He shifted, sat upright and then made himself stand. Slowly, his head cleared and he remembered where he was.

Inside the hut, the screen had come to life. 'Matt. You there?' said Decker.

'Yeah, yeah,' said Mathias. Then he stepped forward and turned the microphone on. 'Yes, I'm here,' he said.

Decker stared out of the screen. 'I got your message,' he said. 'Hey, don't you guys ever sleep?'

'Huh? Oh, not often,' said Mathias. 'We get called up on TV in the middle of the night.'

Decker laughed and said, 'Boy, I wish I could see you – you sound near dead.'

'Hmm. Listen, I called you because I'd like to know what you're doing out there. Are you making any progress?'

'Some,' said Decker, non-committally.

'I've been wondering about how to tackle it down here,' said Mathias. 'It seems Sukui isn't in any hurry to let people know about the situation. He's waiting for the right time to tell the Prime but he's doing too much else at present.'

'The Prime. He's like your king, right? *El Presidente*?'

'Hmm. Listen, Decker: I think Sukui's wrong. This isn't the kind of thing you put in the hands

177

of a powerful minority – it should be spread from the bottom up. We have to break it to the people.'

'*Vive la révolution*,' said Decker. Mathias let it pass. 'How you going to do that?'

'I don't know,' said Mathias. 'Listen, is there any way you can land? Do you have shuttles that could get you down? The people here are pragmatic, they're stuck in ancestral ignorance. The only way to make them believe is for you to be here and show them. I've thought about it a lot and I really believe that's the only way.'

The set of Decker's shoulders had changed a little, but Mathias couldn't read anything from his fuzzy expression. 'Yeah, we've got shuttles that could land. I might even be able to get hold of one, but . . .'

'Decker, I know it's a big thing for you, landing on Expatria, but the people have to see you. We can't get them out into orbit. Will you think about it? It's our one big chance.'

Decker shrugged and laughed, a little uncertainly. 'Sure, Matt. I'll look into it.'

Mathias signed off feeling tremendously relieved. At last something was being done. He had been positive instead of hanging on Sukui's every instruction. He settled down on his heap of blankets in one corner of the hut and sleep took him easily.

Lui woke him with a mug of coffee. 'Any news?' he said.

Mathias came round instantly, feeling refreshed. 'I spoke with Decker,' he said. 'Sukui doesn't know, of course. Decker says they're going to try for a landing – then Sukui will *have* to tell the Prime. I think it's the best way.' He drank from his mug.

'It's dangerous ground,' said Lui. 'You tell Decker to make as if it's his own idea.'

That had been Mathias's plan anyway. 'Or give Sukui the idea to invite him,' he said. 'Yes, I know: I should have been a bureaucrat.'

There was a knock at the hut door and a woman came in, tall and clad in black trooper's leathers. She glanced at Lui and then said to Mathias, 'Mathias Hanrahan? The Prime requests your presence at the conference chambers.'

She stepped outside and waited for him to follow.

Mathias looked at Lui and shrugged. Today's was scheduled to be the final session and he had been looking forward to Alabama City returning to normal. He followed the trooper out.

The streets were warm and dusty. There had been little rain for the past few days; Borodin had blamed what he called the Niño current for stalling the clouds out to sea. Watching the dust rise and fall, Mathias asked why he had been summoned but the soldier ignored him.

They approached the Merchant Chapel and then, instead of climbing over the seated peace protesters and entering the gallery, the trooper veered off and led Mathias across the Alcazar Square and through an inconspicuous gate into the Capitol grounds. Mathias nodded when he realized what was happening. The conference in the Inner Chamber was just for the bureaucrats, for haggling over detail. The real discussions were taking place in the Prime's grand palace, the Capitol.

Outside a pair of high wooden doors a gaggle of officials congested the corridor. Sukui was there, and one or two others Mathias knew from Alabama City. There were also a number of strangers, their clothing looser and of a cruder cut. One of them was Captain Anderson, looking greyer, his face deeply creased. He nodded at Mathias and then looked away.

Sukui broke away from a discussion with a junior and hurried over to stand by Mathias. 'I told you not to mix with Axelmeyer,' he hissed. 'The Prime is greatly displeased.'

Sukui stopped and took a deep breath. Looking around, he adjusted his skullcap and stood up even straighter. 'It is time,' he said aloud. Everybody looked around and a guard opened the double doors. Then, to Mathias, he whispered, 'I have done what I can. You must be rational.'

The conference room was much like every other room Mathias had seen in Salvo Andric's palace. It was wide and tall, its walls were painted brightly, there were decorated columns and pilasters, and heavy velvet blinds were drawn back from the windows. Set in the centre of the room was a vast table; seated at one side was Andric and at the other, Edward Olfarssen-Hanrahan, looking stangely accustomed to his Primal finery. He had put on weight since Mathias had last seen him, and his features had matured beyond measure.

The attendants filed into the room and sat in banks of chairs at either side of the wide table. Edward glanced along the rows of faces, past Mathias and on along the line. Suddenly his head jerked

180

and he looked back again, finally recognizing his half-brother.

Mathias met his gaze without flinching. He still felt safe in Alabama City, despite Sukui's strange warning of a few minutes before.

Sukui stood and moved to just behind Andric's left shoulder. 'Lords, attendants. I call to order the third and final session of a most satisfactory set of discussions. At Prime Hanrahan's request, there will follow a summary of agreements reached to date. The fishing fleet of . . .'

Mathias stared out of the window at the pale blue sky; still no clouds in sight. As Sukui talked, Mathias worked out the location of this room in relation to the rest of the Capitol. After a few minutes he smiled. He had been right: a dish could be pointed at the correct angle through that window to receive the signals from orbit. He returned his attention to the proceedings.

Sukui was still talking. ' . . . a seven-month conditional posting of an observer unit in each of Alabama City and Newest Delhi, to be commenced upon signature of this Treaty of Accord . . .' Mathias stared out of the window again, wondering why he had been called to attend this session. It seemed that it would consist entirely of Sukui reading from this 'Treaty of Accord' – hostilities would cease, not that they had ever been official, of course; trade would be encouraged; free passage of citizens would be allowed, by permit; and it would all be supervised by an observer unit in each capital. Mathias was pleased that the troubles were over, because it would allow the Project to continue and

181

it would remove the obstacles to Sukui informing Andric about the Orbitals and the ship from Earth. But also it made him even more eager to get back to his work. He sat back in his seat and wondered how long the session would last.

Sukui continued for nearly an hour. It had been a productive summit.

Then he paused and looked across at Mathias. 'Now,' he said. 'We come to a matter raised by the good Lord, Prime Edward Olfarssen-Hanrahan, at last night's closed session. May I suggest the good Lord might continue?' He bowed his head and backed away from the conference table.

Edward tipped his chair back on two legs and looked around the room. 'Yes,' he said. 'The summit has been productive. But I have one last request to make of you, Salvo. It is a personal matter.

'Seated in this room is the man who murdered my father.' Edward glowered at Mathias, then smiled sweetly at Andric. 'This summit would be sealed on a most . . . *positive* note if you would be as good as to grant extradition of this man for trial in Newest Delhi. Although this is not a condition of the treaty, please, Salvo, allow justice to be done.'

Mathias studied his half-brother's face.

Edward had acquired a certain confidence from his time in office, but he was still the same: slippery, underhand. No, it was not a condition of the treaty, but everyone in that room knew the treaty was worthless if this final 'request' was not granted.

Mathias glanced across at Salvo Andric. The Prime was talking quietly with Sukui. He looked up and met Mathias's gaze, then looked at Edward. 'You raised this point last night,' he said, and then paused. 'This individual has caused trouble even here, but that is no confession of guilt. No, no' – he raised his hands to ward off Edward's objections – 'I do not wish to cast judgement on this case.

'This individual has become particularly trouble-some in recent weeks and I confess that it is a great temptation to ship him back to Newest Delhi. I have considered the matter at length, since you mentioned it to me.' He looked at Mathias. 'I am glad you do not make this a condition of the treaty,' he continued. 'Because this individual is an adopted citizen of Alabama City. If his choice is to remain here then I would not wish to interfere.'

Sukui bowed his head to Mathias. This was clearly what he had meant by his warning and the comment that he had done what he could.

Edward was looking at Mathias as, it seemed, was everyone in the room. 'Of course,' said Edward, 'this is no *condition*. But it would greatly ease relations between our two great nations. A fair trial in Newest Delhi would remove one remaining source of conflict. What do you say, Mathias Hanrahan? Have you acquired the integrity to stand up for what you have done?'

Andric was looking at him, too. It was clearly expected that he should reply. He had not expected the Prime's backing, even as strained as it clearly was.

A voice was clamouring in the back of Mathias's mind, telling him that he could stay in Alabama City.

He wanted to laugh, the tension inside him was so great. He could stay! He thought of the Project, of the need to disclose the existence of the Orbitals and the ship from Earth. Things were at a delicate stage.

Mathias stood.

'I am greatly indebted to the good Lord, Prime Salvo Andric, for his hospitality and fairness,' he said. 'I feel duty-bound to accept Edward Olfarssen's offer of a trial – I trust it will be fair, as he claims: I have nothing to hide.' The voice was still clamouring in the back of his head, screaming, bouncing around the inside of his skull, demanding to know why he had sealed his fate in such a way.

He shook his head angrily, trying to still the voice, and sat down.

The Project was at such a delicate stage – if hostilities were resumed then communication with the Orbitals might easily stumble at the first obstacle. By returning to Newest Delhi peace would be secured and the Project could continue.

Mathias looked across at Sukui. His self-control had won.

It was the rational decision.

'Decker, we have to talk – I don't have much time.' It was strange how quickly Decker had become the one person Mathias could talk to. But now there was more than just talking to do, he had to try to explain the situation so that his sacrifice would be more than an empty gesture.

Mathias had returned to Dixie Hill. It had been late and the others – Helena and Sunny – had left immediately. Nobody liked the idea of staying with a condemned man.

It was all very civilized. Troopers had not seized him as soon as he had announced his decision. He had been given until dawn, then he would join Edward's delegation to begin the journey back to Newest Delhi. Until then he was free, although he felt sure no-one would let him leave Alabama. Not now.

The summit had not lasted long after Mathias had spoken. Captain Anderson had informed him of the arrangements and then he had found himself in the corridor with Sukui. 'It took a great deal to convince the Lord to offer you freedom,' Sukui had said, still talking in the restrained manner he had employed in the conference room. 'I expected you to take the opportunity. Would you explain?'

'The Project is at a delicate stage,' Mathias replied. 'You know that. If I don't go back Edward will escalate the troubles until I'm faced with the same decision later on.'

'I think you judge your half-brother accurately. Your future is important to him.'

'You have to let people know about the real situation. If I can win you peace for a time, then maybe things will work out. If not . . . well, the ship from Earth will arrive amid a war with no-one waiting to meet them. You have to spread the word, Sukui-san. *That*'s why I did this.'

Sukui had stopped to stare at him. 'Mathias Hanrahan,' he said. 'You have become a rational man.' Then they had parted and Mathias returned to the research hut.

He slept little, that night. He didn't really try. All he wanted was to play the blues with the Mono- tones. He could play the slap drums, maybe relearn the mouth-organ. He would work at it. He knew, now, that he would work at it.

The time just before sunrise was the worst.

Mathias sat with his back to the wooden slats of the hut, watching the sky slowly grow pale. A bank of clouds was riding in from the sea, the Niño finally having given way to more conventional currents; the sun, although still hanging below the horizon, picked out the edges of the clouds, made them silver with tinges of gold. Gradually, colour seeped into the mid-grey of the morning sky, like blood spreading through a puddle.

'Matt? You listening?'

Mathias leapt to his feet and then hurried in to the microphone. Decker was on TV, looking around as if he was trying to peer out. 'Matt, are you there?'

'Decker, I'm here. Thanks for calling.'

'Trouble?'

'You could put it that way. Listen, I won't be speaking to you again. I have to go away.'

'What's happening?'

'It's a diplomatic affair. The details aren't im- portant. You'll be dealing with the others, from now. I guess it'll be Sukui – if you need someone more sympathetic you could ask for a friend of mine: Lui Tsang.' Mathias heard footsteps out- side; time was leaking away. There was so much he had wanted to say. 'Decker, I have to go now. Remember: the only way to make any progress down here is to *be* here. The people have to see you if they're going to believe in you.'

'Sure, Matt. But—'

The door opened and a leather-clad trooper looked inside. There were two more standing on the grassy slope, a short distance away. The trooper looked around the room – her eyes skipping over the face on the TV screen as if it didn't exist – and cleared her throat. 'Mathias Hanrahan?' she said. 'Would you step this way?'

'You know my name, Louisa.' The trooper looked uncomfortable. She stood aside as Mathias stepped past.

Behind him he heard Decker's voice raised. 'Hey! What's going on? What's happening?'

Mathias turned and called to the microphone, despite Louisa's strange looks. 'I have to go now.'

He just heard Decker say, 'Not now! Hey, what was that name? Hey come back! Come—' and then the door shut softly, cutting off his words. Mathias glanced briefly at the blank-faced troopers and then, sadly, he began his journey back to the city of his birth.

# Chapter Fifteen

As he watched Mathias Hanrahan walk away from the last meeting of the summit, Kasimir Sukui bowed his head in disbelief. The Lord Salvo had informed him of Edward's demand the previous night. It had taken great effort to convince the Prime that Mathias shouldn't simply be handed over as a part of the Treaty of Accord. 'He works well in the laboratories,' Sukui had said, struggling to justify himself. 'He has acquired a strong element of discipline in his thoughts. I expect—'

'What of discipline in his *actions*, eh?' The Prime had been walking irritably around the High Office, pulling at his beard and twisting it in his fingers.

'Sir, I fear you overestimate the significance of Hanrahan's behavioural aberrations.' Contradicting the Prime had been a calculated risk, but it had worked. The Lord Salvo had let the comment slip by and, after a moment or two more of brisk pacing, had said that his decision was to give Mathias the choice, even though the treaty would founder if Edward did not get his hands on his half-brother.

And, against all the odds, Mathias had agreed to a trial in Newest Delhi.

Sukui had confronted him when the final session ended. 'It took a great deal to convince the Lord to offer you freedom,' he had said. 'I expected you to take the opportunity. Would you explain?'

Mathias had acted rationally. He had assessed the likely effects of choosing to remain in Alabama City; Edward Olfarssen-Hanrahan would almost certainly be spurred on to greater aggression if he was slighted in such a manner. Mathias had given his life to save the Project.

Now, as Mathias disappeared around a corner in the corridor, Sukui was still stunned. Mathias had asked him to spread word of the Orbitals and the ship from Earth. That would have been the next step anyway, but now Sukui felt there was an added urgency. He felt that he should give Mathias's sacrifice meaning. The vague, emotive term 'honour' came to his mind.

Maybe it was not such a bad term. Maybe it could be interpreted as a rational reason for action; he would have to consider the matter.

Sukui headed for the side office where he was to meet Lars Anderson. He opened the door and the Captain of the Hanrahan Guard was already there, resting against a desk, arms folded across his chest. Sukui noted the reserve etched across Anderson's lined face. The two of them were probably of a similar age, both had reached the pinnacle of their careers within the respective Primal households.

Sukui bowed his head. 'Captain Anderson,' he said. 'I requested this meeting so we could discuss the terms of the observer units – yes, I am aware that Captain Mahler is responsible for sending our unit to Newest Delhi, but I will share responsibility for your unit in Alabama City.' Sukui filled two tiny crystal goblets with liqueur and handed one to the captain. Anderson nodded, but his expression remained unaltered. 'But first, there is a subsidiary matter I wish to raise.' Sukui glanced up at Anderson's face, but the captain was no help. 'The trial of Mathias Hanrahan.' For the first time Anderson's expression faltered. 'You will be aware of the faith he is placing in the judicial system of Newest Delhi, in returning for trial. It would be a great dishonour, not only to Mathias, but to the Prime of Alabama City, if the trial should be coloured by . . . prejudicial influence.'

Anderson waited for him to finish. He drank his liqueur in one swallow. 'Sukui-san,' he said. 'I've not known you for long, but from what I *do* know, you must be aware that you've just insulted the entire power structure of the Primacy of Newest Delhi. But you've done it in private and I'll do you the justice of replying. As Captain of the Guard I have influence but you must know the Prime is *Prime*.

'No, the trial isn't going to be fixed. I knew Mathias well – or I thought I did – and I knew March better. If Mathias is innocent then you can be assured I'll look out for his interests. If not . . . well all I can say is that justice will be done. Now: the observer units.'

Sukui nodded. The units had been his own idea but he had fed it to the Prime; that was sometimes the best way to get things done. To ensure the smooth progress of the reforms stipulated by the treaty there was to be a unit of observers posted in each capital city. Sukui had suggested that the units should consist of trusted advisers, perhaps to be headed by a senior figure from the militias. The leader had to be someone with a shrewd tactical mind, capable of seeing through any subterfuge and also of co-ordinating the unit in its functions. The units should be put in place at the earliest opportunity. Sukui had put forward a convincing case.

'Our unit will remain here when we leave,' said Anderson. 'We have the available personnel. There may be some exchange later, when we can assess the requirements more accurately.' He reeled off a list of fifteen names, along with duties and roles in the unit. They had organized themselves quickly.

'And who will head your unit?' asked Sukui.

'Lucilla Ngota, an attached officer in the Primal Guard. She—'

'I have encountered Miz Ngota,' said Sukui. His heart was beating so loud he thought that perhaps Captain Anderson could hear it. He tried to calm himself. Lucilla Ngota. She was a trusted member of the Primal household, she had been given assignments in foreign territory before, she had a shrewd tactical mind.

She had been the most probable choice.

The following morning, as the sun rose, Kasimir Sukui was out in the streets of Alabama City. He had slept little. He had been plagued by thoughts of Lucilla Ngota and Mathias Hanrahan and strange aliens that landed and said they were humans from Earth.

Walking through a back street in Soho, he spotted broken windows and slogans painted on walls. The vandalised building had housed one of the

Project's laboratories, Life Sciences Experimental. Sukui paused and drew a notebook from a fold in his robes and a pencil from under the rim of his skullcap. The slogans said 'Prime Folly' and 'Dark Practiss' and 'Old Ways Old'. He noted down the details. The Conventists had been out, celebrating the announcement of the treaty with the north. The undercurrent of fundamentalism that had always been a part of Alabama City was surging now, encouraged by the newly forged links with the Prime of Newest Delhi. It appeared that one conflict was about to be replaced by another. It was a situation that warranted close observation. Sukui tucked the pencil back into his cap and the notebook into his robe, then walked on.

For the first time in weeks, he had a few hours to himself. There were no meetings to arrange or attend, no consultations, no need to be in the Capitol just in case the Prime should require him at short notice. He wanted to go to Dixie Hill, but he hesitated. He looked at the sky and noted that the sun had cleared the horizon. Mathias should be under arrest and on his way back to Newest Delhi by now.

He gave himself a few more minutes. He did not wish to see Mathias being marched away under guard; he would leave his pupil that dignity, at least.

Finally, he headed for Dixie Hill. He had to contact the Orbital Colonies; he needed more information before he could consider informing the Prime.

The research hut had originally been quite modest, but two annexes had been added to house the stores of artefacts. The wooden slats had been coated with preservative at some time in the past, but even at a distance Sukui could see several areas that were rotten and crumbling away. The dish, two metres wide, sat atop the hut's roof; it looked dirty and grey but Sukui knew that did not impair the device's functioning.

Through the hut's small windows, Sukui could see that the researchers were already there. He passed through the open door and Sanjit Borodin greeted him with a nod. The atmosphere in the hut was subdued and quiet. Irrationally, Sukui did not want to disturb it by talking so he stood for a time and looked around at what was being done.

Eventually he cleared his throat and spoke. 'Everybody, will you gather around?' They stopped their work and moved closer. 'Our efforts must continue, they must transcend personal feelings. We have two priorities: we must consider renewing contact with the Orbitals and we must, I think, endeavour to complete the visual side of communications. For full communication both sides must be on an equal footing. Does anyone have any suggestions?'

The hut was silent.

'Mathias did what he did so this work could continue,' said Sukui. 'We must do our best.'

'We'd be best to ask Decker for ideas,' said Sun-Ray Sidhu. 'They're centuries ahead of—'

'Decker?' asked Sukui, suddenly realizing that he was at least one step behind everyone else. 'Who is this "Decker"?' But he already knew the most probable candidate for the name.

Sun-Ray glanced around guiltily. The others

studied the ground, except for Lui Tsang, who stared defiantly back at Sukui.

'Who is Decker?' Sukui repeated.

'He's the guy in orbit who you spoke to,' said Tsang.

'We did not exchange names,' said Sukui.

'He called us when you were in conference,' said Tsang. 'He spoke with Mathias.'

Sukui recalled one of his earliest impressions of Hanrahan: *trouble*. He had been consistent in that one respect, at least. What complications had this illicit communication created?

'You must all remember the importance of what is happening in this hut,' said Sukui. 'Our knowledge must be treated with maximum caution.'

'And you are the only one capable of that?'

The interruption had come from Tsang. 'From what has been happening up here, that would appear to be the case,' said Sukui. 'Lui Tsang, you are bitter today. We all feel the loss of Mathias but we must continue: his action must not become without purpose. By all means blame me – as you appear to do – but do not let your emotions interfere with your work. You can be replaced.' He could not. In all his time in the Project, Sukui had never encountered a talent greater than Lui Tsang's; the youth was a hard worker, too. Tsang's shoulders slumped and, finally, he stopped glowering at Sukui. He would grow calmer, after a time: he had backed down at a crucial juncture and Sukui knew from experience that this meant his rebellion was not a serious one. 'I repeat: does anybody have any ideas about the visual link?'

Sanjit Borodin stood and bowed to Sukui. He was a poor scientist but a good organizer; the decision to put him in charge of this team had been a good one. 'Before you arrived, Sukui-san,' he said, 'Lui was talking about the possibility of connecting the trifacsimile into the system. Rather than a face on a flat screen we might manage a fully dimensional face in projection.' Borodin sat down again.

Sukui raised his eyebrows at Tsang.

'It might work,' said Tsang, not looking at Sukui. 'We should discuss it with Decker.'

'It is an innovative suggestion,' said Sukui. 'But not, at this juncture, a practical one. The trifacsimile is in this hut. We already have the capability to receive visual signals from orbit. Our current problem is sending visual signals to *them*. We need some kind of "camera".' He had learnt the word from his reading. 'We do not even know that they would be able to send the correct input for a Toshiba trifacsimile.'

'But there's already a kind of camera in the trifax,' said Tsang. 'Anyway, they're centuries ahead of us – they'll have the capabilities to take whatever we send them.'

'Decker has told you this? I thought not. Lui, I am not dismissing your suggestion. I simply point out that we must work within the bounds of what we know: they send us pictures on a TV screen, therefore they must have facilities for receiving such input.'

Sukui turned to Borodin. 'Sanjit,' he said. 'We must contact our friends in orbit. This Decker may be of use at this stage.'

The response was quick, no more than four minutes by Kasimir Sukui's reckoning. He had been prepared for a longer delay. Decker could hardly be expected to wait by his receiver at all times.

'This is Kasimir Sukui, scientific adviser to the Prime of Alabama City,' he had said. 'I wish to talk with you, Decker.' Then he had waited with his researchers, watching the dancing greys of the screen. Only Lui Tsang had feigned indifference, annotating the pages of a textbook and looking only occasionally at the screen.

Sukui's call was repeated by disc-recording and, four minutes later, the screen flickered and came to life. It was the same man Sukui had spoken to initially, this Decker. He swallowed his distaste for the man; it was irrational, it had no place in the scientific mind.

'You are, I presume, Decker?' asked Sukui. 'My name is Kasimir Sukui, scientific adviser to the—'

'Yeah, yeah,' said Decker. 'I heard your call-up. Would you explain what happened down there? I was talking to Matt and then it sounded like someone came for him and he left. I heard a name mentioned – what's Matt's name? Where's he from originally?'

So Hanrahan was to be an obstacle in this, too. 'His name is Mathias Hanrahan. He vacated his claim to the Primacy of Newest Delhi a little over three and a half years ago amid a degree of scandal. Now he has returned to face the consequences of that scandal.'

Decker was nodding slowly. 'So he *is*,' he said,

to one side. 'What about this Hanrahan clan? How big is it?'

'The political clan is large, the genetic family small. Mathias has a half-brother, now Prime of Newest Delhi.' Sukui wanted to get back to matters in hand; he could see no reason why Decker should be so interested in Mathias. 'They are the end of the Hanrahan line. Mathias's father had a reputation for care in the matter of bastards. Edward's mother taught him that lesson. Edward has produced no heirs, so the line is at an end. Now . . .'

Decker had turned away from the screen. He was talking to someone who occasionally edged into the picture. 'Kasimir Sukui,' he said. 'I'm sorry for my abruptness and what must seem kind of a strange line of questioning. This revelation is of great importance to us. I don't know if Mathias told you of the problems my friends have been having in convincing people out here about the situation. This could just win the case for us. Let me explain. Do you know the story behind Ha'an's – August Hanrahan's – escape from Expatria?'

'I have heard a version,' said Sukui. 'But please continue.' At the mention of August Hanrahan, Sukui had deduced where Decker's story might begin. He sat back and studied the screen.

'August Hanrahan was Prime of Newest Delhi until fifty-seven terran years ago. You know that. From what you say, his son, March, somehow held the Primacy together and handed it on to Edward. August Hanrahan was tough and he was clever. He saw the ways things were going. There were all kinds of cults spouting different versions of the Truth and all of them rejecting the technology that brought us here in the first place. He saw that if that went on there'd only be a bunch of barbarians left on Expatria, if anyone survived at all. He saw that they'd fight themselves into the dust if they could. So he tried to do what you guys appear to be doing: he started people to work on reprocessing the old ways, he started trying to move people forwards. Shit, you know all this – you know that it didn't work and he had to get the hell out.

'His greatest pride was an old landing shuttle that had been mothballed years back; he'd had it cleaned up where he kept it, at a small place outside of Newest Delhi.'

'The place was a village called North Cape,' said Sukui. 'Continue.'

'Yeah. He got away in the shuttle with ten of his friends.'

'In Newest Delhi they say the shuttle was struck down from the skies by a bolt of lightning,' said Sukui. 'I thought, perhaps, it had failed.'

'No,' said Decker. 'August Hanrahan got into orbit. His shuttle was picked up by a rigger from Ark Yellow. They say it was a miracle they even shut the doors on the thing, let alone managed to make it lift off of Expatria. I've seen it – it's still in orbit. Shit, that thing is near falling *apart*.'

'Forgive my interruption,' said Sukui. 'But now you know Mathias is a descendant of August Hanrahan. Why do you hold this to be of importance?'

'He changed his name when he found us, or it was changed for him. What he found was a bunch of hopelessly inbred, ignorant morons. The only reason they located him was the automatic systems of the rigger ship – the on-boards did all the docking and transferrals for them. Most of them were too dumb to learn a name like Hanrahan, they called him Ha'an. I guess some just grunted, or so the stories say.' Decker laughed. 'Ha'an rebuilt the Orbital Colonies. In only fifty-seven T-years we've reached where we are, from where he found us. That's pretty miraculous. He's like a little god to us – no, we don't worship him, although some think we should.

'That generation weren't so much inbred, they'd just allowed themselves to lose what they had. They were apathetic. The arrival of Ha'an changed all that. The people wanted to know how he had come among them. Life on Expatria had made him and his friends strong and healthy. They put a bit of diversity back into orbit.

'I'll tell you why I'm so interested in Mathias: Ha'an is my grandfather. He's grandfather to a good deal of us out here. That makes Mathias and Edward my cousins. They're the closest relatives of Ha'an on all of Expatria. That means a lot to us, it'll mean a lot to the people I have to convince. Family's important out here.'

Sukui stared at Decker's face on the screen. He could tell the expression was an earnest one – Lui Tsang had improved the reception of the signals since Sukui had last been here. Looking at the features of Decker's face, he could finally understand why he had instinctively disliked the man: he look just like a slimmed-down version of Mathias Hanrahan. The hair was the same thick black, the mouth had the same wide, innocent smile. But it was more than just looks: the gestures, the range of expressions, the arrogance and the confidence – they were all there. The likeness was strong indeed.

Sukui sighed. The Hanrahan blood was clearly potent. Was trouble a Hanrahan trait, too? 'Your story is of interest,' he said. 'I see we have much common ground. Now, the reason for my call was to enquire after technical details. We will need your assistance if we are to have full two-way communication. I believe we need what is known as a "camera".'

Decker laughed – so like Mathias – and said, 'Don't take offence, Kasimir, but is there someone there who will be doing the tech-work? It'd be a lot easier if we spoke direct. Hey, Matt mentioned a guy I could talk with. His name was Lui Tsang. Is he there? Is he the right guy?'

Suddenly Sukui felt unbearably weary. 'Yes,' he said. 'Lui Tsang is "the right guy". Lui?' He stood and moved aside to make room for Tsang at the microphone.

He was tired, he had not slept well for a number of weeks. Of course Lui was the man to whom Decker should be talking. Sukui was a scientist no more, he was a bureaucrat. Quietly, he slipped away from the hut. As he walked, the afternoon sun soaked into his aching limbs but he barely noticed; he had things to do.

## Chapter Sixteen

He wanted to head for his apartment in Hitachi Tower. He wanted to sink into his soft bed and let the tiredness seep away from his body. He shook himself and a shudder passed down his spine.

He was losing control.

He could not allow that to happen. He was Kasimir Sukui, man of science, principal adviser to the Prime of Alabama City. He was shivering a little, even though the sun was still warm on his shoulders. He concentrated on lifting and placing his feet in the correct sequence, on walking slowly through the jostling streets of the city.

Gradually, his breathing steadied itself and he began to feel refreshed. His mind was disciplined; from past experience he knew that sufficient concentration could make his body feel however he desired it to feel.

He still wanted to return to his apartment and sleep, but now that desire was isolated in a remote part of his mind: it existed but he paid it no heed.

His position demanded such discipline of him.

Passing through a wooden archway, he stepped out on to Grand Rue Street. A glance at the position of the sun confirmed what a public timepiece above a small Harrod-store told him: he was due shortly at the Capitol. Prime Salvo had commanded a dusk consultation. The Prime's equerry had passed on a warning with the message. 'The Lord is insistent,' he had said. 'Things are tight in the Capitol – the Lord is causing havoc among the domestics.' Sukui had chastised the equerry for his loose tongue, but privately he was grateful for the warning. He had planned to broach the subject of the Orbitals this evening; now that would have to wait until the Prime was in a more receptive mood.

Grand Rue Street took Sukui into the heart of the city, through the fringes of Soho and then on to the Route Magnificat that fronted the Capitol. The streets here were even busier than the rest of Alabama City. Sukui surveyed the excited faces, wondering what had awoken the crowd. Soon it became hard to move for the press of bodies. Spicy, sweaty scents drifted on the air, along with bawls and screams and cascades of laughter. The faces were quizzical and happy, mostly looking up at Canebrake House, a tall building that faced the Capitol across the Magnificat. The people were merely curious, there was no hysteria to this crowd. Sukui relaxed and waited; the currents of bodies had drawn him to the heart of the gathering and he could barely move. He drew out his diary and then tucked it back inside his robes – writing would be impractical within such constrictions.

Canebrake House had a fourth-floor balcony, wide and overgrown with flowering clematis, fronted by a bowed metal railing. A big-bodied man stood on the balcony; there were others in the background, but this man was clearly the focus of attention. He was tall and broad shouldered, his hair rusty brown and standing angrily out from his skull. His face was clean-shaven and flushed and he was waving expansively at the crowd.

He was wearing a violet robe, tied with a chequered sash, and a matching skullcap.

They were the clothes of a scientist.

Sukui forced a path through the crowd but there was no need. He already knew what the closer view confirmed: the man on the balcony was Siggy Axelmeyer.

Axelmeyer was holding something in front of his face and, with a start, Sukui recognized what it was: a microphone. He thought of the Project. What if Axelmeyer knew of the Orbitals?

But then Sukui relaxed. The microphone was only part of a voice amplification system, what Mathias had once called a 'PA' system. Axelmeyer was talking into the device and his voice was being blurred and distorted and thrown out in a jumbled torrent. Sukui tried but he could barely make out Axelmeyer's words. Only the occasional phrase came through – words of dissent and revolution – but somehow it was enough to feed the crowd's curiosity.

Axelmeyer continued to gesture and wave for a time, and the listeners continued to laugh and talk over his words. He did not appear to be put off by this reception, in fact he looked to be in his element.

Unable to move, Sukui watched the Prime's cousin. No matter how hard he tried, he could find little in Axelmeyer's nature that he liked. He was the only person Sukui knew that irritated him even more than Mathias Hanrahan.

With Hanrahan it had been a conflict of egos: Sukui had tried to instil discipline into a potentially able scientist and he had succeeded, at least to a degree. But Axelmeyer was different: he had turned to the Project purely for access to power. Science, for him, had merely been a way to win the Lord Salvo's favour. He had used the Project, he had used Sukui; it was inevitable that he had failed.

Squashed between hot bodies, Kasimir Sukui concentrated on slowing the pattern of his breathing. No-one had the ability to make him angry in the way Axelmeyer did. He inhaled and counted, exhaled and counted, inhaled, exhaled. Inhaled. Exhaled. As his pulse returned to normal he surveyed the crowd again, noting expressions, the faces he recognized. All would be entered in his notebook when he had the time and the space to record them.

Up on the balcony, Axelmeyer was coming to a conclusion, or so it appeared. His arms were held wide and his voice boomed out of his crudely assembled loudspeakers. ' . . . a position of power to one of defeat,' he said. ' . . . time to get together and . . . *play the mother-fucking blues!*'

Sukui jerked to attention. Had he just said . . .?

Up on the balcony, Siggy Axelmeyer pressed something to his mouth and the sound of music came out of the loudspeakers. First there was a rising and then descending chromatic scale, then a 'One, two, a one-two-three-and-a.' Axelmeyer played his mouth-organ and some of the people behind him must have had instruments too, for the sound was that of a full band.

The music was ragged and undisciplined. There

was none of the precision Sukui knew well from the streets of Orlyons. But there was something, there was most certainly *something*.

The tones were fuzzy and distorted, but the PA system was better suited to music than to words and the sound held together remarkably well. There was an energy to the music, a flood of raw aggression. Sukui looked around at the gathered faces, their attention finally focused on the onslaught of sound and rhythm. The crowd was beginning to take on a mood of its own, fed by the music. Sukui felt himself caught up in it, too, his hatred of Axelmeyer coming to the fore once again.

The crowd was moving. Spaces were opening and people were dancing. Sukui slipped through the gaps, plagued by the thought that Axelmeyer probably did not even have an entertainments licence, but then, looking around at the manic faces of the people, the masks the crowd had given them, he wondered if this could really count as entertainment.

Gratefully, Sukui broke free of the mass of people and found himself only a few tens of metres from the Capitol gates. He presented himself to the guard who waved him through with an impatient flick of his bayoneted rifle. He glanced at the colouring sky and was relieved to see that it was not yet dusk, he was not late for his appointment.

'Have you seen what that worthless cluck of a cousin of mine is doing out there?' demanded the Prime, when Sukui entered the High Office. 'He's mad! They're all mad. Tell me, Kasimir: do you think

I'm mad? Everyone else is, so why shouldn't I be? Will you answer me that? Will you? No, don't. You are an honest man, I don't want your answer.'

Prime Salvo marched around the large office at a frantic pace. He kicked a chair at the central desk and cursed when its back splintered under the impact. 'What did they make it from, anyway?' he mumbled, as he resumed his pacing.

His long, red beard hung in tangled strands on his chest from where he had been twisting it through his fingers, pulling at it and smoothing it with food-greasy hands. 'I tell you, Sukui, he's pulling the mat from under his own feet – he won't get my continued support now. He must know that!'

Sukui thought that as Axelmeyer was being so open in his dissent he would, at least, be aware that the Prime would no longer pay his endowment.

Prime Salvo took a bottle from his desk, proffered it to Sukui, and then drained it himself. 'Have you seen him? Have you seen him out there?' Sukui bowed his head and waited. 'He's taken up rooms in Canebrake House. He's got himself a balcony and he stands on it, whingeing at the people, telling them I'm no good. And they listen! After all I've done for him, after all I've done for *them*. I've given them street-lighting, haven't I? Hmm? We have a fishing fleet that catches three times as much as when I came to the Primacy. We have farms that grow *four* times as much. We have the grandest capital city on all Expatria! Hmm?'

'Sir, it is not me that needs convincing.'

The Prime glared at Sukui and then grunted. 'You're right, Kasimir. As ever. Did you know there are Conventist chapels springing up in Alabama City? They came with the Hanrahan mob and some of them have stayed. They're moving damned fast. Captain Mahler tells me they've linked up with some of our own churches – the smaller ones – and there's a lot of scope for them. Cousin Siggy has been stirring them up, too. He marched into their inaugural Gathering and told them to pick up their weapons and fight if they wanted to get anywhere. They picked up their weapons and they threw him out of their chapel, but that won't stop him. Listen, Kasimir: why is he mixing with them? They're fundamentalists and he's a scientist – opposite extremes. Why is he doing it?'

This was all disturbing news to Sukui. Was this the peace Mathias had sacrificed himself to preserve? 'Sir,' he said. 'I fear young Axelmeyer is looking for someone to fight. I feel certain that the Primacy's least positive move would be to rise to his bait and offer him such conflict.'

Prime Salvo sat heavily on his big desk. 'You're right again, Kasimir: he wants to fight. And by the gods will he get one! *He cannot do this in my city*. I cannot let him challenge the Conventists – that would only lend them some sort of credibility among the people of the city. I think it is time my young cousin learnt something of his real place in this world.'

Sukui bowed his head even lower. The Prime was trapped: by his own nature he could not sit back and let things fade away, as they would, but by intervening he would only escalate matters. That way he would be giving credibility to Axelmeyer and then the struggle for power would become genuine. 'Sir, were there any matters that we should deal with now?'

'Huh? No, no. Nothing that has to be done now. It seems my cousin has rearranged my schedule. Very impolite.' The Prime laughed loudly, but it was forced. 'You can go,' he said. Then: 'Oh, there was one small matter. Tell me: what is it that commands so much of your attention up at Dixie Hill? Hmm?'

'The finds from our last trip to Orlyons.' He had not meant to lie. It would only make things more difficult in the long term. 'My best team works at that installation – we have a number of projects in hand.' The words slipped of his tongue so easily.

'Hah!' The Prime had found another half-full bottle and he took a long swig from it. 'Hmm. You're lying, Kasimir. I bet you really brought that whore back with you from Orlyons and you've got her hidden away in that hut. Hah! Ha Hah!' He took another drink and Sukui gratefully slipped out of the High Office and into the still coolness of one of the many corridors of the Capitol.

As he walked, his heart beat slowly and calmly. He was thinking, running through the endless possibilities and permutations arising from what he had just learnt about the political upheavals occurring all around. He would have to consider matters carefully. The Project must survive. Progress must continue, at whatever cost.

'We've met before.' The tall, dark-skinned woman dismissed Sukui's junior with the casual wave of one big hand.

A night's sleep had refreshed Kasimir Sukui. His head had been clear, his responses reasoned and rational.

And then Lucilla Ngota had entered the office he was using in the Merchant Chapel.

Her voice sent ripples of tension across his skin, her eyes pinned his own in place and he felt that she could read his thoughts as clearly as if they were printed across his forehead. Over the years of monitoring the functioning of his own body, Sukui was certain that he had never felt this way before and he did not want to feel it now.

But her eyes drew him on and he gestured to a seat and offered her a small glass of minted mulberry. 'You asked to see me,' she said.

Sukui nodded. 'You recall faces well,' he said.

'The Woodrow Gates, Greene Gardens, Orlyons.' Lucilla smiled, a strange expression in such strong features. 'You made me remember. An untrained mind out-manoeuvred me.'

'Untrained in a military sense, perhaps,' said Sukui, wondering why he had summoned her from her work with the observation unit. 'I hope the incident will not impair our relationship.' He felt his face flush, something he was not accustomed to. He resisted the impulse to seize a notebook and write it all down.

'At that time we were on opposing sides,' said Lucilla. 'Now we are not. And anyway, justice is being done and I will return for the trial. A grudge would serve no purpose; it would be irrational.' She looked around the small office. 'Is this a social invitation, or did you have something to tell me?'

'Let us label it a social call in the cause of our respective duties,' said Sukui. 'If we are better acquainted then both our jobs will be more straightforward. I trust you are receiving adequate co-operation in your duties? I will arrange a tour of our scientific establishments for you, if you require. Unless, of course, you object on . . .'

'On religious grounds?' Lucilla laughed. 'No, I'm not a cultist – I have little preference as far as the old technologies are concerned. I live in whatever world I am put in, technology or no. Greta calls me a pragmatic bore.' She shrugged.

'Perhaps I can convince you of the value of the scientific view of life,' said Sukui. 'Or maybe *I* am the bore.' He wanted to stop but could not. This woman was corrupting the self-control he had taken years to accumulate. He talked on, about nothing in particular. He poured Lucilla a liqueur and had one himself. She told him what it was like to be a successful figure in government, coming from a backward valley in the Massif Gris as she did.

After a time, she stood and replaced her glass on the drinks shelf. She smiled at Sukui and said, 'I'm glad you invited me, Kasimir. You must show me your Project and try to win me over. I have to go now.'

She went.

He was desperately glad that she had gone. He could have taken little more. The first time he had met Lucilla Ngota she had made him feel tiny, insignificant. She could have killed him and it would have meant nothing to her. Now she was charming and diplomatic; he felt at ease with her pragmatic view of the world and the discipline of her thoughts.

A genuine friendship was in prospect. And she made him feel terrible. He felt weak, he felt empty when she left the room, he felt totally under her power when she was with him.

Worse still, he liked it, this animal urge that was clouding his senses.

He stopped himself. He stood and walked around the small office. Lucilla was clearly unattainable; he should forget her. But he felt constricted – he had no outlet for his feelings, no Orlyons to drain his urges and help him regain his self-control.

For long minutes, Kasimir Sukui paced around that borrowed office in Merchant Chapel, wondering what he should do. Then a repeated cry from the Traders' Gallery finally filtered through the layers of his confused mind.

'Chet Alpha's Pageant of the Holy Charities has come to Alabama City!'

Sukui hurried across to the window and looked out over the packed trading place.

'Your munificent host, Chet Alpha, invites you all to come and see his Glorious Pageant!'

There was a horse-drawn caravan inching its way through the masses, the same brightly painted caravan Sukui knew from Orlyons. Alpha's women were sitting in the caravan and on top of it, staring out at the writhing shapes of the crowd.

Sukui spotted the man who was doing all the shouting. Chet Alpha had come to Alabama City.

Sukui smiled. Maybe things were beginning to work out in a positive fashion, after all. He left the office. It was, perhaps, an appropriate time to renew some old acquaintances.

*

The tightly packed bodies and the curious expressions reminded Sukui uncomfortably of his last encounter with a crowd, below Siggy Axelmeyer's balcony. This time the people were looking at the gaudy little caravan being pulled in their midst by a pair of bony horses, they were looking at the confident little man who pushed his way through, shouting, 'Come around and see what's here – it's Chet Alpha's Pageant of the Holy Charities and it's setting up right here in the Traders' Gallery!'

Immediately, Sukui noted the differences in Alpha's appearance. He was wearing a long, dark cloak, tied around his bulging waistline with a length of cord. His hair was cleaner and longer, flowing in blue-silver strands to his shoulders, and his face had been shaved accurately, without the occasional missed tufts of stubble that had been his fashion in Orlyons. The women were wearing pastel-coloured robes and were clean-faced; not the exotically clad, painted whores of the Rue de la Patterdois Sukui had frequented before. Alpha had cleaned up his act, a sensible precaution when arriving in a new city.

Chet Alpha turned and put his hand out to stop the horses. 'Here, girls,' he barked. 'This is the place. I can feel it in my bladder.' The procession came to a halt and the girls busied themselves removing boards and cases from the caravan and giving corn to the horses.

'Chet Alpha, I see you have taken up my offer,' said Sukui, emerging from the crowd. 'You have come to Alabama City.'

Alpha turned and squinted at Sukui, then he

nodded and smiled. 'Sukui-san,' he said. 'A familiar face, that's nice.' Alpha's skin was flushed, his eyes wide, but he did not smell of alcohol. That was something else that was new, since he had been Orlyons's foremost Purveyor of Pleasure. 'Offer?' he asked. 'What offer?'

'Your memory fails you,' said Sukui. 'In Orlyons you were concerned about the political climate and I suggested that you come to Alabama City in order to continue your trade. I told you of the Lord Salvo Andric's interest in the arts. Do you recall?'

'Mister Sukui,' said Alpha, patting him jovially on the arm. 'I remember what you said, but I'm not here because of that. I'm here because the hand of fate has brought me here.'

Alpha smiled and accepted a mug of beer from one of the women.

Sukui remembered her and nodded. Her name was Larinda and, despite her sharp tongue, he liked her. He had money with him and for once he had time to spare. Larinda smiled meekly and returned to grooming the horses.

'Chet,' he said. 'Are you in a position to begin business at the moment, or shall I make an appointment?' He smiled politely.

'Business? You mean . . .?' Alpha laughed and slapped Sukui's arm again. 'Excuse me, Sukui-san,' he finally said. 'It's good to be reminded of the old times in Orlyons. You see . . . you see my purpose in Alabama City is more of a *recruitment* campaign. We are looking for people to join us.'

'Business is expanding?'

Alpha laughed again. 'Would you like to join us,

Sukui-san? The girls will give you all the training you need.'

Sukui was not accustomed to Alpha joking in this manner. Then he realized that it had been a serious suggestion. 'Me?' he spluttered. 'But . . .'

'You see, Sukui-san, I am here to pursue a higher goal. I've seen the light. I had this dream one night. I was being spoken to. First I thought it was Larinda, then I thought maybe the chillis – my old mother used to blame everything on the chillis – and then I saw the Truth.

'I was *chosen*, Mister Sukui. Chosen to spread the Word. In my vision I learnt that my function in the current life is to travel the settled lands of Expatria, telling people . . . well, telling them the *Word*. You want a beer? Benasrit brews it in a tank under the Caravan of the Holy Charities. That's what they are, you see. The girls, they're not whores no more. No, they're *Charities*, consorts of the gods. But the goddesses must need consorts too, so I'm looking for a few boys as well. You'd get a nice robe if you joined, Mister Sukui. You want to try out for a trial period?'

Sukui glanced across at Chet Alpha's Charities. Suddenly they seemed so pure, in their pastel robes and their unpainted faces. He looked back at Alpha and tried to decide if he had been driven entirely insane or if it was only a temporary setback. 'I would need to understand your theology,' said Sukui. Alpha looked blank. 'Your divine purpose. Tell me, what is this message you have been chosen to spread? What is this *Word*?'

Alpha looked smug. He grinned broadly and then

took another swallow of his beer. 'Sukui-san,' he said. 'You are truly a man of wisdom. Your intellect shines through like a . . . well, it does, anyway. You are—'

'What is your Word?' prompted Sukui.

'God didn't tell me that.' Alpha shrugged. 'He just told me to spread it. Said He'd tell me the Word some other time. Shit, I'm in no hurry, Mister Sukui. The Guy wants time, I *give* Him some time.'

Sukui smiled; he bowed his head and made ready to leave. He had business that required his attention.

'Now,' said Alpha. 'Which of the Charities was it you wanted to fuck?'

Lui Tsang had acted against Sukui's directions but now Sukui was eager to see the results. Sukui had told him to concentrate on a simple visual link; Tsang had wanted to be more innovative. Tsang had wanted to use the Toshiba trifacsimile as the basis for their communication system.

'You've got a trifax?' Decker had said, as reported by Sanjit Borodin. 'Then we're in business. And it's a *Tosh*? That's amazing. I'll tell you what to do and we'll be fixed up in zero time. OK?' It appeared that the Toshiba unit was the basis of the standard means of communication in orbit – 'It's kind of like a quasi-hologrammatic real-time simulator,' Tsang had said, one time when he had failed to explain it to Sukui. The initial broadcast had only utilised TV to keep things simple.

Now, half of the hut had been transformed into what Lui Tsang was calling a 'Com-studio'. The windows had been covered over – darkness improving the clarity of the trifax – and the adapted Toshiba had been arranged on a four-legged stand, cables trailing across the floor in an unruly tangle.

The TV screen was filled with a face Sukui had not seen before. 'Hi, I'm Decker's and Mathias's and Edward's cousin,' she had said, when Sukui had enquired. 'Who are you? You've gotten a screwy voice.'

'He's OK,' Sun-Ray Sidhu had said over Sukui's shoulder. 'He's the boss.' Then to Sukui he had added, 'She meant she liked your voice, sir. By when she said "screwy", I mean. She's cover for Decker. He's working on the trifax.' So was everyone in the hut with the exception of Sukui.

Sukui said, 'Call me,' and then went outside and sat on the damp grass. He drew the diary from his robe and the pencil from his skullcap. There was much to add, he was growing lax. Soon he was adrift in the world of memory, sorting, sifting, deciding what was important and what could be forgotten.

He paused to push the lead further out of his pencil stalk and noticed that there was no noise emerging from the hut. He turned just as Helena Lubycz emerged and waved at him. 'It's time,' she said, then turned and vanished inside the hut.

Sukui felt nervous as he brushed himself down and headed for the door. Everyone looked up as he entered. 'Stand there,' said Tsang, pointing to an open space in one corner of the hut. 'This is your camera, you have to look at it here.' He pointed to a trio of lenses, each directed at Sukui.

Sukui stood straight; it was a proud moment. Tsang flicked a switch and Sukui noticed a gasp come from the TV screen. Decker's cousin was staring to one side. 'Look at the camera,' hissed Tsang.

Decker appeared on the TV, looking in the same direction as his cousin. 'Lui,' he said. 'You've done a good job. Hello. Hello, Kasimir Sukui – you've now got yourself a twin, here in Orbital Station Blue. How does it feel?'

It felt vaguely disappointing. Sukui was still in the hut, looking at the TV screen. At least Decker appeared pleased with the results at his end of the link.

'Will you move a bit?' said Decker. 'No, not that much, you'll get out of range. You just lost an arm for a moment there. Right. OK. You'll like to know that we now have a full visual link this end. We can see you. I'll need to fix up your colour a bit – you look a little green – but that's easy enough. We'll fix your end up in a few minutes.'

'It is good that you are satisfied,' said Sukui. 'Do you have any news?'

Decker looked serious. 'How are you doing with putting word about? We've got us a definite fix on the GenGen ship. Their blue-shift has dropped drastically and they're close enough for us to look for parallax. ArcNet puts them a little over eight months distant, but that's still inspired guessing. We have to decide on our response, Kasimir. Time's running out. And I'll tell you another thing. They've started broadcasting at us again. Only this time it's different, it's propaganda. They're telling us how GenGen has improved the lives of millions, how they're so wonderful that now they want to improve

217

life for *us*. I'm not so sure about wanting to be improved by them when they don't even know us. Listen, we've got to do something.'

'In your conversations with Mathias you must have discussed the options,' said Sukui. 'What do *you* think?' He was stalling. With the Prime in his present frame of mind, the only thing possible was to delay.

'Mathias wanted us to land. He asked if we had shuttles that could take the trip.'

'And have you?' Sukui had not considered this possibility – it could cause problems, but on the other hand it could well be the answer to everything.

'Yes, but . . . it wouldn't work, I'm sorry. The shuttles could take it, it's the people that couldn't. You see, we don't live at gees out here. There are a few stations with low gravities scattered around, but they're just for industrial use. We don't need it. So you see, there's none of us who could take the gravity, it's not possible.'

'Then we must think further,' said Sukui. 'You mentioned completing the trifacsimile link. Shall we continue?'

'Yes,' said Decker. 'Yeah. I've told Lui: we're going to end this transmission and send you down a looped holo sequence, one that will repeat over and over. It'll let you set your equipment up how you want it – you set it for that and everything'll be fine. OK?' The picture on the TV cut out and Tsang deactivated the camera that pointed at Sukui.

Sukui stood to one side and watched Tsang and Sender moving about, positioning what Sukui recognized as another part of the trifacsimile, the

218

projector. It was all very cumbersome, but he knew that, given time, they would grow accustomed to the equipment. He would have to direct the team's work towards such a goal. The way things were going, they would have to be ready to move out of the hut at short notice. Watching them set up the holo, Sukui decided that he must suggest that Tsang and maybe Sender would have to devise a wholly portable communicator, even if it took two or more people to transport the device. It was a necessary precaution.

'Ready?' said Tsang. Sun-Ray Sidhu nodded. 'Right.' Tsang made a final adjustment and stepped back from the projector.

At first Sukui thought they had been tricked. A figure appeared in the centre of the hut, looking around but not meeting anyone's gaze. Was this the onset of an invasion?

Then Sukui forced himself to be rational. He studied the figure and made himself see that it was merely a projection, an image. It had no substance.

He looked at the face and saw that it was the face he knew from the TV screen. It was Decker, his features still blurred, sparks of varicoloured light flashing excitedly around his image. His body was thin and weak; Sukui could see clearly why the Orbital peoples could not land on the planetary surface. Their wasted muscles would never resist the gravity, their atrophied bones would snap under their own bodyweight. Decker's feet were twisted under him, a few centimetres clear of the floor, and he drifted occasionally, shifting position without the impediment of gravity. One hand was outstretched, holding a ghostly rail, fixing Decker's position against the perturbations of freefall.

Sukui glanced at the others, trying to read their expressions. They were excited and nervous, but above all else, Sukui could see that the apparition scared them. Its ghostly green hues, the strange angle of lighting and the 'wrong' shadows, the way it hung unattached in the air.

Tsang was looking at Sukui; he appeared less intimidated than the others. Sukui nodded, remembering that Decker had mentioned refining the image. He held his breathing steady, trying to remain rational, but this image, this *ghost*, was a potent thing.

Tsang adjusted one of his controls and the trifax wavered and split into a double image. He made another adjustment and the images merged, then split again.

Sukui moved over to stand behind Tsang, then impatiently he said, 'Lui, move over. I will make the necessary adjustments.'

Tsang vacated his seat without protest.

Sukui looked at the controls and allowed Tsang to show him which ones Decker had told him to set. They were simple knobs. Twist them one way or the other until the image was satisfactory.

He turned one, noted how it separated the images as Lui Tsang had done. He turned it the other way and then adjusted it minutely until the image was single again. Another control threw the trifax into blurred confusion and then back into a clarity Sukui had not expected from a mere projector. Over the ensuing hour, Sukui experimented with each control, testing the trifacsimile's range of capabilities.

It was a powerful tool. He could create an image so convincing that he could barely believe that it was *not* Decker, floating in the middle of the hut; Mags Sender actually tried to touch the image at one point, but her hand passed through without even causing a ripple.

But there was more that could be done with the image. Sukui found that he could selectively alter its colouration, adding light to the eyes and skin. He could blur and twist the features into an animate snarl, twisting Decker's face to such a degree that even he, Kasimir Sukui, scientific adviser to the Prime of Alabama City, was filled with a tremulous, pathetic fear.

Eventually he gestured for Tsang to close down the power. In an irrational moment he jumbled the dials, losing the setting for the last, most powerful figure he had created. The trifacsimile was truly a potent device.

Quietly, he left the hut, not wanting to stay and hear the inevitable discussions among the team. He had a lot to consider.

## *Chapter Seventeen*

Lunch with the Lord Salvo was not Kasimir Sukui's greatest desire, but he could not refuse. The Prime was in a sensitive frame of mind.

Heading for the Capitol, Sukui had just turned off Ruby Way when he heard the voice.

He paused to listen.

Ever since Siggy Axelmeyer had started to cause trouble, the boldness of the street entertainers had grown, particularly in back-street Soho. Wherever a space was to be found, it was a juggler, a musician, a dancer, who found it.

But this one was different.

For a moment Sukui could not put a face to the voice. Then he remembered and wished he had not.

He stood like a rock in a stream, people pushing past him this side and that, nudging him, jostling him, dragging at him, but he would not shift. A face was floating in his mind, framed with drifting, blue-black hair.

Mono had come to Alabama City.

Sukui started to walk again, heading for the voice. He didn't recognize the tune, a complexity of half and quarter tones, words that were bland and mostly indistinguishable. Sukui had never been keen on music, it was too indefinable. You could write down the notes, calculate the timing intervals and still there was something more. It was like the sea, and the behaviour of crowds: too much for a single mind, too much for a mere bureaucrat.

Closer to Mono, the crowd was impenetrable. Sukui considered moving on.

He had an appointment at the Capitol.

But suddenly that did not seem so important. He was listening to Mono's voice and it stirred up a curious mix of emotions in him. Even a day or so before, Sukui would have fought the feelings, pretended they did not exist. But now he could see that if he did so, he would be denying a part of himself. He remembered lying by Mono's side, in her claustrophobic room in Orlyons's Gentian Quarter. He remembered wanting to bring her back to Alabama City.

And now she was here and he was standing alone in a tightly packed crowd, listening to her, unable to see any but the nearest heads and bodies and a swathe of grey sky.

He realized he did not want her any more. Not in the way he had. The very thought made him feel dirty, self-abused. He shook himself, tried to snap himself into a more rational frame of mind. He had an appointment at the Capitol but a strange torpor had overcome him and he could not move.

Mono's song finally wound itself down into a faint, repeated groan, and the crowd stirred and began to shift. Sukui pushed his way forward, desperate to catch her before she vanished. Some-one cursed him and thumped him on the back, but he continued. The populace of Alabama City had become more aggressive recently – Sukui had recorded numerous examples in his diaries – a trend for internal conflict which had easily replaced the national antipathy towards Olfarssen-Hanrahan and his northern territories. As the congestion thinned, Sukui's progress became easier.

When he found her she was sitting on a sack of grain, shoulders against a wall, scanning the faces of the dispersing crowd. She saw him and smiled as if she knew he would be there. 'Sukui-san.' She nodded her head.

'Mono,' he said, crouching down in front of her. 'You have moved south.'

She was hugging herself, her skin dimpled. 'It's colder down here,' she said. 'Nobody told me that.'

'We are farther from the equator and so closer to the ice-caps,' said Sukui. 'You should have asked a scientist.' That made her smile and Sukui felt a little better. 'Why have you come?'

'Last time in Orlyons, Matt asked me to come here with him. I said no. I was stupid.' She paused, searching Sukui's eyes.

'Go on,' he said. Talk of her relationship with Hanrahan did not affect him now.

'Orlyons is full of Newest Delhi militia, now,' she continued. 'They say it's part of some treaty and they're there to stay. They've banned gatherings on the streets. No more than four together at a time, they say. Shit, that made the 'tones illegal for the first. You sing on the Patterdois – even alone – and more than four people stop to listen and the troops are in there, boots and fists first. I lost three teeth one time. I think maybe soldier-boy lost more than me though.' She smiled.

It was true. The Treaty of Accord had stated that current occupations marked the new official boundaries. Alabama City had gained part of the Massif Gris and a twenty-kilometre coastal strip. Newest Delhi had gained all of the island of Clermont. 'Do you have accommodation?' asked Sukui.

'That's why I'm singing: I've just arrived in Alabama but I know people here. People only stay in Orlyons to fight Newest Delhi. Rather than search a strange city I thought people could come find me, so I sang and you found me. Where's Matt living? I thought maybe he'd have some room for me, if he's still interested.'

She knew nothing. Sukui looked at her, wondered how to tell her.

'So it's true,' she said, studying his face. 'I heard it in Orlyons but it was only a rumour an' there's lots of rumours. They've got him, right? In Newest Delhi, right? He's still alive, isn't he?'

Sukui swore never to underestimate Mono again. He admired her self-control and stopped himself making a mental note. 'Yes, it is true,' he said. 'Come along, let's walk – I have an appointment.'

He didn't know how to explain. 'It was part of the Treaty of Accord: peace, as long as Mathias returned to Newest Delhi for trial. I have used whatever influence I have to ensure that the trial will be fair, but the odds of that are poor, to say the minimum.'

'Why did he go?'

'There is a Project here in Alabama City, of which I am the nominal head. It was important to Mathias. He saw that the troubles would disrupt it and he sacrificed himself in order to secure peace for the Project.'

'And you let him go.' Her voice was toneless.

'Yes, Mono. I let him go. It was Mathias's choice, but I could have stopped him. Blame me, if you wish.'

'When is the trial?' asked Mono. 'Or . . . has it already been done?'

'My best information puts it at two weeks hence, but delays are probable.' They stopped outside the Capitol gates. 'You can stay in my apartment,' said Sukui. 'There is a guest suite. I would be honoured.'

Mono shook her head. 'I don't think so, Sukui-san. I'll find something.'

'Then go to Merchant Chapel – the Traders' Gallery. Chet Alpha has taken over an entire length with his so-called Pageant of the Holy Charities. Alya Kik is said to be there. She will take care of you. Good luck.' He kissed her on the forehead and nodded to the guard. From the other side of the gates he glanced back, but Mono had already disappeared into the crowd.

Passing through the seemingly endless corridors of the Capitol, Sukui knew that this was finally the time to inform the Prime of what was happening on Dixie Hill.

He had already left it for too long.

It must be handled carefully – he could not let the Prime know that so much had occurred behind his back. More by his side, than behind his back; that was the phrasing Sukui would use if Prime Salvo challenged him on the matter. Hopefully, it would not come to that. He would simply explain that he had news of great importance. A message had been received. There were people living in orbit. He would have to ensure that these people would not appear as a threat. He would inform the Prime that they could not land. Maybe he should leave the GenGen ship out of it, at this stage. The Prime would not react positively to an outside threat of such proportions.

Sukui knocked on the door of the White Suite, the room where Mathias had first been introduced to the Prime. A bellow came from within and he entered.

Seated at the table was the usual Primal coterie. Rampraketh Osk, his face painted and his long, bangled hair trailing into his bowl of food; Pom-Pom MacGrew, picking daintily at her loaded plate; Andrei Klowski, Naomi Klowski-Hill and Chop Hill, all rolling about in the heaped cushions scattered beyond the far end of the table, Chop giggling and clutching at his bodice.

The Prime sat at the head of the table, glaring at his companions. 'Pom-Pom,' he growled. 'You're not enjoying yourself.'

'Oh, I am. I *am*,' she said, forcing laughter and tossing a grape at Osk in what she evidently hoped would appear a playful manner.

'Get out,' growled Prime Salvo. 'You're lying.' He raised his voice for the benefit of the others. 'You hear? You're here for *fun*. Now *laugh*!' He turned to Sukui, as Pom-Pom MacGrew ran tearfully from the room. 'You're not laughing, Kasimir. Should you leave too?'

'Sir, I fear I came in part-way through the amusements. I am sure I would have been entertained if I had been here earlier.' Sukui bowed his head. For the first time in his life he was angry with the Prime. How could he sit there, insisting people have 'fun' when his empire was crumbling all around him?

Prime Salvo accepted Sukui's explanation and gestured for him to sit in Pom-Pom's vacated chair. Sukui diplomatically filled a bowl with food and ate a little.

'I'll smash him,' said the Prime. 'And I'll hang him from Merchant Chapel for all to see.'

'Siggy Axelmeyer?'

'He's no cousin of mine. Do you know he burst into Merchant Chapel and climbed to the roof? He stood there and pissed on the crowd, then he played that damned mouth-organ of his. When they called for more he managed another piss. And do you know what, Kasimir? He's even applied for an ents licence.'

Sukui had heard something of Axelmeyer's games and they irritated him intensly. What annoyed him most was the way Siggy had managed to carve disorder out of the most promising opportunity for peace that had occurred in decades.

'He thinks he can overthrow me,' said the Prime. 'He thinks that by causing mayhem on the streets he can push me into making mistakes.' The Prime leaned forward in his seat. 'The only mistake I ever made was allowing him the chance to work for your Project. It gave him time to plot against me. Nobody does that, Kasimir. Nobody works behind

228

my back. I hope you are listening, Kasimir: I will smash anyone who conspires against me.'

Prime Salvo took a handful of cashew nuts and crunched them one by one in his mouth. 'You're not laughing, Kasimir. You're not having fun. Leave. Go and do your business. And remember what I said.'

Sukui left.

'Alya Kik! So it is true.' After his lunchtime encounter with the Prime, Sukui was relieved to see a friendly face.

She was standing on a Soho street corner, studying the people passing by. Wrapped in a pale green robe with a silk sash around her waist, she looked different, somehow: smaller and more fragile, not the coarse old street-trader he knew from Orlyons. A youth, dressed in a matching wraparound, stood vigilantly nearby – a bodyguard, a sad reminder of the city's new turbulence.

'What is it that you say's true *now*, then? Which of the rumours?' Alya looked as if she had been expecting him.

'That Chet Alpha has shown you the light,' said Sukui. 'That you have been converted.'

'You make me sound like some rich kid's house. "Been converted", hah!' She punched him lightly on the chest. 'You old rogue,' she said. 'You look good. I haven't seen you since you brought me on that big boat of yours. Not good enough, eh?'

'You must have been hiding if you haven't seen me, Alya. Or your eyes have gone the way of your teeth. Or have you found other diversions?' He

229

nodded at the bodyguard and smiled. 'Tell me, Alya: what do you make of Chet Alpha's Pageant of the Holy Charities? Do you think he's sincere? He's involving a lot of people – they might not like it if they find that he is not genuine.'

'Kasimir, come with me. See for yourself. That's why I'm here anyway: Lucilla wants to see you.' She took his arm and began to lead him back through the streets of Soho towards Merchant Chapel. 'But let me tell you, too. I've known Chet since he was that much of his daddy' – she held her hand so there was a tiny gap between thumb and forefinger – 'and a bit more of his mamma. He started out on the streets of Orlyons before he went up to Newest Delhi with that Peep Show of his. He's a drifter, never known what he wanted. I tell him so many times. "Chet," I say. "You got no direction. You got to have something to live for." I tell him again and again, but always he drifted. Now, Kasimir, I tell *you*: he believes in that dream of his. Chet Alpha, he's never had a purpose in life until he had that dream. Now he's different, it's changed him. And anyway,' she shrugged, 'you get Chet, you get the Holy Charities, you get some bottles and some bits to eat and you got the finest damn party you could hope for.' Alya Kik bustled on, cackling away, and Sukui followed, smiling.

Their guard melted away as they climbed the wide steps at the front of Merchant Chapel and passed between the columns of the entrance. This part of the gallery was the same as ever, packed with stalls and traders, the air full of spices and calls and the unchanging murmur of the crowd. But the western gallery had been transformed. The stalls had gone and the floor was covered with flower petals and streamers and empty bottles. Chet Alpha's little caravan was standing on wooden blocks part-way down the gallery; its wheels had been removed to be strung from the wall by ribbons. Elsewhere there were tents and simple little huts, as if the place had been overrun with refugees. The inner wall was covered with streamers and ribbons and bright splurges of paint and chalk, some of it in abstract patterns, other areas depicting people and animals in crude, bold strokes, as if drawn by a genius or a child. The open side had yet more streamers and ribbons, wrapped around the white columns and strung between. The gallery appeared more spacious than when it had held traders and their stalls, but still there was a multitude of people sitting, standing, swirling. Many wore the pastel robes of the Pageant, many more looked as if they had been dragged in off the streets or as if they had arrived by mistake, still expecting the gallery to be full of market-stalls.

Sukui was stunned by the scale of Chet Alpha's takeover. It was only a matter of days since he had brought his Pageant to Alabama City and already it had grown into *this*.

'Come on, come on,' said Alya. 'We're missing the party.' She left him in front of a small tent. 'In there,' she said, and then she was off among the crowd, seizing a bottle from a nearby man and then seizing the man as well.

Sukui looked at the tent. He cleared his throat. 'Lucilla?'

Since their first meeting, he had maintained contact with Lucilla Ngota and their friendship had flourished. She was a strong woman who knew her own thoughts and he admired that. Also, he admired the way she could balance things in her mind, making decisions rapidly and accurately.

But he had been unable to understand why she had become involved with Chet Alpha's Pageant of the Holy Charities. She had attended as an observer, at first; then out of curiosity. For the last two nights she had slept in the Traders' Gallery, presumably in this cramped little tent.

A flap lifted and Lucilla smiled out at him. 'Kasimir,' she said. 'Come in.' He crouched and then crawled in, squeezing past Lucilla as she held the flap open for him. She still had a most extreme effect on him; brushing past her made his heart race and he broke out into an impolite sweat.

The tent was cramped and when they sat facing each other their knees touched. 'It's private here,' she said. 'I can meditate here. Chet says we have to pursue our inner spirituality any way we can and I get it best meditating. I'm glad you came.'

Sukui listened to the sounds of the people outside; he could see their movements through the gap between the tent's entrance flaps. 'I was curious,' he said. He had not spoken to her since she had moved in with the Pageant. 'You are a strong, rational woman. Chet Alpha is sincere, but he is misguided. I thought I was getting to know you but then you joined his Pageant. I would appreciate enlightenment.' He bowed his head and stared at Lucilla's horn-like toenails.

'Everyone has something spiritual in them,' said Lucilla, wriggling her toes. 'Even you, Kasimir. Chet can't be misguided – he hasn't even been guided. All he knows is we're here for a purpose and we're just as well having a good time while we find out what it is. He's not feeding us shit, Kasimir. Each of us is here because we think there's something *more*. Can you see that?'

Sukui shook his head slowly. 'I am a man of science,' he said.

'It's an extension of how I've always seen things,' said Lucilla. 'You take everything for what it is. If someone's worth hating, you hate, if they're worth loving, you love.'

'You loved March Hanrahan?' said Sukui suddenly. He did not know why he had asked.

For a moment there was anger in Lucilla's eyes, then it was overcome by sadness. 'You observe people, Kasimir. You don't need to ask. I was with March a long time and, yes, we were in love. But I had a second reason for pursuing Mathias. Greta Beckett. She was destroyed by what happened. Before, she had been happy and carefree; afterwards she was cold and withdrawn. I loved her, Kasimir, and I watched Mathias break her. After Mathias, she built barriers around herself. She loved me but she loved *him* more. I don't think he ever knew what he did, or understood why I hated him. I will go back to Newest Delhi for the trial; I don't know if I want to go. It'll stir up what I'd rather leave untouched. I don't know . . . ' She was crying, her head and folded arms resting on her knees.

233

Sukui put a hand on the back of her head, felt the tight coils of her hair. Lucilla placed her hand on his and looked up, her face wet. She smiled again. 'Kasimir,' she said. 'I'll understand if you say no, but you're a kind man and you've been good to me and I guess I'd appreciate it if we could make love.' She looked away, apparently scared of rejection. Sukui kneeled, embraced her clumsily and she kissed him hard. It was cramped in the tent and Sukui wondered what would happen if they dislodged one of the ridge-poles, but he found that he didn't care any more, the world could – as Alya Kik had once so aptly said – go suck.

Sukui felt uncomfortable at the head of the procession. He was not embarrassed or worried about what onlookers might think; it was more a pragmatic discomfort, a rational one. With no precedent, he had no idea how the Prime would react if he was to be told that his principal scientific adviser had led the Pageant of the Holy Charities through the streets of Alabama City. He might be angered or, equally probable, he might simply laugh at such a preposterous notion.

Thinking back, Sukui could not really work out how it had come about.

He had emerged from Lucilla Ngota's tiny tent in mid-afternoon, feeling complete at last. Tucking his robe loosely around himself, he had put aside his fears and his doubts of the previous days and gone looking for Chet Alpha. It was time to set up an experiment and Alpha was the obvious candidate: a simple man, honest and deceitful in similar

234

proportions; in a moment of clarity, Sukui had seen that if Salvo Andric had not been born of Primal blood then he could easily have been another Chet Alpha.

He had found Alpha at the far end of the western gallery. He was standing on an up-ended barrel, a wine bottle in one hand, the other hand stabbing and waving in the air. ' . . . my old mother, she said I was here for a reason. She said we *all* were. Shit, it's empty.' His bottle was tipped up and only a few drops had fallen out. He had looked around. Nobody had been paying attention anyway.

Sukui had nodded to him and held out a hand to help him stagger down from the barrel. 'You are to be congratulated on the success of your mission,' Sukui had said. 'And before you ask: no, I am not ready to join. I feel that I should wait, at least until you know what your "Word" is.'

'You're laughing at me, Sukui-san. 'S not nice.' Alpha had tossed his empty bottle aside.

'Chet,' Sukui had said. 'Do you have some time to spare? I have something to show you, something that may prove of interest to you. If you could come with me I would be grateful for your opinion.'

Chet Alpha had turned to Larinda, who had been passing nearby. 'Hey, Larinda, d'you hear that? Sukui-san's got something to show us. Hey, Pom-Pom! Sukui-san's got something to show us! Where is it, Mister Sukui? Huh?'

Thrown offguard by Alpha's enthusiasm, Sukui had muttered, 'Dixie Hill. I have some people there.'

'Hey, *Pom-Pom*. Put that guy down and get us some banners and some streamers and something more to drink. Mister Sukui's taking us up on Dixie Hill!'

And so, now, Kasimir Sukui was at the head of a procession of assorted Charities from the Holy Pageant. Chet Alpha was marching by his side, swigging from a fresh bottle of wine and hanging on to Sukui's robe with his one free hand. The Pageant trailed back a good fifty metres, sometimes more, sometimes less, as followers lost their way and others joined on. Some were singing, others dancing, as they processed through the narrowing streets of the urban fringe. Many wore the pastel robes of the Charities, others wore brighter or darker robes in the same casual style, Alabama City's supplies of pale-tinted linens having been exhausted. Sukui put his shoulders back and marched. If he was to be seen then at least he would look proud and not as if he was trying to squeeze into the cracks in the road.

Alya Kik tugged at his sleeve and said, 'Hey, y'old rogue. What're we going to see?' She had been smoking hash and her robe hung loosely over her generous body.

Sukui had been trying to work out what he should do. He had certainly not planned for *this*. 'This was a private invitation to Chet Alpha,' he said. 'I requested that he share an opinion on a certain matter.' He smiled; Alya had taken offence. 'Although it delights me to have the company of my old friends, that is how it must be, at present. Alya, have you ever seen Dixie Hill? The grass is thick and the views would probably be considered

236

impressive – it might be a good site for a party.'
Alya cheered and slapped him on the back, then
she was part of the procession again and Sukui had
to seize Alpha's arm to stop him from taking the
wrong turning. They were nearly there.

The Pageant spread itself out on Dixie Hill but
Sukui led Chet Alpha directly to the research hut.
As they drew closer he could see Sanjit Borodin and
Mags Sender staring out of the window, their faces
pressed close to the glass. When they recognized
Sukui they disappeared and, moments later, opened
the door. Sukui saw Mags pushing a heavy beam
away across the floor and he raised his eyebrows at
Borodin.

'We thought . . . well, we're the only ones here,
apart from Decker, and we saw *them*' – he nodded at
the fifty members of the Holy Pageant on the lower
slopes of the hill – 'so we thought we'd better—'

'OK,' said Sukui. 'Your caution is noted and
approved. Now,' he continued, turning to Chet
Alpha. 'I wonder if you would be so good as to
give me a minute or two with my colleagues?'

'Sure, sure,' said Alpha, already turning and sur-
veying his partying followers and then glancing at
the sinking sun. 'I think it's time to pray.'

Sukui followed Borodin and Sender into the hut
and closed the door behind him. 'So you're *back*,'
said Decker's trifax. 'I can hear you but you're not
on view. What're you doing?'

Sukui could see that Borodin wanted to speak,
probably to demand an explanation for what was
happening, but the team-leader's discipline was
winning. 'Decker,' said Sukui. 'I apologize for

causing you any confusion.' He stepped into the range of the trifax-broadcaster. 'Is that better?' Lui Tsang had been working on a portable communicator, but it was still under preparation; when completed it would cast a trifacsimile, but it would send only TV pictures out to orbit. In the hut they still used the full trifax link-up.

'Yeah,' said Decker. 'Now will you tell me what's happening?'

Sukui bowed his head. 'You have been very insistent that we "get the show on the road", as you phrase it. That is what I am currently doing. Outside I have a man who is in complete innocence of the situation. I would like to bring him in here and show you to him. I wish to observe his response. It is the first step in the spreading of our knowledge. Will you co-operate?'

He saw Decker begin to grin broadly, glad that things were finally happening. 'Well blow him in then,' said the trifax. 'Let's see what he says.'

Sukui nodded and backed away. 'Fetch Chet Alpha,' he said to Mags Sender, and she went to the door and called for Alpha. 'I think this might prove interesting.'

Chet Alpha poked his head warily around the hut's door. 'Can I bring the Charities too, huh?'

Sukui spread his hands and said, 'I think not, Chet. We have little enough room as it is, and I would value your opinion more if you were alone.'

Alpha shrugged and closed the door behind him. 'So what's the deal?' he said, peering around the interior of the hut. 'Hey, have you been to Merchant Chapel recently?' he said, looking at Mags Sender,

238

then at Sanjit Borodin, and finally at Decker. 'Have you spent some time with the Pageant of the Holy Charities? Everyone's welcome, even the sick.' He nodded at Decker, his eyes on the trifax's twisted feet and atrophied limbs. 'The Charities'll look after you,' he said.

'I can't see you again,' said Decker.

Sukui led Alpha further into the hut.

'Blind too, huh?' said Alpha. 'Ain't life a shitter, sometimes, huh? Huh?'

'No, Chet,' said Sukui. 'He can see you now, can't you Decker?' Decker nodded. 'So what do you think, Chet. Be honest.'

'Think? 'Bout what?'

'About our friend Decker. You see, Chet, Decker is not here in this room. This is an image, a *shadow*. He is not even of this planet. He lives high above us, orbiting Expatria in one of the ancient Ark Ships. What do you think of that?'

Chet Alpha did not appear to be impressed. 'Of course he's here. I can *see* him, right?'

'Kasimir Sukui is telling the truth, Chet,' said Decker. 'What you see is no more than an image, a fiction of light. Touch me. Go on.'

Chet Alpha stepped forward and reached out. His hand passed straight through Decker and he snatched it away and stared distrustfully at it. 'It's a trick, a trick!' He looked again at Decker and his face had been transformed by fear. 'What did you do?'

Sukui had observed the exchange quietly. Suddenly he was struck by an idea, a vague hunch. Sukui did not believe in hunches – the best ideas came from hard work, not so-called inspiration. But this time . . . this time he felt in his heart that he should at least try. It would be a good way to gauge Alpha's reactions. He moved over to the trifax controls and drew up a stool to sit on. He reached for the first knob.

Kasimir Sukui had experimented with the tri-facsimile on a number of occasions. He knew precisely what to do. First he blurred the image: fractionally around the face, more so around the wasted limbs, obscuring them, making them look suddenly more complete, more substantial yet also more ethereal. He amplified the basso of Decker's voice, adding in tones below the normal hearing range, so that his words made the very flesh tremble. Finally he altered the colour balance, casting Decker in a more favourable light, giving warmer, rosier, tints to his face, drawing light from his eyes to make them look like beacons. The light from Decker's face cast itself upwards, illuminating his hair in a kind of halo. The image was a powerful one. Even Sukui had to quell a surge of unthinking awe. He sat back from the controls and resumed his observations.

Chet Alpha was on his knees. 'Oh my . . . oh my sweet mother-fucking gods. Oh!' He rocked back and forth, hands gripping his thighs tightly. He looked at Sukui and then back at Decker's image.

'Will somebody tell me what's going on, again?' said Decker. 'Chet, what's up with you?'

Alpha stared at the holo. 'I had a dream, you see. It made me see there was something to live for. You look . . . you look . . . I don't know.'

'Chet, I'm only a man,' said Decker. 'Just like you. Kasimir brought you here to see me. You're the first guy he's brought here. I want to tell you about us, about why you're there. Will you listen?'

Gradually, as Decker described the background to the situation, Chet Alpha began to regain control of himself. When Decker finished, Alpha stood and then he said, 'Look, I'm a simple man. You can tell me all you like, but all I see is someone that's a little bit more than human, floating in front of me. You can explain all you like, but it's still just like magic to me.'

'Chet, will you do something for me?'

'Like I said, I'm a simple man. I'll do anything.' Chet Alpha was shivering, still in shock from what he was experiencing.

'Chet, will you tell the people what I've just told you? Will you spread the Word?'

'Yes.' Chet Alpha's voice was faint but his eyes were suddenly alive with a zealous fire. He turned to Sukui. 'Thank you, Sukui-san,' he said. 'Thank you so much.' Then he hurried over to the door and stepped outside. 'Hey, hey, hey!' he called.

Sukui moved to the doorway to observe. Somehow he had been outwitted again. Decker had used Alpha to bypass his efforts to tell the Prime. Why had he not foreseen this? Now things were rapidly moving out of his reach. He would have to consider his options quickly. The time for action was close.

Alpha was jumping up and down on a ridge just below the hut. 'Listen, all my lovely Charities. Come and listen. I've just had myself a goddamned *vision*. I've just spoken to an angel! There are angels living in the old Ark Ships, angels living in orbit! Will you gather around?'

Sukui groaned and pressed a hand to his forehead.

Alpha straightened himself, pushed his chest out and held his arms wide. 'Pageanteers, Charities, Friends. This is a momentous occasion. It's *big*. Chet Alpha's Pageant of the Holy Charities has received its Holy Orders. Soon it'll be time for us to move, but now I feel it's time to . . . well, I guess it's time to *party*!'

# Chapter Eighteen

The decision had been a hard one, but Kasimir Sukui could come to no other. Despite Decker and Chet Alpha, despite Lucilla Ngota, he was still a rational man.

He had lived through six Primacies before Prime Salvo; he had served under three of them. He had seen these six Primacies crumble away under pressures internal and external. He knew the presages.

Salvo Andric's days were numbered.

Civil unrest was spreading from street corner to street corner. Acts of apparently undirected crime were becoming manifest. Cults and lobby groups were proliferating and becoming both vocal and active. The body politic of Alabama City was undergoing a convulsion.

And now Kasimir Sukui had decided that he should hedge his loyalties. He would never turn against the Prime, but this was certainly a time to cover all possibilities. Striding towards the Capitol, he veered away from his normal route up to the main gates. Instead, he stopped before the door of a building just across the Route Magnificat, a tall building with climbing vines and a fourth-floor balcony that overlooked the street. The placard by the door read 'Canebrake House'.

He disliked Siggy Axelmeyer intensely but, weighing all the odds, he had to see him. The Project must be preserved – that was his foremost objective and he knew that he must put all else aside.

Of all the rabble-rousers and orators and cult-leaders, Axelmeyer was the most charismatic, the most popular and, above all else, he had the best claim to the Primacy of anyone who might dare to oppose Salvo Andric. That was central to Sukui's reasoning but equally important was the fact that Axelmeyer had spent three and a half years as part of the Project. He had a scientific mind – even if his control was absent for the present – and if the Primacy should fall then Axelmeyer was Sukui's best hope. Others would destroy the Project at a stroke, either through their inability to control the powers of the throne or through sheer vindictiveness. Sukui knew that he stood at least a moderate chance of guiding Axelmeyer back to some sort of balance.

Now that Decker had spoken with Chet Alpha, things had gone beyond Sukui's control. No longer could he hope to direct the dissemination of the knowledge that Decker had given him. It was out of his hands. All he could do was hope to guide some of the forces that had been released.

He knocked on the big front door and immediately a stub of a woman opened it. 'My name is Sukui-san,' he said, standing tall. 'I wish to converse with Mister Axelmeyer.' He pushed the door and stepped past the startled woman.

'Oh, can't do that, sir, he's practising, sir, and he don't like as to be disturbed when he's *practising*. Says as he's letting his soul speak with the cosmos and how it makes him feel at peace, sir, and he says as it makes his blood pulse too, sir, and I can vouch for that, sir. Maybe you should make an appointment, sir, he's very . . . '

Her words trailed away, under the force of Sukui's glare. 'I wish to see him,' he repeated.

She scuttled away, up a flight of stairs and out of Sukui's sight.

A few moments later she reappeared on the landing. 'If you'd be following me, sir, he'll see you straightaway, sir.' She waited for him and then turned and led him up three more flights of stairs.

The sound of Axelmeyer's mouth-organ came floating through an open slatted door. 'He's in there, sir,' said the woman, unnecessarily, and then she hurried away.

Sukui stood in the doorway. The room was wide and airy, low sofas and cushions scattered about, half-opened bottles and items of food spread wherever there was space. Axelmeyer stood at the far side, playing his mouth-organ and staring out of the tall french windows. In that light he looked very much like his cousin. His hair was thick and fiery, his figure tall and muscular; all that was absent was the tangled red beard. After a few seconds he turned and then he stopped playing and threw his arms into the air. 'Kasimir!' he called. 'Come in, come in. She said it was you but I didn't believe her. What brings you? Has Salvo demoted you to errand-boy? Are you running his messages?'

Axelmeyer was the only Project member to have called Sukui by his forename; the others all knew their position. 'Prime Salvo does not know I am here,' said Sukui. 'I am merely satisfying my own curiosity. No more.'

'So? What is it?'

There was no diplomacy with Axelmeyer. He knew nothing of the ways of high government. Sukui bowed his head. 'Please, let me move at a pace dictated by my own judgement.'

Axelmeyer shrugged and played a quick trill on his mouth-organ. 'Fine, fine. Tell me when you want to know anything.' He moved across and opened the tall windows, stepped through and surveyed the street below. 'One day, Kasi,' he said. 'One day, this will all be free.' He spread his hands, embracing Alabama City.

Sukui looked at Axelmeyer's broad back. Standing, as Axelmeyer was, against the low railing of the balcony, it would be an easy matter for a man of slight build – Sukui, for instance – to push him over. Sukui had always been a man of peace. He had never physically hurt a person in all of his life. But now, if there was one person he could guiltlessly kill it was Siggy Axelmeyer.

Sukui took one step forward. Looking down he saw that the ground below was paved; the odds of surviving such a fall were not favourable.

Axelmeyer turned, laughed, slapped Sukui on the shoulder and the moment had passed. 'Did you ever think it would come to this, Kasimir?' he said. 'Cousin fighting cousin – don't look so shocked, Kasimir, there's no pretence now. I'm challenging Salvo for the Primacy. The way things are, if I don't then someone else will.'

'Please,' said Sukui. 'Credit me with a little more.

You cannot innocently claim to be stepping in to fill the void; you cannot claim to be saving Alabama City from a worse alternative. Not to me. You have manufactured this situation, you have guided the forces of the city to your own purposes.'

'Perhaps you're right, Kasimir. Perhaps not. But this is how it is and I am the best person to harness the energies of the city. Salvo is out of touch. The treaty with Hanrahan was wrong. He sold us and he sold us cheaply. Now Alabama City is riddled with cultists from the north, Conventists and Jesus-Buddhists and Nano-Hippies. We need a strong Primacy.'

'You have been talking to the Conventists,' said Sukui.

'They threw me out of their meeting!'

'And since that day they have been mobilising their support. Prime Salvo would have defused your challenge but *they* responded, they have given you someone to fight. They have given you an opportunity to make the Prime look weak.'

'Only the *Prime* can make himself look weak, Kasimir.' Axelmeyer shrugged. 'Maybe you're skirting around the edges of the truth. Conflict is a necessary element of government, it keeps the cogs turning. You're a *scientist* – you, if anyone, should see that.'

Sukui stared across at the Capitol. It was late afternoon and servants were flowing in and out, changing shifts. Soon it would be dark and the streets would be unsafe again. 'There are alternatives,' he said. 'There is always an alternative.'

'You said you wanted to move at your own pace,'

said Axelmeyer. 'Kasimir, you're transparent. If you wish to side with me then say so. That's why you came here, isn't it? Yes? I thought so. Or was there something more? You're playing safe. Very *rational*. Looking out for yourself.'

'I came here to tell you something,' said Sukui, then he stopped himself. His plan had been to buy the safety of the Project with the information about the Orbitals. He had planned to tell Axelmeyer everything. He looked at Siggy's face, full of the passions of power and conflict. 'But,' he corrected himself, 'I feel the time is inappropriate.'

'I don't like you, Kasi. Not one bit. But I recognize your value. I could have you interrogated but I doubt your information is that important and, anyway, I would prefer that you came to me of your own freewill. Come here tomorrow evening, if you're going to come at all.'

'I will be here,' said Sukui. It was the rational choice, but he was glad it had been deferred for another day. At that moment all he wanted was to be away from Siggy Axelmeyer. He did not like the feelings the man inspired in him. 'I will return and give you my decision then.'

Kasimir Sukui descended the last flight of stairs and smiled as Axelmeyer's small servant hurried to open the door for him. 'Thanks, sir,' she said, refusing to meet his gaze. 'Thanks for being s'nice.'

He felt disturbed by the way she hurried about so. It was indicative of unfair treatment. 'Run away,' he said to her, impulsively, 'and start anew.' She just looked at him, confused and smiling. He was suddenly glad that he had refrained from giving Axelmeyer the information he had intended. Surely there must be a better alternative? As the door shut behind him, he hoped he had underestimated Salvo, that the Primacy would ride out the current disturbances.

Sukui paused on Canebrake House's front steps and surveyed the ever-moving crowd, its patterns always a mystery. He shook his head slowly. A rational person must always face the truth, if he wishes to retain reason. Standing, across from the Capitol, on the steps of Siggy Axelmeyer's rented house, Kasimir Sukui admitted that truth: finally, he was lost. He had run out of options.

He did not know what to do.

The admission felt strange to him. Always, he had been guided by his calculations, his information, his rigorously determined facts. But now his path had become one of those unfathomable mysteries. He did not even know where to begin.

There was only one person he could turn to, one like-minded person who might shed some light upon his dilemma. He would go to Lucilla Ngota, he would tell her everything. Maybe the simple process of talking would free the cogs of his mind and help him see what he must do.

It was all that remained.

He set off across the Route Magnificat, feeling better already. Traders' Gallery was less full than the norm; Sukui had little trouble pushing his way through to the western gallery and the Pageant of the Holy Charities.

Chet Alpha was there, his head buried in Alya

249

Kik's chest. 'Chet,' said Sukui. 'Tell me: where is Lucilla Ngota? I have to speak with her.'

'He don't want to speak,' said Alya, holding Alpha's head in place. 'He's not happy.'

'Where's Lucilla? Please.'

'She's out with Larinda and some others but it's no good. They're spreading the word but people don't like it, they don't listen. Chet, he gave a sermon on Grand Rue Street. He say there's people living above us, he say there's *angels* and all they want is to talk with us and make us be happy, but they don't listen, it's no good. There were Conventists there an' they started singing Golden Life-Fountains an' throwing eggshell crosses, an' the street kids started throwing 'em back an' we were lucky to get out of the middle of it all. So Chet, he's not happy now. He needs a mamma.' She rubbed the back of Alpha's neck and nodded, agreeing with herself.

Sukui turned and made his way out of the gallery. He would stand little chance of finding Lucilla in the darkening streets of Alabama City and the risk to his own safety on any but the main thoroughfares would be too high if he stayed out for much longer.

It was as he turned down a quieter side street, making for Soho, that Kasimir Sukui realized he was being followed. There was a figure he had spotted outside Canebrake House and dismissed, a face he knew vaguely, a military man, a trooper. That was not unusual in the vicinity of the Capitol. In Merchant Chapel he had seen the man again; that had been notable, but not highly improbable.

Now there was no doubt. There were only about fifteen others passing along this particular side street. The probability of such an occurrence by chance was minute.

Sukui was being followed.

He searched his memory, recalled the man's name and rank. Jan Gromyko, Lower Lieutenant, private attachment. He could be a bodyguard, posted to protect Sukui during these troubled times. Even as he snatched at this hope, Sukui dismissed it: he would have been told, there was no reason to keep a bodyguard secret.

The answer was simple: the Prime must have Canebrake House under surveillance. And now, in consequence, Sukui.

He walked on, not allowing his pace to falter. They would achieve nothing by following him. He had done nothing wrong; he had nothing to fear.

But then he remembered his last encounter with the Prime. 'Nobody works behind my back, Kasimir. Nobody does that. I hope you are listening, Kasimir: I will smash anyone who conspires against me.' No, he thought, he was not conspiring against the Prime. But he was working behind his back, he was trying to save the Project. And now he was linked with Axelmeyer. The Prime was in a sensitive state. *Unbalanced* was the word that came to mind.

Sukui swallowed drily. He could no longer rely on the Prime for support. All he had was himself and a small amount of time.

He came to the junction with Ruby Way, joined the mindless flow of the crowd. He sensed Gromyko behind him. Maybe there was more than just the one of them. He stopped himself from looking around. He passed in front of a mule-drawn wagon, loaded high with cheeses and flies. He quickened his pace, lost himself in a knot of people and stepped through an open door.

'Good evening,' he said. 'Please do not get up. The Prime sends his greetings.'

He was in a private dining room, well-dressed merchants gathered round a well-dressed table. He passed through another door and was in a hallway. He heard voices raised behind him but refused to panic.

The door at the far end led on to a compact yard where hens pecked in the dust. He shut the door behind him, gathered his robes and climbed on top of the poultry hut. He swung his legs over a high brick wall and then dropped to the other side. His ankle gave a sharp twinge, but he was still able to walk.

He was in another yard, a little bigger than the first. He stepped through a doorway and into a kitchen, his mind working frantically, trying to locate himself on a street plan of Alabama City.

He felt faintly absurd, limping through the busy kitchen, but nobody complained. He hurried through the eating area. He was in the Happy Hobo Eaterette.

He hurried out into twilight Soho and paused a few doors away.

After two minutes he knew that he had deceived his pursuers. It was likely that they had been caught unawares, thinking an old bureaucrat such as himself incapable of action. He straightened his robes and headed for Dixie Hill, smiling and breathing rapidly. The rush of adrenalin had picked him up, cleared his head.

He had only a matter of time; whatever happened to *him*, Decker must be informed of the situation. From now on everything would depend on Decker.

At the back of his mind was the thought that it had all been too easy. What if Gromyko was merely toying with him? He emerged on Grand Rue Street and turned south towards Hitachi Tower. Let them think he was returning to his apartment.

After a few minutes he turned off the thoroughfare and down an alleyway towards the docks. There were less people here to hide him, but there were also less to hide Gromyko or any of his associates. He was heading away from Dixie Hill but that was not important. The last thing he wanted was for them to guess his destination.

A baby screamed from a nearby doorway and a dog barked. Sukui hurried onwards. He came to the end of the alley and glanced over his shoulder. People going about their business, shadows long and dark. He stepped out and headed north again, relieved to be free of the alleyway. Dixie Hill was normally no more than ten minutes from Soho, but it was near to an hour before Sukui emerged from the trees at the bottom of that long, grassy slope.

An electric light was on in the hut, its steady illumination spilling out over the surrounding grass, highlighting the evening's insects and other flying invertebrates. The team would still be working and Sukui hung back for a time, not wanting to disturb them.

He took his first step up the hill and then was struck by the possibility that Gromyko could be waiting for him in the hut. It might not have been difficult to guess Sukui's destination.

He quashed the impulse to turn and run. The Project was his first consideration. If there were troops in the hut then Sukui must be there to assess the damage. He needed to learn the facts of the situation so that he could weigh the probabilities and so have some idea of the best course of action.

As he walked towards the hut, holding himself upright and proud, he thought of Mathias Hanrahan. *He* had put the Project first and so must Sukui.

He opened the door and there were no troops, no Gromyko. Lui Tsang, his back to Sukui, was talking to the trifax of Decker. Sun-Ray Sidhu was taping a bundle of wires together. Sanjit Borodin, observed glumly by Helena Lubycz, was sweeping a fistful of playing cards off a small table and hissing at Mags Sender, who was counting out a pile of coins.

'I warned you not to teach people the cards,' said Sukui, nodding at Borodin. 'They will only take your money.' He smiled at Mags and Helena, and then at Lui and Sun-Ray. He was out of range of the trifax.

He stepped further into the hut, feeling strangely calm. He knew that soon everything would change. He did not know *what* would happen, but the probability was almost unity that something major would occur.

Decker grinned his infectious grin and said, 'Hi, Kasimir. I can see you now.'

Sukui nodded to the camera. Then he said, 'Colleagues, we have little time. I am afraid I committed a tactical error in being seen in the presence of Siggy Axelmeyer. I have displeased the Prime.' The team looked blank. Sukui knew that it was not his normal manner to be this open with his juniors. 'The trend was there, however. I do not think I have accelerated it by more than a day, two at most,' he continued. 'Whatever should happen to us as individuals, we must remember the Project. The most important thing is that we retain our link with Decker and his friends in orbit. Lui, how is progress with the mobile unit? Could we vacate this hut at short notice and retain the link?'

Lui waved a hand at the items on a nearby workbench. 'We've got the rudiments,' he said. 'Decker's been telling me what to do. There's supplies everywhere once you know what you're looking for. But I need more time.' He shrugged. 'Six hours, maybe a day. I was planning on working through tonight at any rate. If Sunny or Mags stay then things might be quicker. Can you hold them off?'

Lui did not need to say who he meant by 'them'. In the space of an hour the Prime had become the Project's principal enemy, and it was all because of Sukui's mistakes.

'I will do what is possible,' said Sukui. 'Decker, how are things developing in orbit?'

'People believe you're down there,' said Decker. 'Lui and Sun-Ray have been here in holo. They've started to convince people. There's a pressure building up, though. There's a lot of people who want to meet the only remaining Expatrian descendants of Ha'an. That's become more important out here than the ship from GenGen. All they want is Mathias and Edward.'

Sukui thought for a moment. 'Decker, it would be best if you were to regard Mathias as unavailable. Permanently. He is on trial for murder. Execution is the penalty and a fair trial is hardly possible, given the cir—'

Sukui noticed that the door of the hut was open. He was sure he had closed it.

A man stepped inside. He was tall and thin and he was wearing military leathers. Two more stood beside him, and it was apparent that others were assembled outside.

The trooper squinted at Sukui's face and nodded to himself. 'Kasimir Sukui,' he said. 'You're arrested. Come on.' He grabbed Sukui's arm and tugged him roughly to the doorway.

'Hey,' said Decker, looking around, but clearly not able to see what was happening. 'What's going on?'

'You'd better get that geek under control,' said the trooper, nodding at Decker and talking to the rest of the team. 'Or he comes too. OK?'

'Decker,' said Sukui, brushing his sleeve where he had been held. 'I am under arrest. Control yourself. Lui will take over.'

'You should be moving!' barked the trooper. 'Or d'you want us to burn your hut, as well? Hey, guys, you got any matches?' He laughed and pushed Sukui from the hut.

'I don't *enjoy* being like this,' said Prime Salvo

256

Andric. 'It's not in my nature. But you've been irresponsible, Kasimir. What else can I do?'

Kasimir Sukui gazed into the Prime's face. All kinds of strange emotions were rushing through his head – fear, confusion, pain – but he ignored them. All his doubts of the past few weeks were nothing to him now. He was controlled, he was rational. He was a scientist. 'You are Prime,' he said, his face aching. 'You must follow your judgement.' He bowed his head.

They were in a small room, somewhere in the security block of the Capitol. The windows were wide and glazed, with curtains and external shutters. The door was of lightweight wood and appeared to be without a locking mechanism. It was more of an office than a cell.

Sukui was strapped to the wall, naked and cold. His arms were bound above his head and tied to a hook in the wall. His legs were bound at the ankle, wide apart, so that he hung forward, supported by his wrists and the strap across his chest. He had been in that position since shortly after arriving at the Capitol some time before. Sukui had a disciplined time-sense but now it told him he had been there for only around forty minutes and that could not possibly be correct; it felt closer to half a day. His face hurt from where one of the troopers had cuffed him for losing balance as they bound him. He wanted to ask for a drink of water but that was one of the thoughts he suppressed.

'Tell me, Kasimir. What were you doing at Canebrake House?' The Prime shrugged and raised his hands. 'I don't like this, Kasimir. But you have to talk. You're lucky I'm here – the boys wouldn't be so restrained if I was gone.'

Sukui could read all the signs on Salvo Andric's face, he could interpret the subtext of his words. Whatever he did now, his place with the Prime – and almost certainly his life – was forfeit. Salvo Andric had finally lost his sense of equilibrium; unguided, he would destroy himself and all around him.

Much as he abhorred the thought, Sukui recognized that the future of the Project was now safest in the hands of Siggy Axelmeyer. He resisted the wave of hatred that came over him at the memory of Axelmeyer. It was the only way.

He steeled himself, renewed his self-control. He was a rational man, a scientist. He must take what was to come and, in so doing, preserve the Project. The pursuit of knowledge would outlast these petty disputes, these meaningless lives. Including his own.

He knew the end was near. He was strong. He would accept what was about to happen.

Kasimir Sukui smiled and he saw Prime Salvo look at him in disbelief. 'You are Prime,' he repeated. 'You must use your judgement.' He bowed his head, but his body remained proud, supporting itself against its bonds.

Salvo Andric left the room.

Some time later there was a sound from the doorway and Sukui looked up. Two men had entered the room, one carrying a big wooden case which he placed on a chair and carefully opened.

Implements of torture gleamed in the candlelight. There were scalpels, tongs, thumb-screws, clamps, rasps, files. The tallest of the two men drew a pair of needle-point tongs from the case and held them over a candle's flame. 'Stops infection,' he said to his colleague. It appeared to be an old joke between them.

Sukui was a scientist. He steeled his quivering nerves, monitored his breathing, his heartbeat.

By his internal clock, it was twenty minutes before he first begged for mercy. He would never have believed a person could bleed so much and still be alive. Three minutes later, he said, 'Please, call the Prime. I can . . . help him . . . I have something to tell him. Someone he should . . . meet. Please.'

The Project could look after itself – Sukui *hurt*.

# Chapter Nineteen

It was well into the night before Mathias Hanrahan saw the bulking landmass that marked the cliffs around Newest Delhi. He remembered seeing Alabama for the first time, the city a smear of amber light picking out the horizon against the star-speckled void; the image had lodged itself firmly in his memory.

There was a faint glow to Newest Delhi – candle-light and public street fires – but it was the outline of the cliffs that Mathias recognized. He had seen this view many times from a fishing boat but now it seemed strange, somehow, out of place.

He had never expected to see these cliffs again.

Sitting in the prow of the barge, militia guards nearby, he wondered if it was all worth it. He had no illusions about the 'trial' that Edward had promised: he was going to be executed. He tapped out a rhythm on his leg and thought back to days spent playing the blues with the Monotones. He felt for Mono's opal pendant around his neck. Life could be so easy.

The barge was painted brightly in regal golds and blues. Its sails were cut from the finest canvas and banded with matching colours. Early in the voyage, Mathias had learnt why he had not simply been locked in one of its holds: they were crammed with goods from Alabama City. Linens, leatherwear and woodwork of the highest quality; nothing that too obviously incorporated the forbidden practices, although most items had been made with technological assistance. Mathias had smiled at that. The fundamentalist influence was clearly strong in Newest Delhi, but ignorance was also firmly in place.

He sat and watched the waves lapping gently, picked out by the light of Expatria's moons and the lanterns on the other two barges. Edward's barge was even more extravagantly decorated than Mathias's. The banded sails bore a simple image of a huge sceptre while a variety of flags and pennants decorated the rigging. The Primal barge was well lit and sounds of laughter bounced across Liffey Bay to taunt Mathias. Edward was celebrating the success of his trip. The third barge of the convoy was tied up on the far side of Edward's and a host of smaller vessels were tied to the two.

One of the guards brought Mathias a cup of coffee and then left him to his solitude. It tasted bitter, unsweetened. At least it was warm. Mathias drank it in a single gulp and tossed the cup aside. He wondered what his guards had done to be the only ones not invited to the party. Maybe they were just unlucky.

He straightened his legs, rubbed them, trying to renew the circulation. He had to coax himself into a better frame of mind – the least he could do was be positive. But it was no good. Why think like that when you're almost dead?

He noticed a change in the sound of the waves as they lapped at the barge's hull but thought nothing of it. They had probably hit a drift of weed, it was nothing unusual for Liffey Bay.

It was the clunk of wood against wood that made him realize something was happening. It came from the blind side of the barge, the side sheltered from the view of the rest of the convoy.

Mathias's heart started to pound, but he made himself stay where he was. It would only be a row-boat from one of the other barges, probably drunken bureaucrats unaware of what they were doing.

A hand appeared over the side of the barge, then another. 'Are you gonna give me some help or d'you want me to just go away?' A head appeared, rope gripped between grinning teeth, and then a leg swung over and into the barge.

It was Idi Mondata.

He hadn't changed. He could never change, he was that kind of person.

Mathias sat and watched his old friend pull the rope taut and loop it around a bulk-pin. He thought his own grin must be even wider than Idi's. He couldn't move. All he could do was sit and watch. 'I've been waiting,' he said. 'You're getting slow.' Finally something shifted inside him and he clambered to his feet and embraced Idi. 'Idi,' he said. 'Idi, you don't know how good it is to see you.'

Idi pulled away, gesturing at Mathias to keep his voice down. 'D'you want me to go over to Olfarssen's boat and tell him I'm here? Or shall we keep it a private party for now?'

Mathias looked around, reminded of his circumstances. 'Sorry,' he said. 'I suppose I'm not all here at the moment. I forgot myself. You're looking well, Idi. What about the guards?'

'Oh, don't you worry 'bout Jerzy and Jilly. They're screwing in the back hold and anyway they're OK – they know I'm here and they say they'd rather fuck. And anyway' – he grinned so that his teeth shone in the darkness – 'this is a Mondata boat. It's only leased out. I got a right to be here, though Olfarssen might not like it if he knew. I tell you one thing for free.' He scratched at a nearby bulkhead. 'They can strip this damned paint before they get their put-down back.'

'Idi,' said Mathias. 'Will you tell me what's happened in Newest Delhi? How's Greta? How strong is Olfarssen's grip?'

'Greta's a difficult one,' said Idi. 'You going away was the final twist – she really believes you killed your father. I guess her heart is bust, or however they say. You won't get any sympathy from her – she won't influence Olfarssen, if that's what you're hoping.' Idi shook his head. 'All Greta is is a way for the Conventists to get at the Prime, climb their way back up. That's what she uses her influence for. Olfarssen's crazy – I don't know how to put this, Matt. Greta's gone off men. Word is she hasn't let Olfarssen touch her since their wedding night. I guess once was enough.' He smiled uncomfortably. 'And Olfarssen is crazy about her – she can use him however she wants and at the same time it's the Conventists that use her to get at *him*. The whole set-up is mad. You won't get anything through Greta.'

Mathias accepted all this numbly. He had hoped that Greta might be a calming influence on Edward. 'The Conventists are strong then?' Talk would occupy his mind, stop him dwelling on what he had just heard.

'Shit, they're all strong. Conventists, Death Krishnas, Jesus-Buddhists, Black-Handers, Masons. Olfarssen is weak. I don't know how he's held on for so long. You've got to do something, Matt. The whole place is falling apart.'

Mathias knew why Idi had come out to meet him on the barge. He was going to suggest they lock the back hold and float away into the night.

But the thought had to be resisted.

Why escape when he'd come this far? He would gain nothing. Edward would automatically blame the Andricci, even though it would be obvious that they had done nothing. It would be a cue for greater hostilities, maybe full-scale warfare. The Project would be destroyed. The Project, itself, didn't matter – the quest for knowledge would always re-awaken – but what *did* matter was that communications with Decker and the Orbitals would be lost. The terran ship would arrive unannounced. The consequences were unforeseeable; all Mathias knew was that if anyone suffered it would be the people of Expatria.

'Idi,' he said. 'Let me tell you why I'm here.' Idi had been about to speak but he closed his mouth and listened. Mathias told him of Decker, he told him of the approaching terran ship and the broadcasts by the Holy Corporation of GenGen. After a while Idi stopped shaking his head in disbelief and his shaded face grew serious. 'I can't do anything that Olfarssen could blame on Alabama City,' finished Mathias. 'That would make everything go to waste.'

There was a moment of silence.

'I was going to shut Jerzy and Jilly in the hold and—'

'I know.' Mathias grinned. It was good to be with Idi again, even in the present circumstances.

'You want to die, that's your choice,' said Idi. 'But I don't like the idea that the only people who know about your Orbitals are in the south. Matt,' – he leaned closer – 'I guess it's time we set about evening up that imbalance. There's people would like to hear what you've just told me.'

'Idi,' said Mathias. 'I'll do anything that will spread the knowledge. I'll do anything that will fuck Edward's plans. But, Idi, I don't want to do anything that can be blamed on Alabama City. Do you hear?'

Idi grinned. 'I'm hearing,' he said. 'Got to go. I've things to sort.' He stood and swung himself over the side of the barge and down into his row-boat. 'Be ready, Matt. I guess I won't be able to give you much advance notice.' Then he began to row and Mathias sat back against the blue and gold bulkhead. Seeing Idi again had left him with misgivings. He hoped his old friend was not as impetuous as he had once been. Things had to be kept under control

Mathias didn't bother to count the days they kept him in their various prisons. The barges stayed out in Liffey Bay for the entire night and, from the sounds, it had appeared that Edward's party was

265

going strong enough to continue into the next night too. But in the morning the sails had been unfurled and the barges had drifted slowly into Newest Delhi harbour.

Mathias's barge was the last to dock and by the time he set foot in the city of his birth the Primal party had been swept away in a convoy of horse-drawn carriages. He couldn't see much of the docks through the gaggle of guards that surrounded him and hustled him at a quick march through the lock-ups and boat-houses. But then they spread out on the steps of West Wall and Mathias was able to survey the scene.

He did not know what to expect, but it was not this. Nothing had changed. The docks were alive with the returning fishing fleet, ice-trays filling every spare space, crates of fish being thrown up from the newly moored boats.

From the top of the wall Mathias could see into Newest Delhi itself.

He paused to look out over the canopied market-stalls, then a guard prodded him with a bully-stick and said, 'No sightseeing.' Mathias bowed his head, smiling graciously, and continued on his way.

The market had changed, but only to a small degree. It looked the same but the sounds had been transformed. Wailing mommas cried out for the mercy of Jesus-Buddha, or maybe just a few bucks for a holy statuette; Conventists mumbled and chanted from beneath a swathe of white canopies, sounding like a swarm of meth engines on idle; Death Krishnas sang 'Hari-Hari, Hari-Hari' and danced and swallowed swords and fire and wine.

Drugged Nano-Hippies drifted to no pattern. From the sound alone, it appeared that the market had been overrun by the battling cults and sects, but in his brief look Mathias had seen the traders and he had smelt their spices on the air. They were crammed into less space than before, but still they persisted.

The guards led him north along West Wall, past a line of scaffolds, their nooses dangling loosely, stirring in the occasional breeze. There had been no hangings in March Hanrahan's day. Descending into Newest Delhi, they passed through the winding city streets to the Manse.

Handed over to the Primal Guard, Mathias was put in a cell, deep in the Guard rooms that were set behind the bulk of the Manse. The following day he was transferred to a cell in a militia post on the northern side of Newest Delhi. From his window he could see Gorra Point and, in the early morning light, he thought that perhaps he could see the Pinnacles.

On the third day he was transferred to more permanent accommodation in the guest wing of the Manse. The windows had been reinforced especially for him and the door had two new locks, top and bottom. The room was compact and smelt musty and damp.

They brought him food; they led him to the washroom that he shared with scuttling, masked servants; guards always answered when he called but rarely did as he asked. They would not let him walk in the gardens that he could see, so close, through the window. They would bring him no books to read and none to write in. 'Books?' the guard had said. 'Haven't seen one since . . . Well, since I seen one. The Conventists have been burning them, you know. Books, that is. Along with the Masons. There was a time when they was burning *mad*. Conventists, Masons, Jay-Buddhists – they all had something they wanted to burn. Me, I just left 'em to it. The Guard wasn't allowed to interfere, you see.'

The guard brought some playing cards, next time he was on duty. It passed the time, but Mathias won too often and the guard soon lost interest. After that, Mathias constructed pryamids and houses from the cards.

A number of days later – Mathias didn't count – the door opened and Sala Pedralis walked in.

As she closed the door, Mathias saw the guard beyond her, standing upright and staring at the wall ahead of him. It was as if he had not seen her, but then he glanced nervously along the corridor, betraying himself. Mathias looked up at his old mentor. It all seemed rather familiar.

She looked much older than he remembered, her hair lank and streaked with grey, her skin pale and lifeless. Her movements were sharp and unsteady, her eyes darting to the corners of the room. Time had taken its toll on her; life under Edward Olfarssen-Hanrahan had clearly been an ordeal.

'Sala,' he said. 'I'd hoped you might have been in the delegation to Alabama City. I looked for you. I had things to tell you.' Sala was the person to inform about Decker's news; she would be a counterbalance to Idi Mondata. Mathias could die peacefully if he knew Sala was in control.

'Cut the small talk, OK?' Her voice was rough and strained. 'I have to tell you that I've been a fool, Mathias, and now I'm suffering for it. I helped you get out of this city once before and *if it kills me* I'm going to—'

The door swung open and Sala stopped. Her jaw sagged as she saw, first, who was entering the room.

It was Edward.

Wrapped in Primal robes that had been the favourite of Mathias's father, he was grinning broadly. 'Take her.' He gestured at Sala and two guards swept in and seized her arms. 'Miz Pedralis. Until now you have been the model of diplomacy. I have been waiting for your mistake and now you have confessed. Your trial will follow that of my half-brother. It is treason to aid the escape of a suspect of the Prime's murder; the penalty is death by suspension.' He nodded sharply and Sala was led away. 'A woman of such qualities,' he said, shaking his head. 'Yet it does not occur to her that she will be under observation at a time like this.' He straightened himself and turned to face Mathias. For a long time they were silent, each studying the other's features. Then Edward looked away. 'Your hearing has been put back until the end of the week,' he said. 'Administrative matters.'

Mathias was still recovering from the shock of seeing Sala in such a state. Things must be bad indeed if she was so ready to revolt against Edward. Sala would *never* go against an incumbent Prime.

'It would be far simpler if you would make a complete confession,' said Edward, heading for the door. 'It would be so much more tidy.'

'Our agreement at the summit in Alabama City was that I would return for trial,' said Mathias. 'Not that I would make false statement. You have no evidence, Edward. You're going to fix the trial because you don't dare do anything else. Anything that resembled justice *too* closely might implicate *you* and you wouldn't want that, would you? Why play games, Edward? Why not kill me like you killed March? It would be much more "tidy".'

Edward paused in the doorway. He shook his head sadly. 'It's over, Mathias. Can't you accept that?' The door shut behind him and Mathias sat back on his bed, annoyed that he had let Edward get to him so easily.

After the incident with Sala, security was increased. Guards were changed more often and the one who had let Sala in never returned to duty. Mathias took to inventing new forms of solitaire with his set of cards.

He sat by the window a lot, peering through the bars and watching the butterflies and the crawlers and the sparrows, each living life as only they could. Sometimes he saw Edward, marching through the gardens, alone or tagged by advisers and servants and senior clan-members. There were people Mathias didn't recognize, too, others with faces he knew but could not place. For some strange reason he kept expecting to see March slowly strolling by, taking in the evening scents that he had once enjoyed so much. After a time Mathias refused to look out of the window. He kept trying to tell himself that nothing mattered any more and for much of the time he succeeded.

The guards came for him early one morning. He had not slept the previous night, choosing to play solitaire by candle-light instead. 'Is it my trial, or has Edward decided to dispense with that kind of formality?'

One of the guards seemed pleased that a person in Mathias's position could still joke and smile; his occasional light spirits had disconcerted some of the others. 'No, sir, no,' she said. 'Of course you'll get a trial. The Prime's fair if he's nothing else. This is your Preliminary Hearing. It's like a warm-up. Is there anything you want explaining?'

This guard seemed better than the others and Mathias liked her instantly. 'No,' he laughed. 'Tell me: do you play cards?'

'Of course, sir. I'm a *Guard*.' She grinned and led him from his room.

The hearing was a farce. Mathias sat for an hour in a cell in the militia block set at the southern end of West Wall. Then he was led into a room and made to stand before a seated row of officials, two from the military and two from the Primal Service.

A youth with a fuzz of moustache and the sash of a junior Primal Equerry stood by Mathias's side and read the formal charges. 'That on the night of the Dumandee Ball, seventh of eleven, twenty-six, the accused did forcibly and intentionally end the life of Marchoise Eusebio Hanrahan, Prime of Newest Delhi and the amalgamated regions of influence. That he did avoid lawful arrest on that same night. That he did wrongfully deny the charges against his name. That he did refuse co-operation

271

in the investigation of his crimes. That on the night of the ninth of eleven, twenty-six, he did escape custody and flee the jurisdiction of Newest Delhi. That he did spend three years, ten months, eighteen days, in contradiction of a formal warrant of seizure, beyond the jurisdiction of Newest Delhi. That he did not return during the aforesaid period for the pursuit of formal justice, despite that he was at liberty to do so. So reads the charge inventory of Mathias August Hanrahan, filed by the office of the Primacy and formally recommended for trial at the earliest possible et cetera, et cetera.' The Junior Equerry smiled at the head of the judicial panel. 'The rest is the same as they always are, Uncle Tobias.'

The panel head waved his nephew away. 'According to the Code of Legality, the Efficacy Amendment thereof, you may plead now if you so wish.' He waved a sheaf of papers at Mathias. 'It would save a great deal of trouble if you were to do so.'

'I am not guilty.'

The panel head sighed and squared the papers on the desk. 'The evidence is compelling. This panel recommends guilty and a plea for mercy.'

'I am not guilty.'

'That's it then. Evidence and hearsay will be heard at formal trial in eight days' time. No counsel may be appointed in cases of treason. Your case will be heard by a panel of judges headed by myself. I don't like it when people use delaying tactics – a trial should be succinct, it keeps the facts fresh. Anything to say? No? Good. Dismissed. Liqueurs, gentlemen?' Mathias was led away by a member of the Primal Guard as the head of the judicial panel poured himself a tall glass of something red and sticky-looking.

Outside, part-way along the wide walkway on top of West Wall, there was a disturbance. Death Krishnas were waving burning swords in the air and running the blades across outstretched tongues. It was basic street-ents material, except the Krishnas always claimed that it was divine proof that they were holier than anyone else and so the world could go screw.

One of Mathias's entourage of guards stepped forward and tried to clear the Krishnas from the path. 'Out the way,' she said. 'Out the way.' A tongue of flame leapt from one of the Krishnas' mouths. It didn't reach the guard, but it was enough to make her flinch and glance back at her colleagues for support.

Two more troops went forward and suddenly a chaotic crowd descended on Mathias and the three remaining guards.

Mathias felt hands on his arms, pulling at him. The guards shouted and lashed out at the crowd, but gradually Mathias was eased away into the confusion.

He didn't want to go and he struggled at first, but the flow of the crowd was too great and the confines of West Wall too restrictive. He went with the flow, and then, when he saw a gap, he pushed himself, levering past the surrounding bodies, heading for a low arch that he knew opened on to one of the balconies that overlooked the market-place. If he waited there, then the crowd would thin and he could find his guards and Edward would have no chance of blaming anything on mythical agents from Alabama City.

Idi Mondata was waiting on the balcony.

'Stay cool, Matt. We'll get you back and we've put word on the street: this is strictly local business. Olfarssen will look an idiot if he tries pinning anything on Alabama City. You OK?'

Mathias leaned against the wall, feeling a little dizzy. He nodded.

'I've got some people here'd like to hear what you told me on the barge.' Idi waved a hand around. There were four people standing on the balcony, smiling at Mathias and waiting. Two were orange-clad priests, Death Krishnas, and the other two wore more ordinary street clothing. 'We've got plants in the crowd. They're primed, they'll do all the right things.'

Mathias wondered what his old friend was talking about. He stared at the smiling orange priests. Then he realized that Idi had not been waving at his four friends on the balcony, he had been indicating the market-place beyond. Gathered around the stalls and the canvas chapels and the wailing mommas there was the usual crush of people, but they were all standing still, looking up at the balcony. And in the hand of one of the priests was a microphone that looked just like the one Mathias had used four years before.

'We've got the PA set right,' said Idi. 'And everybody's ready for you. You've just got to tell 'em.'

Mathias jerked upright, suddenly full of energy. This was his one chance to do something positive and it would be impossible for Edward to blame it on Alabama City.

And maybe, into the bargain, Mathias could save his own life. Before, he had always resisted such thoughts, but now . . .

Idi and his four friends were looking at him expectantly. Mathias pushed himself clear of the wall and took the microphone in both his hands. There was a hiss of static from the loudspeakers mounted on either side of the balcony. 'People of Newest Delhi,' he said. The crowd did not panic as it had the last time he had spoken in this marketplace. Every face was focused on the balcony and Mathias tried to sort through his thoughts. His mind had been numb ever since the peace summit and now he had to squeeze something out of it, something in the form of words that would stir the crowd into action. 'People. My name is Mathias Hanrahan.' A ripple went through the crowd and a woman cheered. 'I was reared to be your Prime but that's all gone . . .' It was difficult, so difficult. 'The reason I'm doing this – talking to you like this – is that I've got news from the south. No, not from the south, it's from further away than that.' He wished he was closer, that he could see the people's faces and not just the seething blur that was the crowd.

'You see, there are people living in orbit around Expatria, people descended from the first colonists of our planet. They're living in the old Arks. And they've heard from Earth, too. Or from a ship that's coming from Earth. We have to decide how we're going to respond, we have to stop all this pettiness, all the squabbling factions. *None of that matters any more.*'

He didn't understand the crowd. They were listening to his words, his explanations, they were hanging on everything he said. But he wasn't getting through to them.

It would take more than words to convince the people of Newest Delhi. He could see that clearly now.

'The people of Expatria must unite with their allies in orbit. We must present a single voice when the ship arrives from Earth.' They were listening to his voice, not his words. He could imagine them telling it to friends and relatives who had not been present, how they heard the Prime-killer talking at the market-place, how loud his voice had been but how they couldn't remember what he had said – that hadn't been important, it was who he was that mattered.

He turned away from the microphone. 'It's no good,' he said to Idi. 'They don't want to know.' People were stirring, assuming, from the pause, that he had finished. Watching the twisting, convulsing shapes of the crowd, Mathias realized that he had. There was nothing more he could say. They were a pragmatic people; not ignorant, as he had once thought. They would never believe his words, only the fact that he was *there*.

'Shit, Matt,' said Idi. 'You didn't say it right, you didn't say it like you told me.' But Mathias could see in his friend's eyes that he knew it too.

They had failed.

There was a disturbance at the archway that led from the balcony back on to West Wall. 'Time we moved,' said Idi, snatching the microphone with a

276

whistle of feedback. He slapped Mathias on the arm and said, 'Stick around,' and then he was gone into the confusion that still filled the walkway beyond the balcony.

Two Primal Guards pushed through and seized Mathias roughly. They held him against the wall until a third came through, a lower lieutenant. 'You've just fucked my promotion,' he said. Then he punched Mathias in the stomach, leaving him wheezing and gasping, racked with pain and heaving for breath. Mathias looked up and the guard struck him again, in the chest.

*Body blows* was all he could think. Hurting him where it wouldn't show in court.

'He has been disciplined,' said Edward. 'And the two that helped him.'

Mathias was sitting on his bed, leaning forward so that his room-guard could bind his battered chest. She grinned at him as she tied the knot. It was Jeanna, the friendly one. He was glad it was her.

'Will you tell me who organized it? I have to know.' Edward was pacing about the small room. Mathias had been surprised to see him so soon after the trouble at the market-place. He must take his duties as Prime very personally, always on the scene; modelling himself, presumably, on March.

'Edward, a deal: I won't patronise you by pretending I don't know who set it up if you don't patronise *me* by pretending there's any chance I'd tell you. Fair?' Talking hurt his chest, especially talking to his half-brother in circumstances such as these.

'As we're being frank,' said Edward, 'I'll tell you this much. Stunts like the one you tried today are a destabilising influence. They are unproductive. They will not be permitted. You are not going to leave this room until you go for trial.' He looked around and sniffed at the stale air. 'I will see that you are brought a bucket.'

Edward paused by the door and looked back. 'Will you tell me something?' he said, feigning indifference and feigning it badly. 'How much of what you said today is true? Your little balcony speech.'

'Everything,' said Mathias. 'I have nothing to hide. In ten years, maybe as little as a month – I don't know – you'll see. I've spoken by radio to a man called Decker. He lives in what he calls a personal biosphere, linked into a kind of modular setup of living units. No, I don't understand it all either – he rambles, he doesn't explain well.'

'You would be most unwise to play games with me,' said Edward.

'I've got nothing to gain by that,' said Mathias. 'Just wait and see.'

'You cannot make me look a fool.' Edward opened the door. 'Confusion causes unrest – yes, I listened to our father, too, even though he despised me. I will see you at your trial. You should grow up, Mathias. I don't have time for your games.' The door slammed shut.

# Chapter Twenty

'That on the night of the Dumandee Ball, seventh of eleven, twenty-six, the accused did forcibly and intentionally end the life of Marchoise Eusebio Hanrahan, Prime of Newest Delhi and the amalgamated regions of influence. That he did avoid lawful arrest on that same night.' Glumly, Mathias Hanrahan surveyed the High Court of All Justice.

He had woken that morning to the sound of bird song, with rays of strong sunlight breaching the dusty panes of his window. He had looked out and butterflies had been flying, crawlers crawling, trees blossoming in delicate hues with birds snatching flies from their branches. The guards had come for him early and they had led him out through the corridors by August Hall to where the court marquee had been set in the Playa Cruzo. Already, the traders had gathered: buskers sang dissonantly, finely clothed stall-holders yelled aloud about their jewellery and their commemorative plaques, wailing mommas cried for Jesus-Buddha and all the time people hurried on by, eager to get to the best seats.

Now they were crammed into the marquee, hushed as the first words were spoken, the charges against Mathias. 'That he did wrongfully deny the charges against his name. That he did refuse co-operation in the investigation of his crimes.'

The observer delegation from Alabama City was assembled on the front row. There was Nina Annawhal-Crosky, military leader of the group; there was young Johnny Petrograd, listening closely and making notes of everything that happened and was said, his face serious; there was Egon Petrovsky, middle-aged and still one of Kasimir Sukui's juniors, destined forever to be an assistant to his betters, a secretary to committees; and there was Benazra Kawabata, fiddling with her fingernails and looking bored. As Mathias looked, Benazra stood. He watched her weave her way through the reserved seats and then up an aisle to haggle over trinkets with the vendors and traders gathered in the marquee's entrance.

'That on the night of the ninth of eleven, twenty-six, he did escape custody and flee the jurisdiction of Newest Delhi.' Mathias watched Benazra return to her seat and there he spotted a new arrival in the front row.

As far as Mathias had been aware, Lucilla Ngota was in charge of the observer delegation in Alabama City. But she had returned for the trial.

Maybe she was to be the one to place the noose around his neck.

Lucilla had been looking around the crowded marquee but at that moment she looked straight at Mathias, standing flanked by guards in front of the panel of justices. She had changed a lot since he had last seen her: she was wearing a pastel robe instead of her usual military leathers and she had allowed her hair to grow longer, less formal. But one thing had remained untouched by her transformation. As she stared at him the fury in her eyes made him want to shrivel up and surrender. He had never encountered anybody who could do so much damage simply by looking. She couldn't have expressed her hatred more clearly if she had stood up in court and screamed it at him. Mathias looked away, stared at the hard mud surface of the Playa Cruzo.

'That he did spend three years, ten months, eighteen days, in contradiction of a formal warrant of seizure, beyond the jurisdiction of Newest Delhi. That he did not return during the aforesaid period for the pursuit of formal justice, despite that he was at liberty to do so. That he continues to deny the aforesaid charges and so incurs the expense of the city of Newest Delhi, and the amalgamated regions of influence. So reads the charge inventory of Mathias August Hanrahan.' The Prime's Equerry bowed to the panel of justices and then marched away and took his seat by Lucilla.

There was a commotion towards the back and the justices stood, gesturing for the rest of the court to follow suit. The Equerry hurried back to the open space at the front and said, 'High Court of All Justice, the Prime of Newest Delhi.' He returned to stand by his seat.

A panel of canvas lifted and a line of Conventist Guards, clad in dark grey bodices and leggings, filed into the marquee. Then, after a slight pause, Edward led a small group into the court. As they took their seats by the panel of justices, Mathias saw Greta Olfarssen-Hanrahan for the first time. She sat behind Edward and to his right, present but not in the way of the Prime's advisers and consultants. Her

hair was tied tightly back from her face and she
wore a simple grey gown. Her features were set and
unchanging and she kept her gaze fixed on the back
of Edward's neck; Mathias watched her for long
seconds – he couldn't keep his eyes off her – but
she wouldn't look in his direction. Her face was pink
and her eyes reddened, as if she had been crying.

'Tobias Macari, Senior Justice.' Mathias looked
round. The head of the panel was announcing himself to the court. 'The preliminary plea was of innocence,' he said. 'Has that changed?'

Mathias looked again at Greta. She looked broken.
He had grown away from her long ago but, for an
instant, he wanted to plead guilty, to spare her
from reliving a painful period from her past. 'I
am innocent,' he said. 'Nothing can change that.'
He could not let Edward win so easily, he wanted
his people, at least, to know that the trial was fixed.
He had no doubts of the outcome.

The Equerry stood forward again and recited the
state's case. 'Prime Marchoise Eusebio Hanrahan
was found dead in his private office on the night
of the seventh of eleven, twenty-six. He was found
by a servant, one Rab el O'Ahim.'

'Call the witness,' said Justice Macari.

'In the intervening period, sir, the witness has
been lost in the troubles.' The Equerry continued
with his recital. The Prime had been rendered
unconscious with an unidentified implement and
then strangled with a length of heavy-duty electrical
cable.

The case dragged on. Considering that there had
never been any actual conflict in Newest Delhi, a

remarkable number of witnesses had been lost in the troubles. At times Mathias wanted to plead with the audience: couldn't they see what was happening? At times he wanted to plead with the observers from Alabama City, but the Treaty of Accord had made it clear that they were to be non-interventionist. If he involved the delegation then that would just give Edward an excuse to renew hostilities with the south.

The only witness that was actually called that morning was Raphael Agrozo, a lieutenant now, honoured for his heroism in the ongoing fight for Clermont. He repeated what had happened when he waited in Mathias's bedroom and Mathias had climbed back in over the balcony. He told of how a mask, stolen from the absent servant, had been found on the balcony. Mathias could argue with none of it. It was true.

After three hours, Justice Macari glared around his marquee. 'This is the longest damned trial I've sat on in years,' he said. 'I propose we break for something to eat. Reconvene in, oh, let's say an hour. Court suspended.'

Mathias didn't get anything to eat. His guards wouldn't let him through to the vendors and caterers who had gathered outside when the word had spread that the trial would last into the afternoon. During the interval, he sat in an enclosed area to the rear of the marquee. He stared at the ground, he stared at the high canvas roof, threadbare and patched, he stared at his guards but they didn't care.

When the hour was up, Mathias was led back into the court and everyone had to stand up while first the panel of justices and then the Primal group strolled in and took their seats.

Justice Macari wasted no time in the second and final session of the High Court of All Justice. 'I've consulted with my co-justices,' he announced. 'Equerry tells us there's more to come but we don't think it's worth it. We've heard all we need. I move that the case be brought to a verdict.'

'Second,' said a justice to Macari's right.

'Approve,' said the other two.

'Right, that's that, then,' said Macari. 'Hanrahan has no defence, no corroborative evidence. This court finds in favour of the state. Mathias August Hanrahan is guilty on all charges. With Primal approval we move that the punishment should be death by suspension.'

Mathias looked across at Edward. He was a little stunned by how fast Macari had moved but the verdict was what he had expected all along. For a moment Edward met his gaze.

'Seeing you standing there, Mathias,' said Edward, 'you are a pathetic sight. I have always sworn that justice would be done in the case of my father's murder, but now that the time has come a part of me wishes there was an alternative. I wish it had never happened and that we could still be part of the same family.' Edward shook his head. 'But that cannot be. Even a Prime must accept the word of his courts.' He smiled and nodded towards Macari. 'You have formal Primal approval.' Edward gestured to his entourage and strode out through the back of the marquee.

Mathias looked around the court, the audience already shifting and filing out. The people should be protesting at the unfair way Macari had brought proceedings to a close but instead they had been won over by Edward's pretty little speech. Mathias grinned wryly to himself. His half-brother had certainly learnt a few of the tricks of Primacy.

A guard stopped before Mathias. 'Let's go,' she said. Mathias went.

Mathias was led away from the High Court of All Justice with the party just beginning. The seating in the marquee had been dragged to one side and within minutes a host of stalls had taken their place. A wailing momma had approached him outside the court; she had bestowed her blessing on his holy soul and then spat at him and said he needed all he could get, the place *he* was going.

Mathias was broken. The people of Newest Delhi believed that he had killed his own father. As the guards led him away he heard sounds of merriment and music coming from the marquee. It was too good an opportunity for the people of the city to miss, a chance to party.

They shut him in the cramped ground-floor room that had been his cell for so long already. Jeanna was on the door but she wouldn't look at him, she must have been informed of the court's outcome.

With the door shut, Mathias sat on his bed, then stood and moved across to the window. He pressed his head against the cold iron bars and watched flies bouncing repeatedly off the glass, each insect convinced that *this* time its way would be clear.

He heard the door open and so he turned. A stocky woman in the dark grey of the Convent was staring at him. Her hair was a short and spiky grey, her face square and heavily lined. She looked around the room, studying every surface, every corner. She stepped further into the room and made space for another grey-clad Conventist to enter.

Greta.

Finally, she had come to see him. 'Greta,' he said. He could think of nothing better to say.

'Matti.' No-one had called him that for almost four years.

'Greta,' – the name felt right on his lips, but all his old feelings had gone; he was sure of that now – 'why have you come? It only makes problems.'

For the first time, Greta met Mathias's look. He didn't like what he saw. Once, she had been full of lightness, full of energy and laughter. Now, her eyes were like the eyes of a corpse. No feeling, no compassion, no life.

'Curiosity, I suppose. I wanted to see if you were the same old Matti.'

'Am I?'

She looked at him again, this time really studying his face. 'You're older,' she said. 'Inside, I mean. You're not angry any more, not even now. Am I right?'

Mathias nodded. 'Perhaps,' he said. 'Maybe I've just improved my act.' The sight of Greta, so close, had disturbed him deeply. Idi had warned him of how events of the past four years had affected her, but now he could see it for himself.

He blamed himself for everything. There *must* have been an alternative to the way he had acted, there must have been a way to minimise the damage but he had thought of no-one but himself. 'Greta,' he said. 'I've lived through a lot since I was driven out of Newest Delhi. I've thought, over and over, about what happened. Will you do one big thing for me?'

'What?' He couldn't read Greta's face.

'Leave Edward Olfarssen.' He had to explain to her. 'It was Edward who killed the Prime, not me. He's the one who's gained everything since then; I'm the one who's lost. He manufactured the whole situation. He deceived you, Greta. Can't you see that now?'

All the time that she was in the room, Greta had been standing. Now she turned and stepped unsteadily towards the door. Her Conventist companion hurried to open it. 'I was wrong,' said Greta. At first, he thought she was crying; then she turned and he could see that her face was dry and angry. 'I was wrong about you, Mathias Hanrahan! You're not old inside, you're still the obsessive little boy that I dumped four years ago. Out of my way!' She jostled her companion aside and marched out of the room.

Mathias sank on to his bed and wished he knew how to cry, that it had not been drummed out of him when he was little. Primes don't cry, his mother had always said, before she had been killed in Abidjan. Not even *little* Primes.

He screwed fists into his eyes, he bit down on his tongue, but nothing could assuage the feelings that

287

were swirling about inside his head. Nothing could remove the guilt.

He could see it clearly now, how Greta must have felt when she had been forced to accept betrothal to Edward, when all the evidence had pointed to Mathias's guilt. What else could she have thought? And then he had fled Newest Delhi, confirming his guilt in the eyes of everyone. He had broken her heart and the situation had forced her into the arms of Edward.

And now he had just told her that she had been mistaken. Her heart had been broken for no good reason and she had married the man responsible for the entire situation. That was the cruellest thing, and it was all Mathias's doing.

How could he have treated her so badly?

After a time he lifted his head. He could hear laughter from the Manse gardens. It was a laugh he had not heard for a long time.

It was Greta. Her voice was unmistakable.

He rose and moved across to the window. Through a tangle of vines, he could just make her out, a tiny figure in dark grey, her golden hair drawn back and highlighted by the sun. She tilted her head back and laughed once again. There was another figure in the gardens, too. Bigger build, dark-skinned and wrapped in a flowing lilac robe. Lucilla Ngota. He heard a lower-pitched chuckle, now, Lucilla joining Greta's good spirits.

Mathias watched them together in the gardens, talking and throwing handfuls of petals over each other. Then they kissed. For long seconds Mathias's heart pounded madly, until they pulled apart and

Lucilla strode away with a parting wave, leaving Greta to wander, slowly, out of his sight. He lay down on his bed and stared at the cracked ceiling, wishing life did not have to be so confusing and all the same so painfully simple.

# Chapter Twenty-one

It was a dream.

Kasimir Sukui knew that it was a dream: the emotions were magnified yet somehow remote; the colours, the perspectives, were unreal, distorted. He wished it would stop.

Siggy Axelmeyer was before him on the balcony of Canebrake House. He was playing his mouth-organ, his back to Sukui, a microphone cable trailing down over the crook of his right arm.

The two of them were alone, except for the voice ringing in Sukui's head, the Good Lord Salvo booming, 'It's me or him, Kasimir. Me or him!'

The balcony railing came only a few centimetres higher than Axelmeyer's knees and now Siggy was leaning out, playing one-handed and gesturing to the crowd with his other hand.

'*Me or him, Kasimir!*'

Why could the Prime not be quiet? Sukui knew that Salvo wasn't here, on this balcony at Canebrake House, yet the voice was so loud inside his skull.

He took a step toward Axelmeyer.

He knew what would happen next. He had lived this dream before. He took a deep breath, raised his hands in front of him.

And Axelmeyer turned, his eyes swelling, his mouth dropping open, his harmonica tumbling away and lodging itself in the clematis that must be all that held the balcony's railing in position. 'It's me or him, Kasimir,' he said, his voice a strangled imitation of the Prime, Salvo Andric talking to Sukui through the mouth of his cousin.

Sukui took another step and pushed but Axelmeyer was ready for him, his legs braced, his arms raised to fend off Sukui's hands.

They struggled but Sukui found that he possessed a strength he had never suspected and he was edging Axelmeyer slowly, relentlessly, backwards. 'We have to spread the Word,' hissed Sukui, and then he focused all his energy, his strength, and heaved Axelmeyer backwards.

Axelmeyer looked at him, aghast. Off balance, his legs came up against the railing and he tried to brace himself against it, to retaliate.

And then the railing broke.

Axelmeyer cried out, windmilled his arms as he began to tumble backwards, but it was no good, his fall was relentless. Below, the crowd that had been listening to the music gave a collective gasp as the Prime's cousin, along with the harmonica his fall had dislodged from the creepers, fell untidily to the ground.

Sukui sat up in his bed.

The night was still dark but his apartment in Hitachi Tower possessed large windows and so starlight illuminated the room. He shook his head, hoping to free his mind from that awful image.

But it was more than a nightmare. As the dream fragments seeped away from his wakening brain they were replaced by memories, transient images from four days before.

He had introduced Decker to the Prime in the morning; Salvo had been scared, he had said little – he had not wanted this extra complication added to his struggle to retain power. It had been a start, though, and it had been enough to distract the Prime from Sukui's recent activities.

And so, later that day, he had gone to Canebrake House. 'I have something to tell you,' he had said.

Axelmeyer had cleared the room of his entourage of supporters and sat with Sukui. 'Then tell me, Kasimir,' he had said. Sukui had told him about the Orbitals and Axelmeyer's response had been succinct. 'They have no jurisdiction. They interfere and we'll blow them out of the skies.' In response to Sukui's open-mouthed expression, he had added, 'We have a world to tame, a nation to propagate: they are irrelevant, these Orbital has-beens, can't you see, Kasimir? Is this all the information you had for me?' And then he had laughed and dismissed the subject.

How could he be so *blind*?

Sukui had sat for a few moments more, as Axelmeyer went out to his balcony and played his mouth-organ for the ever-present crowd below the balcony. Sukui felt betrayed. He had gone against his Prime, aligned himself with this misfit scientist Axelmeyer, and now he had been accused of irrelevance. Axelmeyer had laughed at him.

Sukui had tried to work it out but had given up. He had sensed that events were beyond him, somehow all control had slipped beyond his reach.

He had stood and walked out to the balcony.

The railing was low, barely centimetres above Axelmeyer's knees. He had wanted Axelmeyer to turn so that he could argue with him, try to persuade him, but instead Axelmeyer had started to play a distorted version of a tune Sukui knew from Orlyons, a song made familiar to him by Mono and her Monotones.

A rage had overcome him and he had taken another step towards Axelmeyer's broad back.

Now, in the bedroom of his apartment in Hitachi Tower, a violent shudder passed over his body and tears began to flow. The feelings were alien to him: had he really wanted to kill Axelmeyer? To push him over that railing?

He had stepped forward and Axelmeyer had sensed him, half turned, cried out in surprise as his foot caught on the railing that could only have been held in place by the creepers and a layer of rust. The railing gave way and Axelmeyer lost his balance, reached out as Sukui had instinctively reached out, their fingers brushing, Axelmeyer's body falling away, arms windmilling, harmonica flying out, matching the rate of his descent to the cobbled street below.

He had wanted to – intended to – kill Axelmeyer. Had he pulled his own hand away as Axelmeyer had reached out for him? If Siggy had not fallen, the railing given way, Sukui would most probably have pushed. He recognized that fact, he was honest with himself, he was rational. Sitting in his room he could see that there was no distinction between intention and fact: Axelmeyer was dead. Sukui had killed a man . . . he could see no other way to put it.

He hugged his knees to his chest and wished the thoughts would leave him, the memories.

He had nowhere to turn. He was alone. Lucilla had left several days ago to attend Mathias's trial; although that was rumoured to have taken place – and Mathias executed, another terrible black mark on Sukui's conscience – there was no word yet of her return. In his state of despair he had lost track of everyone else: all his friends from Orlyons, the pageanteers, his colleagues in the Project.

He had been back to Salvo Andric only once since Axelmeyer's death. One phrase lingered in his memory. 'You have proven your loyalty, Kasimir; but how can I ever trust you again after *this*? You killed my cousin.' He had been unable to deny the Prime's accusation and so he had left straight away.

He could see that it had all slipped away from him. The Prime was desperately in need of guidance which Sukui was now unable to provide. The hut at Dixie Hill had been seized and all the trifacsimile machines impounded. How could the Prime be diverted from this suicidal course of action?

He did not know. Thinking hurt his head. He wanted to sleep but he knew what awaited if he were to close his eyes. He rose, dressed, and left his apartment for the first time in three days.

The streets of Alabama City were dangerous after dark but Kasimir Sukui no longer cared for his own security. He breathed the cold air deeply.

Leaving his apartment, he had possessed no clear plan. After a few minutes he realized that he had been heading along Grand Rue Street towards Soho. He recognized a small side street and his sub-conscious intention suddenly became clear to him.

The building's crooked door swung stiffly on its hinges and Sukui entered, pausing in the dark corridor in an effort to find his bearings. He climbed some uneven steps and paused again. The pale glow under the door before him, the door of the room Lui Tsang shared with Mags Sender, was a certain giveaway.

He knocked and the glow cut out instantly.

'Sukui-san!' cried Mags, as she opened the door. 'We were worried about you. Nobody knew where you were.' Then she peered more closely at him. 'Shit, you look ill. Are you OK?'

He bowed his head and entered the room. Lui Tsang was sitting lotus on the floor below the single, shuttered window.

'Please,' said Sukui, 're-activate the trifacsimile.' He allowed himself a faint smile at the expression on Lui Tsang's face. 'It was the rational thing for you to do.'

Tsang dragged a blanket away from beside him, revealing a back-pack about thirty centimetres in each dimension. He flicked a switch and a trifax of Decker sprang up in the middle of the room. 'It's the only one we could get out,' said Tsang. 'They locked the rest up on Dixie Hill. They're scared.'

'It is possible to construct this apparatus in quantities?' asked Sukui.

'Sure,' said Decker, joining in. 'Once we'd shown Lui what he needed, he knocked up fifteen inside a day. You guys have so much stored that you don't know what to do with, it's crazy: you're almost better equipped than we are.'

'He's right,' said Mags. 'We figured they must have used trifax a lot when they first landed, before the revolutions, that is.'

'But all that's locked up now,' said Lui.

Sukui straightened himself, smoothed the creases in his robe. 'Decker, do you have any news from orbit?' His mind was beginning to function again.

'The terran ship is due in months as opposed to years,' said the trifax. 'ArcNet still hasn't given us a definite fix as yet. Listen, we've got to get ready. We have a loose kind of consensus up here now – at least everyone believes that it's happening – but you guys have to get moving. We're waiting for you, but you don't have much time.'

Sukui thought of Prime Salvo; he had obviously dismissed the same argument. He looked at Tsang, at Sender. 'Come along,' he said. 'We have no time to waste.'

'What are we going to do?' said Lui Tsang.

'We are going to visit a friend of mine: we will lend him your trifax.' The expressions on their faces were almost comical. The answer was clear yet they could not see it: 'We are going to see Chet Alpha.'

# Chapter Twenty-two

Mathias Hanrahan had a day and a night to live. He knew he should prepare himself. He must go with dignity and for that he would need the sort of rigid discipline Kasimir Sukui had tried so hard to instil in him. He wished he could go out to Gorra Point and sit for a time amid the Pinnacles. The sea would calm him, as it always had. He would watch cutters skimming the waves, plunging for fish and then preening their furry bodies as they flew on. He would turn crawlers and watch them resume their initial direction in an ever-tightening arc. He would let the light breeze cool him and remind him of happier times.

But that was not to be. The fantasy calmed him a little but was no substitute for the reality.

There was a light tap on the door and Jeanna slipped into the room. 'I'm on for the rest of the day, sir,' she said. 'Anything I can get for you?'

She sat on a stool she had brought in earlier and began shuffling the set of cards on a cleared bedside table. She looked at him and her expression faltered slightly. 'Or I could just go,' she said. 'If you'd rather be alone.'

Mathias smiled. She was doing what she could. 'You deal,' he said, and swung his legs off the bed so he could be closer to the table. She concentrated intensely on the mixing of the cards; it was a skill she had only recently acquired. Mathias studied the lines of her frown and wondered if she was attracted to him, if that could be her reason for treating him so kindly.

'Cut?' she said.

He cut the pack and she dealt him six cards, straight from the top, then six for herself. He decided she must feel no real attraction towards him, there were no lingering looks, no comments heavy with implication.

He examined his cards. He tapped the table and she dealt him another, a trading Jill, face up. He left it where it was.

Jeanna was small and broadly built, all wisps of mousy hair and narrow lips and nervous flutterings of her hands. She was not unattractive, but Mathias felt nothing physical towards her. In a flash of insight he recognized that he was treating her as a sister, a replacement for the family he had never really had. He tapped and Jeanna dealt him another, a seventh heart. 'End,' he said, and she dealt one to herself.

She was good with the cards. She played intuitively, she had a natural flair for spotting the right moment; her manipulation of her hand was not so good, though – that was something that came with experience – but already, in so short a time, Mathias occasionally lost. Jeanna thought he was being generous and maybe a little patronising – he could see it in her eyes – but Mathias never fooled with cards these days, he always played to win.

Mathias won the first game and then shuffled the

pack. As he dealt, Jeanna said, 'I tried to get you the paper you wanted. And a pencil. But it's no good. The Conventists have burnt a lot of books since the Prime came to power. I'm sorry, sir.'

'I wish you'd just call me Mathias, or Matt – that's what my friends call me.' He had wanted the paper so he could write down his memoirs, his own version of what had happened. Then, when Edward's empire crumbled, as Mathias knew it must, there would be a written record of the truth. He had no idea who would read it, if anybody, but the knowledge that it was *there*, on paper, was the one thing that might make his death easier to face. But the opportunity was not there.

Jeanna won the next two rounds. 'You're too kind, sir, you're too kind,' she said, as she swept up the cards from the table. 'I have to get back to my post,' she said. 'Dinner-time inspection, you know.'

'Jeanna, will you be on duty again? Before . . . tomorrow?'

She nodded.

'I'd like to talk to you.' Mathias grinned and shrugged. 'I'd like to tell you about myself, I'd like to tell you what's happening in the south. There'll be some big changes soon.'

Suddenly he knew what he must do. Jeanna was bright, she was quick and understanding. If Newest Delhi could provide him with no paper then *Jeanna* would be his paper. He would tell her everything. She would hear his own story, but also she would hear about the Orbitals and the ship from Earth. Idi Mondata had been right: such knowledge should not be held only in the south. The first attempt to spread the knowledge – talking to the market-place over Idi's PA system – had failed, but suddenly Mathias knew that a more personal approach might succeed. He had convinced Idi, he had aroused Edward's interest, he could convince Jeanna. Idi and Jeanna could tell their friends and then the process would mushroom. Mathias knew that at least he should try.

Jeanna turned in the doorway and nodded. 'Yes,' she said. 'Of course I'll be here. We'll talk later.'

Mathias ate his dinner, because he knew that lack of appetite would be reported as a sign of weakness, a loss of spirit. Edward would love that.

He stared out of his barred window. It was too early to have eaten: the sun was still in the sky, high enough to cast its light over the Manse walls and into the gardens. The door to his room opened and a hard-faced servant took his empty dishes away. The servants didn't wear masks to deal with Mathias. Maybe the practice had been abolished, since the death of Prime March. Maybe they simply felt that they had no need to hide their faces from Mathias: he was even lower than them, he did not count any more.

He stood staring at the closed door, waiting for Jeanna, rehearsing what he would tell her, trying to order the jumbled mass of his memories. There was so much to say, and so little time.

The door opened and Mono entered the room.
*Mono.*
She was wearing a servant's jacket and trousers,

edged with the tinsel that marked her as an entertainer.

She hugged him so long and so hard that he felt his face and his lungs burning. Finally she relaxed and he breathed in deeply.

He held her at arm's length and studied her tear-streaked face, then he held her close again. 'Matt,' she finally said, the first to speak. 'You dumb shit. Why did you let them take you? You want them to *kill* you? Oh, Matt.'

'How did you get to me?' said Mathias. 'How did you get in?'

'Fuck the right people and you can get anywhere,' she said, her face buried in Mathias's chest. 'And the guard outside, she's OK, she let me through. I had to see you.

'I got here for the so-called trial,' she continued, pulling Mathias down to sit by her on the bed, holding on to his hand as if she would never let go. 'But I couldn't go. Not my scene.' She smiled weakly. 'Anyway, Ngota was there. She was in Alabama, she would have recognized me. She hates you, Matt. She was the one after you in Orlyons, right? You can see it in her eyes. She said she'd found religion, back in Alabama: she joined Chet Alpha's Pageant of Holy Charities—'

'*Chet Alpha*?' said Mathias. 'Religion?'

''S right.' Mono shrugged and moved closer to Mathias. 'I think he's genuine but Ngota, she's different. She hasn't committed herself to Chet's Pageant. She left it to come back here, she just wants to see you swinging, Matt. That's all she wants. One day she's preaching love and peace and the next she's back here, waiting.' Mono was crying again. Mathias had never seen her so distressed, she had always kept her feelings under the surface.

'Lucilla's nothing,' he said. 'Don't let her get at you. It's Edward who's killing me, not Lucilla Ngota.'

'Come on, Matt,' said Mono, suddenly standing and trying to pull him to his feet. 'We've got to get you out of here. It's all worked out.'

'No.' Mathias looked away. He couldn't meet Mono's gaze, it was accusing him, telling him he was cheating her or maybe just that he was the dumb shit she had called him earlier. 'I can't go,' he said. 'It would destroy everything. Edward would blame my escape on Alabama City, he'd stir up the troubles again, probably far worse than they were before. I came here to win some kind of peace, a breathing space for Sukui so he could keep the Project running. There are big things going on, Mono. I can't jeopardise them, not now.'

As he spoke, Mono stared at him. 'Sukui told me all that shit,' she said, her voice sad. 'He said why you'd let them take you, but that's all out in the open now – your Project, the angels. You don't have to stay here now, Matt. It's happening already.' She was pleading now.

'No,' said Mathias, briefly. He reached to his neck for Mono's pendant, removed it, held it out. 'Here,' he said, 'you'd better take this.'

Mono snatched it angrily and turned away. Then she slumped against the door.

Mathias helped her back to the bed where she sat, holding him tightly. 'I'm sorry,' he mumbled, repeating the phrase over and over. 'Will you tell me what's been happening?' he said, after a long interval, trying to change the subject.

'There was a lot of trouble in Alabama City when I got there.' Mono's voice was weak at first, but it strengthened as she spoke. 'The Prime's cousin was trying to start a revolution or something.'

'Siggy Axelmeyer?'

'That's right: Axelmeyer. Well Sukui-san must have thought Axelmeyer would win, and he went to talk to him. Then he was arrested – Sukui, that is – and that was when he told the Prime about the angels.'

'Angels?' Mathias was already working it out in advance.

'That's right. Living in the Arks, up in the sky. That's what they say, anyway. Chet Alpha knew about them too, he'd seen one and it had told him to spread word. They're like people, but Sukui-san says they're just like pictures, they come from projectors – Sukui-san and Lui Tsang have made lots of them. The angels are tall and strong looking and your eyes can't make them sharp. They're difficult to see, normally, but if you see them in the right light they glow, like they really are angels.'

Mathias grinned. Someone had been fooling with trifacsimiles. 'What are these "angels" doing?' he asked.

'Chet's Pageant has split up and the Holy Charities are travelling around the Andricci lands, spreading the Word. You should see it, Matt, the effect the angels have on the people. They don't know what's hit them. People are just dropping everything and going on their knees, you wouldn't believe it but it's happening.

'The Andricci Prime started off by running things. He wouldn't let the angels out on the street at first, but the Pageant got hold of a projector and word got around. The people wanted to know and the Prime had to let more projectors out so he could stop a civil war. The Prime's lost control now, no-one will listen to him – they know about the people living in the sky, they know there's more people coming from Earth.'

'Has the Pageant reached Clermont or the Hanrahan lands?'

'When I left it had hardly got outside of Alabama City,' said Mono. 'The Charities are on foot and they're converting people as they go. They won't even reach the borderlands for another month or two.'

'What did Siggy Axelmeyer do, with all this going on?' Mathias could not imagine Siggy allowing something like this when he had been so close to seizing power.

'Oh, he fell from a balcony,' said Mono. 'He was playing mouth-organ to a crowd, leaning over the edge. Word is that Sukui-san pushed him but I can't see him doing that – he was always so gentle.'

Mathias remembered how Siggy used to irritate Sukui, but he couldn't picture the old scientist as a murderer. Sukui was a peaceable man: that part of the story had to be wrong.

'Can't you see, Matt? It's happening already. You've got nothing to stay here for. Do you *want* to die?'

304

'I have, Mono, I have.' He shook his head. 'You're right: things are starting to move, but that's even more reason to stay. If Edward started the troubles again, everything would be destroyed. Can't *you* see? The Project is working. I can't go.'

Mono slumped against him in defeat. 'Dumb shit, you dumb shit,' she kept mumbling. When she kissed him her mouth tasted of salt. Her servant outfit came off easily and Mathias's clothes soon joined Mono's on the floor. All the time he was thinking that this shouldn't be happening. He was going to die tomorrow and here he was – here *they* were – sealing their bond in a way they had avoided for so long.

It didn't last long, the flow of emotions was too intense. Even as they were – body pressing against, moving against, shuddering against, body – it was not a physical thing, it was a joining of souls, an acknowledgement of something they had always known.

Afterwards they lay in each other's embrace, Mathias ebbing, slowly, inside his lover. 'You have to leave,' he whispered, when their breathing had returned to normal. 'You have to get away from here.'

Mono shifted. 'You're going to stay, aren't you? You're stubborn, Matt, a stubborn, dumb *shit*.' She struggled away from him and pulled her clothes on quickly, keeping her back to him but failing to hide her tears.

Mathias dressed and held the door closed for a moment. 'Mono,' he said. 'I've never really loved anyone before, but—'

'No,' she said. 'I guess you haven't.' She pulled at the door and Mathias let it open without resisting. He wanted to stop her, to hold her again. More than anything he wanted to go with her, but he fought his feelings.

Sukui would have been proud of his pupil.

As Mono hurried away down the corridor, Jeanna looked at Mathias. 'She looked harmless enough,' she said, her voice nervous, unsure. 'I should have asked.'

Mathias shrugged and shut the door, fearful of the day to come, hoping that he could at least give the *impression* of dignity even if, in his heart, he felt utterly worthless.

Turning back into the room, he noticed something glinting on his table. He picked it up. Mono had left the opal pendant. He couldn't work out if that made him feel better or worse. He put it round his neck and tried to forget.

## Chapter Twenty-three

'I don't even know where to start,' said Mathias. 'I've thought about it all night and I don't know what to tell and what to leave out.'

It was early morning, the sky still golden-tinged from the rise of the sun. Mathias sat on his bed, knees pulled up to his chest, Jeanna sitting at his feet. She was tense, studying his face, aware of the importance of her role. She was to be his message to the world.

'What will you do after today, Jeanna?' he asked, deferring the start of his story yet again.

'I don't know,' she said. 'I'm leaving the Guard, that's for sure. It's not my kind of life, I don't like it. Matt, will you tell me what to do? Will you give me some guidance?'

Mathias shook his head. 'I'd hoped you would leave the Guard, but I can't tell you what to do. All I can hope is that you'll spread my words as well as you're able. That's all I can ask.'

'We don't have long, sir. Matt.'

'I'm ready to die, you know. I'm prepared. I'm not going to give Edward the chance to see me suffer. I suppose the place to start is by saying simply that I didn't kill my father; I'm letting Edward kill me because I want to give my friends in the south, and in orbit, some more time to do what they've already started. Let me tell you about a friend of mine, a man called Decker . . .'

And so he told Jeanna all that had happened. He told her of Decker and his people, he told her of the ship from Earth, he told her of a brittle-minded old scientist called Kasimir Sukui and of Lui Tsang and of Chet Alpha, he told her of playing music in Orlyons, of Mono and of why he had refused to leave with her last night.

And Jeanna listened, her eyes growing wide and then narrow, her breathing growing fast and then slow and calm. As he spoke, Mathias knew that his every word was becoming lodged, instantly, in the mind of his guard.

'I heard of your speech at the market,' she said, when he eventually stopped speaking. 'I couldn't understand why nobody was interested in the things you said. When I was small, people used to tell me lies, knowing that I would believe them – I believed *anyone*: why should they tell lies? I feel like that now, sir. I feel like you've just told me the biggest lie anyone has ever told and when I've gone you're going to laugh at me.'

'I've told you the truth, Jeanna.'

'I know,' she said, and shrugged. 'I never doubted that, I'm just telling you what I feel. Stupid, I know, but it's the way I think.'

'I can hear them coming for me.' The door at the end of the corridor had just swung back and hit the wall, a sound he had always associated with mealtimes until now.

Jeanna stood and looked down at him. 'You won't be forgotten,' she said. 'What you've done. I'm going to tell everyone I meet. When the Earth ship comes people will be expecting it. I'm going to spread the Word, sir. Your followers will meet the Holy Charities half-way, I'll make sure of that.'

She turned and opened the door and Mathias swung his feet off that narrow bed for the last time in his life.

Now, he was ready. He had seen the look in Jeanna's eyes and he knew that she would keep her promise. Smiling serenely at the approaching guards, he knew that he had no choice. They would kill him today. But, also, he knew that his death would serve its purpose. 'No need for that,' he said, as the guards grabbed his arms. 'I will go in peace.' Their hands fell away and, dumbly, they followed him out of the small room that had been his cell.

The guards led him through the streets of Newest Delhi, heading for the scaffolds on West Wall. Nobody said a word. The people of the city stopped as the procession passed them by. They stared, they whispered, children ran indoors to fetch friends and relatives. 'Mama mama mama!' he heard one little girl cry. 'The Prime's son – they're taking him past!'

He smiled. Even after four years the people still thought of March as their Prime.

Although individuals would stop and stare, there were no crowds, no tail of children running after Mathias and his guards. Jeanna had told him that it was not to be a public affair, the people were to be kept at a distance.

A street away, Mathias could see the tightly

309

packed market-place, business not halting for a mere execution. A troupe of Death Krishnas hurried past, alike in their orange robes and their shaven heads painted with hearts and swastikas and brightly coloured flowers.

They climbed a set of access stairs, spiralling tightly inside West Wall, and emerged on a paved area that Mathias knew well. He looked seaward. He should have been able to see the fishing fleet dotting the distant reaches of Liffey Bay but there was nothing, only cutters and gulls, and a small school of porpoises breaking surface a few hundred metres offshore. Watching the cutters, he realized that finally he had ceased envying their freedom.

He turned to the sound of voices behind him. The Primal Guards were handing over to an officer in the grey bodice and leggings of a Conventist Guard. Other Conventist troops stood in formation behind their superior and as the Primal Guards headed back down the stairs, Mathias was seized roughly and half-dragged through a stone arch to a wide balcony, the site of his execution. To the seaward side was a low wall and there Mathias saw Greta, hanging on to Lucilla Ngota's arm and staring out at the waves. The other three sides consisted of high stone walls, with two small archways cordoned off and a third, wider one, blocked by a row of Conventists. Beyond, Mathias could see a crush of people who had defied the Primal edict and come to view the proceedings. Mathias wished they had stayed away.

He had not expected the event to be run by Conventists; he had not realized how much influence they had gained, through Greta. In these four years they had risen back to near their former level of power, always ready to throttle any resurgence of the old ways. He looked across at the two women by the wall. Greta looked happy, chatting, laughing, awaiting the death of her one-time fiancé. Lucilla looked more dejected, even nervous; it was the culmination of her vendetta against him – her life would be very different after this morning and maybe she was just realizing that fact.

Mathias was surprised that so few had been invited. He had expected his half-brother to bring along a host of officials and clan-leaders and others he wished to impress. But it appeared that even Edward had opted not to attend. Did it really matter that little to him?

Eventually, Greta glanced around and realized that Mathias had arrived. She smiled and said something to Lucilla. Looking at her, Mathias realized that she was actually pleased for the same reason that Lucilla was tense: an unhappy chapter of her life was finally coming to a close.

She was glad that Mathias was to be executed.

Greta nodded to the Conventist officer, who then barked out an order to the troops holding Mathias. They pushed him up on to a platform that was set against the inner wall. Standing there, listening to the boards settle beneath his feet, Mathias stared at the noose, centimetres from his nose. He smiled at his guards and they looked away, disturbed by his demeanour.

Greta came forward, leading Lucilla by the hand and forever chattering, giggling. Mathias stared at her, at her golden hair dancing in the breeze despite being tied tightly back with a length of black cord.

He felt at peace, he felt happy. He smiled at her, and her chatter faltered and then stopped. He bowed his head. 'I am ready, Greta,' he said. 'Are you going to pull the rope? Or you, Lucilla?' He turned his smile on Lucilla and, for the first time, he saw how her stay in Alabama City had transformed her: at last she bore signs of human weakness. She stared for long seconds at his warm smile and then she turned away, unable to take any more.

Greta opened her mouth to snap an order at the guards, she stopped without saying a word.

Mathias turned to see what had caught her attention.

There was a commotion at one of the small arches and then the guards stepped aside and Edward passed through.

Mathias nodded. He had never really believed that Edward would miss this moment. He started to turn back to Greta and then stopped, his attention caught by the man following Edward into the arena. There was no mistaking that ankle-length violet robe and the matching skullcap.

It was Kasimir Sukui. The old scientist had a kind of pack on his back and was sweating with effort. To one side – emerging from the wall! – was a ghostly image of Decker, floating above the ground, his limbs blurred and translucent, his body and face more tangible, but still somehow unclear. Decker was glowing, even in the sunlight.

Mathias leapt down from his block and strode across to Sukui, the guards too stunned by the appearance of Decker to stop him.

The sight of Sukui had startled him out of his reverie. He didn't want to die. He wanted to live and he wanted to be with Mono and Decker and all of his friends.

Then he remembered Edward and stopped in his tracks. What was going on? He looked from face to face, confused.

'Excuse me, but I must,' said Sukui, and he took the projector unit from his back and set it so that its camera lens had the best possible view of the arena.

Mathias looked at Edward and waited. For once he was at a loss.

Edward stepped forward and surveyed the troops, the scaffold, his wife. He looked at Mathias and said, 'This has gone on too long.' Then louder, he said, 'The execution has been suspended.'

Mathias looked at Sukui, but the old scientist only bowed his head and smiled.

Edward turned back to Mathias. 'I have been in conference with Sukui-san and Decker,' he said. 'It has been most enlightening. You see, August Hanrahan survived. He's a folk hero to Decker's people. He's also the grandfather of a proportion of them. Decker is our cousin, Mathias. He's impressed on me how important it is for people to be in contact with August's only two direct descendants on Expatria. *Us*. He's told me a lot of other things, too. He's confirmed what you said about the terran ship.

'I can never forgive you, Mathias.' Edward shrugged. 'But I can pardon you. Sukui-san says you are of value, and I know you are intelligent. I hereby grant you a Primal pardon, on the condition that you work under Sukui-san's supervision for the foreseeable future. Do you accept?'

'Of course,' said Mathias. It was too much information to digest at one time, so he just stared at the trifascimile of Decker, and nodded to the camera. Sukui had done a good job.

He didn't like it – his instinct had been to demand more: Edward was patronising him – but he had left instinct behind. He knew to accept what little he was offered.

Edward had walked past Mathias and now he was having a heated discussion with Greta. 'You cannot do that,' she hissed at him. 'The court has decided – you have no precedent.'

'Greta,' said Edward, trying to calm her. 'I am Prime. I create precedent. I have talked with Decker, you don't understand.'

'It's a trick, a trick!' She was shouting, now, not caring who heard. 'You can't let him get away now. You agreed: he is an enemy of the State, an enemy of the Convent.'

'You've had your way for far too long,' hissed Edward. 'I think it is time you and your Convent *shut up*. I am Prime. I have made the decision.'

Mathias had never seen such an expression imposed on Greta's delicate features. He would never have thought it possible. It was a sneer, a lip-curling statement of just how little she thought of her husband, Prime Edward Olfarssen-Hanrahan. 'Sewell,' she said, gesturing to the Conventist officer. 'Continue with the execution. The Prime is not responsible for his actions. *Continue*.' And all the time she stared at Edward, daring him to oppose her, daring him to challenge her authority.

Mathias groaned. Realisation was sinking in and he wanted it to stop. He didn't want to think what he was suddenly thinking. Two guards stepped towards him, unsure of themselves, not wanting to oppose the Prime but not daring to disobey Greta.

They stopped as Decker glided forward to float before Edward and Greta. 'You killed March Hanrahan, didn't you?' he said.

The image of Decker was not directed at either of them, but Mathias knew who he was talking to. The image adjusted itself, as Decker was able to see it in his own camera-view.

Decker was facing Greta. 'Please, confirm,' he said, and bowed his head, a gesture he must have learnt from Sukui.

'What is he saying?' asked Edward, stunned, but Greta ignored him.

Suddenly, she appeared scared. The ghostly appearance of Decker had pierced her defensive layers, his questions hurt. 'What does it matter?' she said. 'It's all over now. Guards! Continue with the execution!'

'It's *true*?' Edward had turned white. He looked at Mathias and then at the guards. 'Stop,' he said. 'Stop at once!'

But the Conventists ignored him and moved towards Mathias.

Just as one seized his arm there was a noise from the widest of the three archways, a commotion, a hubbub of raised voices and screams. Suddenly, Mathias could hear amplified music, loudspeakers

315

distorting the sound almost beyond recognition, their circuitry unable to cope with the volume.

Mathias shrugged free of the guard's grip and turned. A line of Conventist Guards were struggling to prevent a crowd of Death Krishnas from forcing their way into the arena. The guards had linked arms, but their efforts were in vain, the pressure of the Krishnas was too much for them. The line broke and a mass of orange robes flooded into the arena, spreading and moving around, suddenly unfocused and lacking in direction. Behind them came a rabble of Black-Handers, yodelling and stamping and swinging their chained bibles over their heads; pageanteers with back-packs and floating trifaxes; neck-tied Masons with clubs and stones; Jesus-Buddhists giving the blood-chilling Cry of the Hellbound as they charged into the fray. Two fazed-out Nano-Hippies came in after the main flow, driving a small motorised kart which had been mounted with the loudspeakers, children racing after them making high-pitched humming sounds in imitation of the renovated vehicle.

'Guards!' screamed Greta, but it was no good.

Amid the flow of oranges and blacks of the cultists, Mathias had spotted some normal clothing, a small, dark figure. *Mono*. And by her, taller, thinner, was Idi Mondata, shouting and waving his arms about, trying to give the Krishnas some sort of direction.

It was over in an instant, the mass of bodies too great for the indecisive Conventist Guards. Mathias snatched Mono from the crowd and headed for the open space.

They paused near to one of the smaller archways and there they saw Lucilla, blocking the way and staring at Greta.

'Please, Lucilla, let me through,' said Greta. 'We can go away together. Please, Lucilla!'

The hippies turned their music down and the arena fell silent, the fighting over. Everybody was watching the two women in the archway.

'You killed March,' said Lucilla, her voice steady and controlled. 'You deceived me, you made me love you even when you'd taken March from me.'

'Please, Lucilla. No! I didn't kill him. It was *Matti* – you heard the judge's verdict.'

'No more lies, Greta.'

'It's true! I didn't kill him. It was the Convent, I just helped, but I didn't have any choice. They wanted Matti out of the way. It wasn't me, Lucilla. Let me through.'

Greta took a nervous step forwards and then flinched as Lucilla raised her heavy hands.

'You've hurt me more than anyone ever could,' said Lucilla. She laid a hand softly on Greta's head. 'But I forgive you.'

'What?' Greta stared at Lucilla, her face quivering. 'What did you say to me?'

'You heard: I forgive you.' Lucilla slumped and leaned on the wall, crying now. 'I forgive you, I forgive you, *I forgive you.*' It was as if she was chanting an incantation, a curse on her ex-lover.

Greta turned away, looked around at the watching faces. She was being torn apart, from the inside out, and it showed all across her face. 'No,' she said. 'No.'

Then she screamed.

'*You can't!*' She took three quick steps, still screaming and then she threw herself over the parapet of West Wall. After a moment her scream broke off, suddenly. Nobody looked.

Mathias stared at Lucilla, sobbing in the doorway, then he felt hands turning him, pulling his face down, a mouth kissing him briefly, gratefully.

He pulled back and Mono was staring up at him. 'Will you come with me *now*?' she said.

Mathias nodded. It was all he could do.


THE END

# KEEPERS OF THE PEACE
by Keith Brooke

'IT HAS BEEN SEVERAL YEARS SINCE A FIRST
NOVEL HAS GRABBED ME THE WAY *KEEPERS
OF THE PEACE* DID. It's a well-crafted, very personal
look at the way war changes (and doesn't change) a young
kid from the sticks . . . It is smooth, clean, and elegant
. . . This is a book worth serious attention'

Tom Whitmore, *Locus*

Jed Brindle is an alien. At least, that's what they call him
on earth. He's really a colony-bred soldier – augmented
with cyborg implants – with the Extraterran Peacekeeping
Force, fighting for control of what used to be the United
States.

When he and his squad are sent behind enemy lines on a
kidnap operation, it isn't long before things start to go
wrong. Marooned in the desert with two wounded com-
rades and his quarry, Jed's mission becomes not just a
struggle for survival but also a journey to rediscover the
quiet, reliable farm boy he was before he became a
machine for killing.

Thoughtful, thrilling and surprising, *Keepers of the Peace*
is a fine first novel from one of the most exciting talents to
emerge on the British science fiction scene in recent years.

0 552 13724 3

# A SELECTION OF SCIENCE FICTION AND FANTASY TITLES FROM CORGI BOOKS

THE PRICES SHOWN BELOW WERE CORRECT AT THE TIME OF GOING TO PRESS. HOWEVER TRANSWORLD PUBLISHERS RESERVE THE RIGHT TO SHOW NEW RETAIL PRICES ON COVERS WHICH MAY DIFFER FROM THOSE PREVIOUSLY ADVERTISED IN THE TEXT OR ELSEWHERE.

| | | | | |
|---|---|---|---|---|
| ☐ | 13549 6 | **Battle Circle** | *PIERS ANTHONY* | £4.99 |
| ☐ | 13548 8 | **Of Man and Manta** | *PIERS ANTHONY* | £4.99 |
| ☐ | 13724 3 | **Keepers of the Peace** | *KEITH BROOKE* | £3.99 |
| ☐ | 13659 X | **The Complete People** | *ZENNA HENDERSON* | £5.99 |
| ☐ | 99478 2 | **Hoffman's Guide to S.F., Horror and Fantasy Movies** | *HOFFMAN* | £12.99 |
| ☐ | 08661 4 | **Decision at Doona** | *ANNE McCAFFREY* | £3.99 |
| ☐ | 13099 0 | **Renegades of Pern** | *ANNE McCAFFREY* | £3.99 |
| ☐ | 08344 5 | **Restoree** | *ANNE McCAFFREY* | £3.99 |
| ☐ | 13763 4 | **The Rowan** | *ANNE McCAFFREY* | £3.99 |
| ☐ | 13642 5 | **Quantum Leap No 1** | *JULIE ROBITAILLE* | £2.50 |
| ☐ | 13643 3 | **Quantum Leap No 2** | *JULIE ROBITAILLE* | £2.99 |
| ☐ | 13584 4 | **Tek-War** | *WILLIAM SHATNER* | £3.99 |
| ☐ | 13682 4 | **Teklords** | *WILLIAM SHATNER* | £3.99 |
| ☐ | 01559 2 | **The Awakeners** | *SHERI S. TEPPER* | £6.95 |
| ☐ | 01784 6 | **Grass** | *SHERI S. TEPPER* | £6.95 |

All Corgi Books are available at your bookshop or newsagent, or can be ordered from the following address:

Transworld Publishers Ltd, Cash Sales Department,
PO Box 11, Falmouth, Cornwall TR10 9EN

Please send a cheque or postal order (no currency) and allow £1.00 for postage and packing for one book, an additional 50p for a second book, and an additional 30p for each subsequent book ordered to a maximum charge of £3.00 if ordering seven or more books.

Overseas customers, including Eire, please allow £2.00 for postage and packing for the first book, an additional £1.00 for a second book, and an additional 50p for each subsequent title ordered.

Name: ..........................................................................................

Address: ......................................................................................

.......................................................................................................